AN IMPERTINENT HEIRESS

THE ISABELLA HARTWELL SOCIETY MYSTERIES

BOOK ONE

SARAH F. NOEL

ISBN: 978-1-972184-00-4

Also by Sarah F. Noel

The Isabella Hartwell Society Mysteries

An Inconvenient Heiress - A Prequel

Tabitha & Wolf Historical Mystery Series

A Proud Woman

A Singular Woman

An Independent Woman

An Inexplicable Woman

An Audacious Woman

A Discerning Woman

An Indomitable Woman

An Intrepid Woman

A Patient Woman

An Enigmatic Woman

A Valiant Woman

An Anointed Woman

A Conspicuous Woman

A Lyrical Woman

A Burdened Woman

A Prescient Woman

The Continental Capers of Melody Chesterson

A Venetian Escapade

Mischief In Morocco

The Amsterdam Enigma

FOREWORD

This book is written using British English spelling. e.g. dishonour instead of dishonor, realise instead of realize.

British spelling aside, while every effort has been made to proofread this thoroughly, typos do creep in. If you find any, I'd greatly appreciate a quick email to report them at sarahfnoelauthor@gmail.com

CHAPTER 1

Isabella Hartwell was sure she knew why she had been invited to Banbury Hall, and she disliked her conclusion intensely. A marquess did not suddenly ask an American heiress he had never met to his country house without a purpose. She was equally certain that declining the invitation would only have made matters worse.

Finally, speaking her concerns aloud, she said, "I shouldn't have agreed to come. I really shouldn't have."

Julia Chesterton, the Dowager Countess of Pembroke, and Isabella's septuagenarian companion, set down the chicken leg she'd been elegantly nibbling on and looked across the first-class carriage at her young friend.

"Why ever not? It is quite an honour, you know. The Marquess of Banbury is a notorious snob and usually invites only those of us in aristocratic circles, or, at the very least, the local gentry. He certainly never invites Americans, of all people."

Someone else might have taken offence. Isabella knew the woman was also a snob. Yet she made an exception for Isabella to her many rules about who was suitable for notice, including a usually ironclad one: no Americans. Contrary to expectations, the dowager had taken an almost instant liking to Isabella Hartwell. While she disliked most Americans, finding them loud and gauche, the dowager found her young friend delightful.

She justified this to herself by deciding that one of Isabella's relatives must be British.

"Have you been to one of his house parties before?" Isabella asked; the dowager's words suggested as much.

It was rare to catch the dowager on the back foot, but somehow Isabella had managed it.

With a tone that almost sounded like discomfort in her voice, she admitted, "Well, as it happens, I have not. My husband was not a pleasant man and was considered an ill-mannered drunkard of a guest who cared only for horses, dogs, and debauching milkmaids on his host's estate. As such, if invited somewhere once, he was rarely invited again. Eventually, he stopped being invited at all. Word does get around about such things."

The dowager didn't talk much about her unhappy marriage. Still, Isabella had learned enough in the relatively short time she had known the woman to realise that the deceased earl's sins as a husband were even worse than those committed as a houseguest.

Her thoughts were interrupted when the dowager asked, "Why do you believe you should not have agreed to come? I can assure you that, despite the unfortunate fact of your birthplace and some ill-advised Americanisms, which I am sure we can smooth out in time, you are a lovely young woman and will be a wonderful addition to even a marquess's guest list."

Isabella smiled and thanked the dowager for what she knew was the woman's sincere and unusual praise. However, her concern wasn't about her eligibility for such a gathering. In fact, it was quite the opposite.

She drew a steadying breath. "I am convinced that the invitation followed a request from Consuelo, the Duchess of Marlborough."

The dowager looked at her in bemusement. "And what if it did? You are friends with the duchess, or at least friendly enough to be her houseguest for some period. Did you not run in the same circles in New York, after all? Why would she not make such a suggestion on your behalf?"

Isabella had hoped the ever-sharp dowager would reach the same conclusion as she had reached on her own.

When she realised that was not to be the case, Isabella sighed and explained. "I would be extremely surprised if the duchess had the idea to make the request on her own. I believe she must have been asked to do so by my Aunt Caro." With this, she raised her eyebrows slightly.

It took a moment, but finally she saw comprehension dawn on the other woman's face. "Oh, and you think that Aunt Caro has made the request to the duchess because she wishes you to catch yourself an aristocratic British husband, as Her Grace did, and believes that such a house party is the perfect place to do so?"

"Exactly. As pleasant as Consuelo is, and as amicable as our time together was, I very much doubt she gave me a second's thought once I packed my bags and said my goodbyes. I certainly cannot imagine she has spent the time since I left considering ways to find an eligible match for me."

The unspoken truth was that the Duchess of Marlborough did not marry willingly and, more to the point, from what Isabella had witnessed, was miserable with her husband. Even though Isabella alluded to this in her letters home to her aunt, she'd been told in reply that some unhappiness was a small price to pay to marry into the British aristocracy.

Despite this explanation, the dowager would not be dissuaded from her view that Isabella shouldn't feel at all uncomfortable about the house party.

"In truth, you are a far more interesting person than most of those I have encountered in the British upper classes," she assured Isabella. "The majority of them are crashing bores at best and pompous asses at worst. I am sure our host and hostess will be thrilled to have you as one of the party. Certainly, I cannot imagine them being anything other than delighted that I decided to break with custom and deign to be their guest."

Isabella suppressed a smile at this last statement. As much as she truly enjoyed the dowager countess's company, and mutual though the admiration was, she was fully aware of who her friend was, for good and for ill. Given this, she wondered whether the dowager's insistence on being Isabella's chaperone would delight the marquess and marchioness as much as the woman assumed.

While Isabella expressed none of this, there was a question she'd been wondering about. "Why didn't you join Tabitha and Wolf in Pembrokeshire?"

The dowager paused for a moment before answering, uncertain how much she wanted to say. Finally, she explained, "Glanwyddan Hall, the ancestral seat of the earldom, holds very few pleasant memories for me. While I did return there with Tabitha and Wolf once, it is not an experience I care to repeat frequently. They are already talking of spending Christmas there this year. That will be sufficient, as far as I am concerned."

Then, with a look of rather sly delight, the dowager added, "And I could not possibly turn down an opportunity to witness for myself how the Banbury marriage is faring. My acquaintance, Lady Hartley, who is the most appalling gossip, has mentioned that there is talk that Banbury's latest love affair is quite scandalous, and that Lady Banbury even threatened divorce at one point. Given this, it will be intriguing to see how they navigate having a house full of guests while maintaining any semblance of marital peace."

Isabella was not nearly so eager to immerse herself in this family drama as the dowager seemed to be. Now, in addition to avoiding whatever matchmaking scheme Consuelo might have been persuaded to set in motion, there was one more reason to dread the days ahead. She knew all too well that a society scandal was rarely the worst consequence of a failing marriage. After the turmoil of recent months, she hoped for something approaching tranquillity. Yet marriages under strain had a way of collapsing at the most inconvenient moments.

The train ride from Paddington Station to Banbury wasn't long, and for the rest of the journey, the dowager and Isabella mostly read or made idle chitchat. Isabella was a practical woman and realised that, regardless of the reason she'd been asked, she'd accepted the invitation and might as well make the best of it. She didn't doubt that she was more than capable of fending off the advances of even the most land-poor, eager aristocrat; certainly, it wouldn't be her first time doing so. Even on the boat from New York, she'd turned down one such proposal.

The marquess had sent a carriage to meet them at the station, and it wasn't far to his estate. They entered through tall iron gates that led onto a long, sweeping drive that meandered through Banbury Hall Park for a few minutes before passing through a small copse and emerging to a view of the house itself.

Isabella had stayed with the Duke and Duchess of Marlborough at their seat, Blenheim Palace, one of Britain's grandest country houses, so she was not primed to be overawed by Banbury Hall. Yet, as it came into view, she admitted to herself that its graceful simplicity was captivating.

Her father, George Hartwell, made his fortune in iron and engineering, and he had taught Isabella to distrust anything built for show alone. Banbury Hall did not clamour for admiration as Blenheim did. Its beauty lay in proportion, restraint, and elegant stonework. George Hartwell would have admired it at once. Isabella smiled at the thought.

As this flickered through Isabella's mind, the dowager looked up at the structure and remarked, "I cannot imagine what the late Lord Banbury was thinking when he built such a plain and boring monstrosity. I have seen prisons with more charm."

Isabella said nothing. Gazing at the simple, composed façade, she wondered whether Banbury Hall concealed its occupants' troubles as perfectly as its symmetry implied.

CHAPTER 2

The inside of Banbury Hall was as elegant and understated as the outside. Again, the dowager didn't appreciate this as much as Isabella.

"My my," she said in a voice that should have been quieter, "has the family fallen on hard times? There are barely any paintings on the walls; have they resorted to selling off the family portraits?"

Isabella stifled a smile; on more than one occasion, she had heard the dowager's opinions of homes she considered overdecorated. Evidently, décor could also be too restrained. Isabella found no fault with it. The art was simple but tasteful, and the absence of endless ancestors and their supposed triumphs seemed no loss at all.

Her own room proved similarly spare, though furnished with obvious expense. Isabella found the clean lines and muted colours to be quite charming. She suspected the dowager's opinion would be somewhat different.

While her lady's maid, Polly, unpacked and arranged her mistress's things, Isabella removed her light cloak and washed her hands and face. Her room had a large window that looked out onto beautiful grounds. In the distance, she saw a lake, and beyond that, woods.

Spring was in full bloom, and the flowerbeds were an abundance of tulips, peonies and early roses. She looked forward to exploring. Isabella hoped the fine weather would hold for their stay. Then, no matter how awful the company, she might escape outside.

Turning back from the window, she saw that Polly was unpacking one of Isabella's lovelier day gowns.

"I thought you should make the very best first impression you can, miss," Polly explained, though Isabella hadn't questioned her choice of gown.

Aunt Caro had employed Polly on her niece's behalf, precisely because the young maid possessed the sense of style that she judged Isabella sorely lacked. As it happened, Isabella was stylish, but in a far less ostentatious manner than her aunt deemed proper for an heiress. For the most part, Polly and Isabella found enough common ground to compromise. When they couldn't, Isabella usually yielded to her maid's wishes.

As Polly helped her mistress into the chosen dress, Isabella considered her reflection and had to admit how becoming she looked in it. However, given her worries about her invitation to this house party being a ruse to find her a suitable husband, she did wonder whether she truly cared to look so striking. Still, Isabella was sufficiently self-aware to realise that her beauty was the sort that would shine through in sackcloth and ashes. More to the point, she doubted that her beauty was the main attraction for the assembled bachelors.

Thirty minutes later, Polly finished restyling Isabella's hair and choosing jewellery. Stepping back to admire her creation, she declared Isabella ready to meet the marquess and marchioness. The housekeeper had mentioned that their hosts would be having afternoon tea with some of their guests and that Isabella and the dowager were welcome to join.

As Isabella descended the sweeping staircase, she wondered what she was about to face. Reflecting on the dowager's snippet of gossip regarding her hosts' marriage, and considering her own concerns about the real reason for her invitation, Isabella felt she needed to stay alert at all times.

Despite her initial mixed feelings when the dowager insisted on accompanying her for the visit, Isabella was now glad to have the feisty old woman by her side. No one would be a better comrade-in-arms than the dowager countess. As it was, the woman approached most social situations as if they were akin to military engagements. There was no doubt that, if she had been born a man, the Dowager Countess of Pembroke would have been a general rivalling any in history.

Isabella paused outside the drawing room door. She heard raised voices that sounded more serious, even angrier, than one would expect over tea and scones. For a moment, she wondered if she should return to her room. Yet, curiosity compelled her forward.

On opening the door, she saw three people in the drawing room: two men and a woman. She assumed that the woman was Antonia, Marchioness of Banbury.

Isabella was a beautiful woman, but her beauty was very wholesome. Despite being American, she looked the part of the quintessential English rose with her porcelain complexion, perfectly formed features, and luxurious golden hair. The marchioness, on the other hand, possessed an ethereal beauty reminiscent of a fairy princess. Winsome, she was so petite that Isabella imagined a man might encircle her waist with two hands. Her hair was so light it almost appeared silver, and her heavily lashed green eyes were enormous.

The older of the two men stood by the fireplace, his face a mask of displeasure. He was in his middle years and of average height and build. The most striking feature about him was his bulbous red nose, which hinted at many years of heavy drinking.

Completing the triangle they formed was a young man of startling good looks. He was tall and slender, with sculpted cheekbones and an aquiline nose. Isabella immediately assumed he was an aristocrat; the man looked born for a pampered life among the highest echelons of the British upper classes. The only thing that marred his perfection was that he was currently sporting a rather unpleasant sneer on his face.

"How dare you make such an accusation, Banbury?" the younger man said.

Well, thought Isabella, that at least clarified which man her host was. The younger man's harsh statement was made just as the trio noticed Isabella's entrance. Isabella couldn't have felt more awkward; she wished she'd followed her earlier inclination to return to her room.

"Please excuse me," she stuttered.

The fairy-like woman rose and approached Isabella, a tiny, pale, delicate hand outstretched. "You must be Miss Hartwell. I am Lady Banbury. Welcome."

Isabella took the proffered hand. "I have walked into a private conversation. I do apologise."

"There is nothing for you to apologise for. Your entrance saved Ravensthorpe from embarrassing himself any further." As the marchioness said this, she glanced at the beautiful young man, who didn't appear at all chagrined.

Was he one of her potential suitors? Isabella wondered. Despite his good looks, she hoped not. The man's face was filled with disdain and arrogance.

At the marchioness's words, Ravensthorpe's lip curled into a snarl. "I believe I should be the one to excuse myself," he said. Without bothering to introduce himself to Isabella, the man stomped out of the room.

With him gone, the tension did seem to ease somewhat. The older man approached and introduced himself as her host, Lord Banbury. Up close, Isabella realised that he was older than she'd originally thought. However, the marchioness looked to be around Isabella's age. Was this nothing more than a marriage of convenience? Again, she reflected on the dowager's gossip: a scandalous love affair and threats of divorce. Why on earth would any man look elsewhere when he had a woman as lovely as Lady Banbury as his wife?

These thoughts were interrupted by the arrival of a middle-aged couple, introduced as Baron and Lady Rice. They seemed pleasant enough, if rather bland. As everyone seated themselves and began introductions, Baron Rice was quick to begin boasting of his hunting prowess, and his wife seemed only to want to talk about her prize spaniels.

The conversation was rather dull, and Isabella was relieved when the dowager entered the room; the one thing the woman could never be accused of was being boring.

Isabella remembered the dowager's explanation of why she'd never been invited to Banbury Hall. Whether it had truly been her husband's behaviour that had made her persona non grata, she seemed to be genuinely welcomed by Lady Banbury, at least. As Isabella considered how long the dowager's husband had been dead, it occurred to her that any potential hostess all those years ago must have been a former marchioness.

"Lady Pembroke, welcome, welcome," the marchioness exclaimed with apparent sincerity. "I am so glad you were able to join us."

What went unspoken was that the dowager hadn't been invited. Fortunately, it now appeared to be regarded as an irrelevant detail by both their hostess and her uninvited guest.

"As am I," the dowager replied sweetly. "And, it goes without saying that I felt duty-bound to chaperone Miss Hartwell. As an American, she perhaps didn't realise the importance of such things, but I am certain that you do, dear Lady Banbury."

If there was any slight intended against the marchioness by this statement, she seemed either unaware or unconcerned.

Instead, she smiled almost beatifically. "You are so right, Lady Pembroke. Such things are often lost on the younger generation. However, etiquette and form still matter, do they not?"

Isabella had to stop herself from chuckling; the marchioness couldn't be more than twenty-six or twenty-seven herself. Who was this younger generation of whom she spoke so sagely?

As much as she'd been regretting her acceptance of the invitation, Isabella was beginning to think that this house party would not be dull.

CHAPTER 3

By the time she returned to dress for dinner, Isabella had met so many people that her head was starting to ache. Banbury Hall seemed full of relations, dependants, and guests, though she could not yet have said where one category ended and the next began. More interestingly, there did not seem to be a single obvious bachelor for whom she might have been invited. Then again, she reminded herself, men in search of a rich wife were not always young.

Polly chose an evening gown that Isabella had never been happy with, but Aunt Caro insisted that she buy and bring to London. The neckline plunged far too low for Isabella's taste. However, when paired with her mother's diamond necklace, even she had to admit the dress was elegant and becoming.

By the time she entered the drawing room, it was rather crowded. Everywhere she looked, people were sipping sherry and gossiping. Spying the dowager seated on a pretty little sofa, Isabella made her way across the room to join her.

The dowager was speaking to a woman who, from what Isabella remembered, was either Lord Banbury's sister or cousin. She was a tiny, bird-like woman. This avian comparison was emphasised when she spoke;

the woman positively twittered. This was just the sort of female the dowager had no time for, and her impatience showed clearly on her face.

"Ah, Isabella, what perfect timing," the dowager exclaimed. "Do you remember Lady Mary, Lord Banbury's aunt?"

"We met earlier," Isabella replied, mentally storing away the woman's identity.

"Miss Hartley, is it not?" Lady Mary chirped.

"Hartwell. Miss Isabella Hartwell."

"And you are an American. What an age we live in, do we not? How astounding!"

Isabella could not imagine what was meant to be astounding and chose not to enquire. There was space on the settee for one more, and Isabella was just deciding whether to join the other women when the dowager stood.

"I see Lady Brinkley by the fireplace and must go and pay my respects. It has been a positive age since I last saw her." For a moment, Isabella thought the dowager might be throwing her to the wolves as she made her escape. Then, she added, "Isabella, you should join me. You and Lady Brinkley share an interest in ornithology."

Isabella had never shown any interest in ornithology and wondered whether it was the first thing that came to the dowager's mind, perhaps prompted by Lady Mary's resemblance to a bird. Whatever the reason, Isabella seized the opportunity, and she and the dowager made their way across the room.

When they were safely out of earshot, the dowager said, "I had forgotten just how empty-headed that woman is. We came out together, and I was forced into her company more times than I care to remember."

Isabella smiled; it was hard to picture Lady Mary and the dowager as young debutantes.

If Lady Brinkley were a bird enthusiast, the topic never came up. Instead, she appeared content to trade London gossip with the dowager.

In a hushed tone, the dowager asked, "And what of our host and hostess? Is it true?"

After quickly glancing around her to ensure she wouldn't be overheard, Lady Brinkley replied, "It seems it is. From what I have heard, the woman in question is a wealthy widow. Word is that he is quite besotted and has been squiring this woman, Mrs Ashwin, around town in a manner that Lady Banbury finds humiliating."

Again, Isabella wondered why a man of Banbury's age and looks, with the exquisite Lady Banbury as his wife, would ever be unfaithful. One would imagine that Mrs Ashwin would have to be a beauty in her own right to begin to explain it.

As if reading Isabella's thoughts, Lady Brinkley continued, "It would be one thing if he were besotted with a young, beautiful actress or the like. But by all accounts, this Mrs Ashwin is past forty and quite stout. I even heard that he was seen at the opera with her, pleading in the most piteous voice for her affection."

For someone who claimed to be above petty society gossip, the dowager seemed thoroughly titillated by Lady Brinkley's words. As the two women chatted, Isabella was free to observe her fellow guests. As she looked around the room, she noticed Ravensthorpe sulking in a corner, still fuming, presumably, over the earlier argument.

Isabella wasn't sure what came over her, but she excused herself and moved to where the handsome lord sat. He had claimed a chair near one of the tall windows and sat half in shadow. A glass of claret rested untouched in his hand. He did not stand up when she approached.

"You do not appear to be enjoying the evening," Isabella said coolly.

His mouth curved faintly, but he made no reply. There was another moment of silence.

"I did not rush past you earlier to insult you," he said at last. "Though I suspect that is how it was received."

"I am accustomed to far more direct insults, my lord," Isabella replied. "If you wished to offer one, I am sure you would have done so plainly. It was evident that I walked into the middle of a heated conversation, and that you were upset. No apology is needed. However, let me introduce myself now. I am Miss Isabella Hartwell."

Now, Ravensthorpe rose and bowed. "I am Lord St. John Ravensthorpe. My father is the Earl of Grantly. And I know who you are. You are the guest of honour!"

What on earth did he mean by that? All Isabella could imagine was that all the single men invited knew she was an heiress of marriageable age. She was tempted to ask, but resisted the urge. However, the thought that this man might be the one for whom Lady Banbury planned her fortune was unsettling; as physically attractive as he was, the idea of being wooed by such a sullen, unpleasant man was not one Isabella relished.

"You are quite unlike what they expected," Ravensthorpe observed wryly.

"And what precisely did they expect?"

He glanced towards Banbury, who was laughing too heartily at something Baron Rice said.

"I suspect that you are not nearly as malleable as anticipated," Ravensthorpe said quietly.

Isabella stiffened. "I beg your pardon?"

He leaned slightly closer, lowering his voice. "You believe yourself invited here because you are charming. Or perhaps because you are wealthy and unmarried. That is the story being told."

"And you imagine there is another?"

"I know there is."

She folded her arms, suddenly irritated. "If this is an attempt to portray our host as some sort of villain, I advise you to choose your audience more carefully." There was something almost indecent about this man's directness. Isabella had already seen enough of British society to understand that its upper classes usually concealed their sharpest opinions behind good manners. Ravensthorpe appeared to feel no such obligation.

"You misunderstand me," he said, and for the first time, there was no mockery in his voice. "Banbury is not a villain. He is a drowning man."

"That is a curious description of a marquess with an estate such as this."

"Estates," Ravensthorpe replied, "can look quite solid while their foundations rot."

"You speak in riddles," she said sharply.

"Because plain speech would be ungentlemanly."

"I am an American and am not nearly as concerned with gentility as the British claim to be."

"Then I shall be plain." His voice hardened. "Banbury's attempts to raise capital have failed. You are his next target."

Isabella felt heat rise in her cheeks. "Target in what sense?"

"I have reason to believe," he said, "that you are here because

Banbury knows you command more ready money than anyone else in this room, and because your father's name still carries weight in industrial circles."

"My father is dead," she said evenly. "And I am not in the habit of rescuing estates I have only just seen."

"No," he said, studying her. "But you might be persuaded to invest in 'modernisation' or flattered into signing something presented as a progressive partnership."

The irritation that flickered earlier now erupted into anger. "You presume a great deal about my intelligence."

"Not about your intelligence," he snapped. "Only about your generosity."

"Which you consider to be boundless?"

"I think it might be exploited."

They had raised their voices, and now all eyes were on them. Isabella was aware of the shift in the room, as people strained to listen to their conversation.

"You speak out of turn, my lord," she said. "If Lord Banbury wished to discuss business with me, he would have approached me openly about it."

Ravensthorpe gave a brief, humourless laugh. "Openly? You do not understand how the aristocracy works, Miss Hartwell."

He placed his glass on the small table beside him, then quickly lifted it again, as if reconsidering.

"Heed my warning, Miss Hartwell," he said, his voice low yet urgent. "You are being positioned."

"For what?" she demanded.

"For an investment opportunity."

The word struck her forcefully, and her anger only increased. "I am not a gullible schoolgirl. You mistake me for someone far more careless than I am," she declared.

Ravensthorpe tilted his head slightly, as if reconsidering her. "Then understand this." He leaned in closer, and she smelled the claret on his breath. "The estate is mortgaged to the hilt. The machinery is financed against yields that will never materialise. If you attach your name to any scheme under this roof, you will be throwing good money after bad."

The sharpness of his words cut through her indignation. "And how," she asked tightly, "would you know any of that?"

"Because I have seen enough," he answered cryptically.

"If you believe you know something, then it is not I you should be addressing, surely. You should be speaking to your friends, Lord and Lady Banbury." Isabella glanced towards Lady Banbury, though she did not mean to. The marchioness stood across the room, seemingly composed as ever, speaking with a vicar. However, Isabella noticed the woman's fingers tighten on her fan.

Ravensthorpe followed her gaze. "It is precisely you."

Before she could respond, Banbury's voice rang out from across the room. "Ravensthorpe! Miss Hartwell! You must join us. We are debating whether steam or petrol shall carry us into the new century."

A ripple of amusement swept through the guests.

Ravensthorpe's jaw clenched. "Do not commit to or sign anything under this roof," he said quietly, with even more urgency. "Not until you have seen every ledger."

"And if I refuse to take your counsel?" she asked, her pride flaring.

"Then you will be precisely what they hoped for."

"And what is that?"

He hesitated for a moment. "The sort of woman who might believe she is investing in progress when she is, in fact, underwriting folly."

The words landed heavily between them.

There was no time to reply. Banbury crossed the room and now stood just a few paces away. "Are we conspiring?" he asked too smoothly.

"Merely conversing," Isabella replied, lifting her chin.

"Then let us converse together," Banbury said, with a smile that did not reach his eyes.

Guests began to gather nearer, drawn by the tension.

Ravensthorpe rose. "If we are to converse," he said coolly, "let us do so honestly."

Banbury's smile faded. "I do not take kindly to insinuations of dishonesty, particularly in my own home."

"Nor do I take kindly to deception," Ravensthorpe replied.

The room had gone quiet now.

"Take care, Ravensthorpe," Banbury warned. "You overestimate your place in this house."

"I care very much," Ravensthorpe said coldly. "That is precisely the trouble."

A murmur ran through the crowd.

Isabella felt her face flush with embarrassment. "I do not require your protection, Lord Ravensthorpe," she said sharply. "And I am insulted by the implication that I do."

Ravensthorpe's expression shifted from frustration to regret. "Remember my words." He picked up his glass, drained it, and walked away without looking back.

CHAPTER 4

As the group filed into dinner, the dowager sidled up to Isabella. "What on earth was all that about? I have to say, you certainly managed to inject some entertainment into what was otherwise looking to be a rather dull evening."

The dowager's gleeful tone did nothing to lessen Isabella's embarrassment. What must her host and hostess think of her?

Isabella did not answer at once and was then spared the need entirely as they took their seats at opposite ends of the enormous dining table. Isabella was seated to the right of their host, Lord Banbury. Earlier, she would have thought nothing of it. Now, she wondered why.

As much as she found Ravensthorpe's warning patronising and melodramatic, she began to wonder whether there was some truth in it. Had she been invited to Banbury Hall for more than a few days of socialising and perhaps some matchmaking?

As the other guests circled the table searching for their names, Lord Banbury settled into his chair. He turned to Isabella and, in an avuncular tone of concern, said, "I am so sorry, dear Miss Hartwell, about that unfortunate scene with Ravensthorpe. He has been a friend of my wife's since childhood, and she insists on inviting him to our home and indulging his petulance and paranoia. I do hope he did not upset you unduly."

Isabella assured him that she was entirely unfazed by the altercation.

"Capital, capital. You young American women are obviously made of sterner stuff than the delicate English blooms I am used to." As Banbury said this, he unconsciously glanced down the table at his wife.

Isabella followed his gaze and couldn't help but notice that Lady Banbury appeared rather perturbed. Was it because of Ravensthorpe's denunciation of her husband? Or was it something else? Looking down the table at the man himself, seated beside Lady Banbury, Isabella saw him downing yet another glass of claret, and then a footman immediately refilling it.

Ravensthorpe appeared even more sullen than before and was studiously avoiding all attempts by Lady Rice to his right to engage him in conversation.

Lady Brinkley, on Banbury's other side, was imploring him to join her campaign to protect the Great Crested Grebe.

"Lord Banbury, while you may not be aware of it, the bird is being shot in dreadful numbers to trim ladies' muffs and hats. Their breeding plumage is quite ravishing, which is precisely the problem. If we do not intervene, our lakes will fall silent. One cannot call oneself civilised while exterminating beauty for ornament. Do you not agree?" It appeared that Lady Brinkley truly was a bird enthusiast, as the dowager had claimed earlier.

As the woman continued her lecture on the importance of avian conservation, Lord Banbury nodded and made the occasional sound that could have been mistaken for interest. Lady Brinkley's attempt to persuade Lord Banbury gave Isabella the chance to observe her fellow guests. She had already realised that the elderly gentleman to her right was quite deaf, which meant there would be no need to engage in polite conversation.

Her first impression, on scanning the table, was that they made a very odd collection of people to gather under one roof. What commonality made their hosts consider this a group that would enjoy spending several days together?

Next to Lady Brinkley sat a slight, younger man who, judging by his appearance, Isabella suspected was Lady Banbury's brother or another close relative. He possessed the same delicate beauty and an almost haunting air. Forcing herself to dismiss Ravensthorpe's claims about why she'd been invited to Banbury Hall, Isabella returned to the question of whether she was being considered as a potential wife. Might it even be possible that Lady Banbury regarded her as a future sister-in-law?

Due to her wool-gathering, Isabella nearly missed Lord Banbury's question. Regaining her focus, she apologised and asked him to repeat it.

"I was just saying that I have heard good things about Hartwell Ironworks. Your father seems to have built an impressive empire before his death." Lord Banbury's tone was one of admiration, and nothing about his words would have given Isabella pause if it weren't for Ravensthorpe's earlier comments.

After a brief hesitation, Isabella decided there was no reason not to accept the man's praise at face value. "Indeed. Ironically, my father was never particularly concerned with building a fortune; his passion always lay more towards engineering and building things that worked well."

"That is quite the fortune to have accumulated by accident," the man said with a chuckle.

The soup plates were replaced with fish mousse, giving Isabella a moment to consider how to respond.

"Accident is probably the wrong word," she said carefully. "My father was an excellent businessman. However, as I said, his primary motivation was to build and innovate."

"How very noble," Banbury replied.

Isabella couldn't decide how disingenuous his words were.

Finally, she chose to take them at face value. "I do not think he was driven by benevolence towards mankind, but rather a scientific drive to understand how things might work better. It was an intellectual challenge rather than a philanthropic one, if that makes sense."

"Quite. Quite. Innovation without sentiment. A most admirable philosophy." Banbury dabbed at his lips with his serviette. "And you retain an interest in the company's affairs, I presume?"

The question was asked in a light, almost casual tone. However, Isabella did not miss the seriousness beneath it.

"I retain full control," she replied evenly.

For a fleeting second, something flickered behind Banbury's genial expression. It vanished almost before she could be certain she saw it.

"How remarkable," he remarked. "One hears so often of heiresses' fortunes placed under trustees and distant advisers. It must be gratifying to steer one's own ship."

"I do not manage the day-to-day operations," Isabella admitted. "However, my father had delegated those responsibilities to a trusted and highly competent lieutenant several years before his death."

Across the table, Ravensthorpe let out a short, sharp laugh. Several guests looked up. It was unclear whether he was sharing a joke with anyone. Isabella noticed that his glass was almost empty yet again. As she watched, he signalled for the footman to refill it.

Banbury, too, seemed to notice, for his jaw tightened almost imperceptibly. "Indeed," he said smoothly, though it was unclear precisely what he was referring to.

The fish plates were removed and replaced with roast pheasant. Across the table, Ravensthorpe declined it and drained his glass. The footman hesitated only briefly before refilling it once again.

Lady Banbury, who had appeared composed until then, leaned slightly towards him. Although her voice was faint, Isabella noticed the tension in her shoulders. Ravensthorpe shook his head, refusing whatever she said. Isabella then observed Lady Banbury making eye contact with the footman and shaking her head firmly.

Isabella felt a flicker of sympathy for the footman standing behind Ravensthorpe's chair, who now appeared torn between his mistress's quiet instruction and a guest determined to ignore her wishes. She noticed the young man she thought might be the marchioness's brother make eye contact with the footman and give him the slightest smile of sympathy. It seemed she wasn't the only person who felt for the servant's plight.

The conversation at the table resumed its hum, though something had shifted, and it was impossible to ignore the tension in the room.

Banbury turned again to Isabella. "I have often thought," he said conversationally, "that England has been slow to adopt certain efficiencies that America seems to embrace with enthusiasm. Agricultural machinery, for instance. Modern irrigation systems. New engines." He paused. "Progress can be costly, but stagnation is ruinous."

Was this a precursor to the request that Ravensthorpe tried to warn her about?

Isabella kept her tone mild. "Progress without prudence can be equally ruinous," she said.

If Banbury understood the full significance of her words, it was impossible to tell from his expression or tone. "Prudence," he repeated. "Yes. A quality in short supply among young men, I fear." His gaze flicked towards Ravensthorpe.

The younger man drained his glass and stood up abruptly. The scrape of his chair was jarringly loud in the high-ceilinged room.

"Forgive me," he said curtly. "I find myself indisposed."

Lady Banbury half rose, then stopped herself.

"Shall I summon a doctor?" Banbury asked with exaggerated concern.

"That will not be necessary," Ravensthorpe replied tightly as he strode out of the room.

At his departure, all conversation ceased; there could no longer be any pretence that his behaviour had gone unnoticed.

Banbury was the first to recover. "I believe our guest may have enjoyed my fine claret a little too much," he said, addressing the room with a forced chuckle.

The conversation resumed, though unevenly. Isabella found she had lost her appetite. Only a few minutes later, as Banbury once again steered the discussion towards machinery and modernisation, Isabella realised that Lady Banbury's seat was empty.

The vicar launched into a lengthy anecdote about parish roof repairs, and most of the company seemed grateful for the comfort of the mundane conversation. Banbury listened politely, though Isabella noticed that his attention seemed elsewhere. He must have noticed his wife's absence by now.

Isabella glanced towards the door through which Ravensthorpe had exited. A curious sensation settled over her. Should she have taken Ravensthorpe's warning more seriously? Their quarrel replayed in her mind with uncomfortable clarity. His urgency. His frustration. The way he had said, "*You are being positioned.*" And then added, "*Remember my words.*"

She attempted to convince herself that the man was already two sheets to the wind and that his words were simply the ramblings of a drunkard.

However, given the direction in which Lord Banbury steered their dinner conversation, was this really the case?

At last, the meal was over, and the ladies withdrew. In the drawing room, the unpleasantness of the dinner interruption seemed to have been forgotten, and the gentle ripple of polite conversation resumed. The dowager appeared quite in her element and was amusing a group of women with a lively account of some long-ago society mishap.

The men lingered over their port and cigars longer than usual. Before they returned, Isabella excused herself, citing a headache. The truth was more complicated; she wanted time to reflect on everything that had happened that night and consider how she might respond to whatever request Lord Banbury might make of her.

The corridors of Banbury Hall were hushed at this hour, lit by discreet gas lamps that cast long shadows across the thickly carpeted floors. As she ascended the main staircase, she became aware of how quiet that part of the house was. She didn't even pass a maid rushing to turn down beds.

At the corner of the landing, Isabella paused. She heard noises coming from the east corridor. She recalled the housekeeper mentioning that it was reserved for the single male guests. Since, as far as she remembered, Ravensthorpe was the only man who had left the dining room during dinner, she wondered whether the sounds were coming from his room.

Isabella hesitated. She knew how inappropriate it would be for her to follow a man to his room. Even in America, such behaviour would be considered scandalous. Yet she felt compelled to throw caution to the wind.

As she moved towards the corridor, she heard a male voice raised in anger, and another quieter voice in reply. Then, there was a sudden scrape, as if a chair had been knocked aside. Silence followed. Her heart quickened, and her decision now seemed unavoidable. She began walking down the corridor.

Then she stopped. Perhaps Lady Banbury had gone to reason with Ravensthorpe, as seemed likely; if so, this was none of her concern. Whatever lay between the two of them was not her business, and she had no desire to interfere in either a private quarrel or a reconciliation.

After a final, uncertain glance towards the darkened passage, Isabella turned away and made her way to her own room. She closed her door firmly behind her and told herself that she had done the sensible thing.

Polly was nowhere to be seen, so Isabella decided to sit at the dressing table and begin removing the pins from her hair. As she sat there, contemplating the evening, she noticed a shadow crossing the light beneath the door.

Isabella froze, one hand remaining raised to her hair. For a moment, she considered rising and opening the door. Instead, she told herself it was just a servant passing along the corridor and forced her attention back to her reflection.

CHAPTER 5

The following morning, Isabella rose early and was among the first at the breakfast table. A buffet stood piled with fresh fruit, bread, kippers, sausages, and the usual breakfast dishes. Isabella wasn't very hungry and accepted a cup of coffee, then asked for some toast.

The morning newspapers were laid out on a sideboard, and Isabella selected one and was glancing through it when Baron and Lady Rice entered the room. They politely wished her a good morning, then filled their plates and took two seats at the other end of the table. Isabella was unsure whether they were avoiding her or respecting her privacy, but either way, she was happy to be left alone.

Over the next half-hour, more guests drifted in. Isabella was on her second cup of coffee and was just considering going to her room to fetch the novel she was reading and then finding a quiet nook to lose herself in it, when Lady Banbury entered.

"Good morning, everyone," she said, greeting her guests. People mumbled replies and went back to their eggs and bacon.

Much to her surprise, Lady Banbury made a point of joining Isabella. "Good morning, Miss Hartwell. I hope you slept well."

"I did. Thank you."

"And how is your headache? I should have offered you smelling salts or some laudanum last night. Excuse me for the oversight. When I returned to the drawing room, you had already retired for the night."

Now that the subject had been raised, Isabella couldn't resist the opportunity to press Lady Banbury about her sudden exit the previous evening.

"My headache is much better, thank you. In fact, I was worried you were unwell when I saw you leave the dining room so abruptly." Isabella did her best to infuse this statement with sympathy rather than any hint of judgement. The expression that flickered briefly across her hostess's face made Isabella worry she had failed in this effort.

"Yes, I apologise for abandoning my guests, but it could not be helped," Lady Banbury said falteringly. "I remembered something that needed to be done before I retired for the night and was eager to do it in case it was a late night and I forgot."

It was a vague explanation, and Isabella didn't trust the woman's attempt at composure.

Isabella didn't want to offend her hostess, but she found herself saying, "I hope Lord Ravensthorpe is well this morning. He seemed somewhat worse for wear last night."

Lady Banbury's jaw clenched slightly. "Ravensthorpe needs to learn to behave himself in company; he is no longer a callow youth. I am sure he slept it off and will emerge later in the day as if nothing had happened."

As she said this, Lord Banbury entered the room and overheard the end of their conversation. "Damn bad form, if you ask me. I promise you, Antonia, it is the last time that man sets foot in my house. I have turned a blind eye to much over the years, but his behaviour last night, including his confrontation with dear Miss Hartwell here, was unacceptable."

Perhaps seeing his wife about to defend her childhood friend, he raised his hand in protest and added, "I warn you, one way or another, our association with Lord Ravensthorpe is at an end."

These words still lingered in the air when the butler entered the room and approached Lord Banbury. He leaned in and whispered something into his master's ear.

"What is that you say, Myers? Speak up, man," Banbury demanded irritably.

In a voice that was only slightly louder, but loud enough for Isabella to catch what was being said, the butler repeated, "Agatha went into Lord Ravensthorpe's room to light the fire just now, and she found, well, that is to say, he..."

"Spit it out for goodness sake, Myers. What did Agatha find?"

"Lord Ravensthorpe is dead, my lord." This was said loudly enough for the other guests to look up in horror.

Lord Banbury looked around the room and addressed his guests. "Nothing to be alarmed about. I am sure Ravensthorpe has overindulged and frightened himself into an unseemly stupor. We all know how hysterical maids can be."

Banbury did not rise with undue haste or alarm. That, above all, stayed with Isabella later. He placed his coffee cup down with deliberate care, unfolded his napkin, and rose as if summoned to examine a misplaced glove rather than a potentially deceased guest.

"This is becoming tiresome," he said mildly. "Ravensthorpe is not a schoolboy and shouldn't be scaring the maids with his antics."

The butler appeared reluctant to contradict his master, but the expression on his face told Isabella that there was more to the situation than just a drunken stupor. While the butler said nothing, his unease was clear.

In a voice filling with irritation, Banbury continued, "Very well. We shall see what ails him." A faint, tense tightening crossed his face, vanishing almost before it could be noticed.

The butler, Myers, turned and left the room, with Banbury close behind. After a pause, Lady Banbury also rose and left.

Isabella had no intention of following. She told herself it would be improper and intrusive. Yet as the small procession moved towards the door, she found herself standing and walking behind them. No one objected; perhaps they didn't notice her, or assumed she was returning to her room. Whatever the reason, she wasn't prevented from ascending the staircase and heading to the east corridor.

Ravensthorpe's door was slightly ajar. It was easy to spot because a young maid, utterly overwrought, stood in the hall outside, being comforted by the housekeeper.

Both women instinctively edged closer to the wall as Banbury drew near, his impatience with the situation emanating from him in waves of irritation.

He entered the room without hesitation, Myers just behind him. Lady Banbury paused for a moment, then seemed to decide to remain in the hallway. Isabella had no such qualms and followed the men into the bedchamber. The very first thing she noticed was a faint but unmistakable metallic tang. Blood.

Light filtered through half-drawn curtains, casting a pale band across the bed where Ravensthorpe lay as if asleep. The covers were slightly disarranged, as if he had turned once during the night. One arm hung over the edge of the bed, fingers loosely curved towards the carpet. His dark hair fell across his forehead. The only indication that he wasn't merely in a deep slumber was a single dark bloom at the centre of his chest, spreading outward into the linen. The sheet beneath him bore a darker stain where blood had seeped steadily into the mattress.

Isabella suppressed the gasp that threatened to escape her lips and summoned all her resolve to remain composed; she suspected Lord Banbury had little patience for feminine distress. To calm her nerves, she forced herself to look around and take stock of the room. There was no furniture overturned, nor any shattered glass. The bedside table remained undisturbed, with a decanter and water glass still in position. There had been no struggle. He had been asleep or too sodden with claret to put up a fight.

She remembered the quarrel she thought she had heard the night before. Nothing about the scene or the body's position on the bed indicated that the murder occurred during such a heated argument. Then Isabella reconsidered. It was possible that the body had been placed on the bed after a struggle. But why make the effort? Nothing about this death could be mistaken for natural.

Then she examined the body more closely than she had allowed herself to earlier; one hand lay half-curled on the coverlet, the fingers drawn inward as though he had grasped at something in the dark. There was nothing there now.

A movement at the threshold caught Isabella's attention. Lady Banbury stood just inside the doorway, her hand lightly resting against the frame, as if to steady herself. For a moment, she stood motionless. Her eyes travelled from her husband to the bed, and then fixed upon Ravensthorpe's still form.

Then, her hand slowly rose to her mouth. She did not scream immediately. Instead, she drew in a long, trembling breath that seemed almost exaggerated in its restraint. Her fingers pressed more tightly against her lips, as if physically restraining herself from wailing.

Finally, Lady Banbury's gaze fell to the dark bloom on Ravensthorpe's chest, and the scream that followed seemed to tear free. It was piercing and almost operatic in its pitch. Lady Banbury staggered backwards into the corridor, clutching at the doorframe as if her knees could no longer support her weight.

"No, no. This cannot be," she gasped.

The housekeeper hastened to her mistress's side, murmuring reassurances. Lady Banbury briefly buried her face against the woman's shoulder, her body trembling as she appeared to be in the midst of violent sobs.

Yet even during the display, Isabella noticed something that did not sit easily. The marchioness's eyes, when they lifted again, remained perfectly clear and dry. They swept the room once quickly, taking in Banbury, the butler, and finally Isabella. Then the sounds of sobbing resumed.

Isabella turned away from the apparently hysterical Lady Banbury and back to the bed. Ravensthorpe's face was slightly turned towards the door. His expression was odd; it held the faintest trace of surprise, as though he had almost woken.

You are being positioned. Remember my words.

A shiver ran through Isabella as she recalled Ravensthorpe's words. He had tried to warn her about something the night before, and now he was dead. Moreover, he had died in a house where she had quarrelled with him in front of witnesses, most of whom had heard their raised voices and sharp words.

Isabella became aware, with sudden and terrible clarity, that she was standing in the doorway of a murdered man's chamber, and that everyone present believed she had been the last person to argue with him.

"Summon the police," Banbury ordered. "Until the authorities arrive, no one leaves the house." Then he paused. "We must consider who among us had cause to want Ravensthorpe dead."

Then he turned, his gaze settling deliberately on Isabella.

Chapter 6

By the time they returned to the breakfast room, word of Ravensthorpe's death had spread. Most of the guests were already gathered there, with rumour outrunning fact.

As Isabella followed Lord Banbury into the room, she caught the tail end of a rather loud conversation between Lady Brinkley and the partially deaf older gentleman she'd been sitting beside at dinner. "Stabbed clean through the heart fifteen times. Can you believe it?"

Isabella was tempted to correct her. One thrust had been enough to kill. However, she caught herself; there was no need to insert herself even more plainly into the centre of this murder.

At the sight of Lord Banbury, the room fell silent.

"It seems that many of you have already heard that there has been an unfortunate incident," he said. "Lord Ravensthorpe has been killed, and the Oxford Constabulary has been summoned. I am sure they will want to interview each of you, so I trust it is understood that no one is to leave the house."

"You cannot possibly imagine that one of us killed him!" Baron Rice exclaimed bombastically. "They should be interviewing the servants. Perhaps he caught one of them stealing from him, and an altercation broke out."

Narrowing his eyes and pursing his lips, Banbury took a moment to compose himself before answering. "You are certainly welcome to share your theory with the police when they arrive. However, until they tell us otherwise, everyone will remain and make themselves available." Then, as if the words had only just occurred to him, he added, "I do agree that the idea that the murderer is someone within this household is unthinkable."

"Shocking, absolutely shocking," the baron muttered to himself.

Isabella took an empty seat next to the dowager. She suspected she would need all her wits about her. It was then that she realised Lady Banbury had peeled off from their group at some point and had not accompanied her husband to speak with their guests. She assumed the woman had taken to her bed after the shock of seeing her friend's dead body.

"Is it true?" the dowager asked her with rather macabre glee. "Lord Ravensthorpe has been stabbed to death? Truly, this house party has become far more interesting than I expected."

Isabella didn't want to be overheard discussing what she had seen in Ravensthorpe's room, so she answered rather noncommittally. When the dowager realised she would gain nothing worthwhile from her friend, she turned to Lady Mary on her right, who launched into a particularly dull conversation about how kippers simply did not agree with her as she aged.

By this point, there were already murmurs among the assembled guests about being inconvenienced. Since they all intended to remain at Banbury Hall for six days anyway, Isabella could not see what the great inconvenience was. However, she kept this thought to herself as she carefully observed everyone.

Inspector Gregory of the Oxfordshire Constabulary was there within the hour. He arrived with two constables in tow. Lord Banbury was informed that the inspector had arrived and went to greet him. Isabella would have loved to be included in the meeting to hear how the marquess described the murder, but Banbury didn't make the offer.

Twenty minutes later, Lord Banbury returned with the three policemen. Inspector Gregory looked every inch the tired, overworked local detective inspector. His suit was ill-fitting, with frayed cuffs, and his hair needed a trim. However, his eyes suggested a keen intelligence, and the set of his jaw indicated he would not kowtow to the toffs in his midst.

"As you may have gathered," Lord Banbury announced, "this is Inspector Gregory of the Oxfordshire Constabulary. I have offered him use of the library for the duration of his investigation. Inspector, would you like to say anything?"

Inspector Gregory neither bowed nor offered condolences. He merely looked around the breakfast room with a steady, appraising gaze that appeared to judge each face in turn. Isabella suspected that this man would rub many of the assembled guests the wrong way and not even care.

"I am sorry to meet you all under such circumstances," Gregory said at last.

Isabella found it difficult to distinguish one British accent from another, but even she could tell Gregory was from somewhere up north, even if she couldn't quite place where. In the time she had spent in Britain so far, she'd learned enough to know that this perceived provincialism would be another mark against the man in the eyes of the gathered aristocrats and gentry.

He continued, "Until further notice, no one is to leave the house. No telegrams are to be sent, and no letters are to be dispatched. I will require statements from each of you."

A faint murmur rippled through the room.

Baron Rice huffed audibly. "Surely you cannot expect to question these ladies as though they were common footpads."

Gregory's gaze settled on him steadily. "I expect to question anyone who may have information relevant to Lord Ravensthorpe's death."

Lord Banbury cleared his throat. "Inspector Gregory has the full cooperation of this household, and I expect that to extend to all of you."

"Thank you, my lord," Gregory replied coolly.

Isabella found herself studying the inspector as intently as he was studying them. Despite the man's appearance, there was nothing uncertain about his manner. If Inspector Gregory felt the weight of aristocratic displeasure pressing upon him, he did not show it. What Isabella sensed was that he would be fair and follow the evidence wherever it might lead.

"I shall begin questioning you all shortly," Gregory continued. "For now, I ask that you remain available and do not leave the grounds of Banbury Hall."

Gregory turned towards Lord Banbury. "My lord, I should like to begin the interviews with the maid who discovered the body."

Banbury inclined his head. "I believe that was young Agatha."

The two men left the room together, followed by the constables. Conversation did not resume immediately. Instead, there was strained silence, as though everyone was uncertain whether they were permitted to speak.

Lady Brinkley was the first to break the silence. "Quite dreadful," she whispered loudly. "We are being treated as if we were common criminals. I would have expected better of Banbury." She paused before continuing in a gossiping tone. "Perhaps it is not surprising that Ravensthorpe came to such an end. Even as a child, he had a terrible temper. It was bound to get the better of him one day."

"Temper?" Baron Rice echoed. "He was foxed, that's what he was."

"Even the most foxed men do not stab themselves," Lady Brinkley replied sharply. "And Ravensthorpe was not the sort to be inclined towards self-harm."

Isabella lowered her gaze as she considered these words; Lady Brinkley plainly knew more than most about Ravensthorpe.

"Well, we all saw his behaviour last night for ourselves, did we not? It was quite clear who Ravensthorpe insulted." This was said by a thin-lipped woman whom Isabella recalled was called Mrs James.

As the woman said this, Isabella was keenly aware of the sideways glances being cast her way. She told herself not to react. She had done nothing wrong. Yet she couldn't shake the feeling that at least some of the people at the breakfast table thought she might have.

Ravensthorpe's words echoed once more in her mind. You are being positioned. Her stomach clenched.

After a few minutes, the butler returned and quietly approached Lady Mary, murmuring something. The woman rose and followed him out. Ten minutes later, the footman entered and beckoned to Lady Brinkley.

One by one, the guests were removed and interviewed. Isabella heard footsteps coming and going, and a door she assumed was to the library opening and closing periodically.

Isabella folded her hands in her lap and kept her expression neutral. If she showed signs of anxiety, it would be seen as guilt. If she appeared too composed, that might be interpreted as calculation. Why hadn't she been called in for questioning yet? After all, she had been among the first to see the body.

Finally, the footman approached her. "Miss Hartwell, the inspector will see you now."

All conversation stilled, and her fellow guests did not even attempt to feign disinterest.

Isabella rose with what she hoped was unhurried grace and followed the footman down the corridor towards the library. The door stood ajar. Inside, Gregory stood by the mantelpiece, examining a small notebook, with his two constables discreetly positioned at the side of the room. Lord Banbury was nowhere to be seen.

"Miss Hartwell," the inspector said, gesturing towards a chair facing the writing desk.

She seated herself, smoothing her skirt, acutely aware that her movements might be interpreted as guilty nervousness.

"I understand," Gregory began, "that you were involved in a conversation with Lord Ravensthorpe last evening."

His tone was mild. Observational.

"Yes," Isabella replied. "We spoke briefly in the drawing room before dinner."

"Briefly," he repeated. "Witnesses describe the exchange as quite animated. In fact, it was described to me as..." he glanced down at his notebook. "It was described as a heated quarrel by at least one observer. I was told that you crossed the room to speak with him in quite a pointed manner, and that a rather intense altercation ensued, such that Lord Banbury was compelled to intervene on your behalf."

Isabella felt heat rise in her cheeks. "I would not characterise it as a quarrel of any sort, certainly not a heated one."

"How would you characterise it?"

She hesitated, considering what she wished to say. If she downplayed the exchange, she risked appearing evasive. If she repeated Ravensthorpe's warning about Banbury's finances, she risked entangling herself in matters she did not yet fully understand. It was clear how others, possibly including Lord Banbury, had depicted the interaction. She needed to be truthful yet cautious in her choice of words.

"It was a disagreement," she said carefully. "Lord Ravensthorpe claimed I had been invited here under false pretences."

Gregory raised an eyebrow. "False pretences?"

"He suggested that Lord Banbury intended to seek my investment in the estate and that he might do so somewhat disingenuously," Isabella said as evenly as she could.

"Did Lord Banbury do so?"

"Not directly."

"Indirectly?"

She considered. "Over dinner, he spoke of modernisation, agricultural machinery, and progress. He did ask me about my holdings in Hartwell Ironworks and expressed surprise at my full control of my fortune."

Gregory's pen moved silently and swiftly across the page.

"And how did that make you feel, Miss Hartwell?"

The question startled her. "I felt," she said slowly, "that I was being assessed."

"Assessed?"

"For my naivety, my willingness, and whether I had the authority to sign away my fortune." The words escaped her before she could stop them.

Gregory looked up. "Did you come to that conclusion on your own?"

"Lord Ravensthorpe first suggested it during our conversation before dinner, when he warned me about the estate's finances," she said quickly.

"And how did Lord Ravensthorpe know the state of the estate's finances?"

"I do not know."

Gregory pivoted abruptly. "How did Lord Ravensthorpe appear to you while you were talking?"

"He had been drinking."

"That does not answer the question."

Isabella met his gaze. "Yes. He was agitated. During dinner, I saw him continue to drink to excess. I was sitting at the other end of the table, but I saw Lady Banbury lean towards him and say something. She then indicated that he shouldn't be served any more wine. Shortly after, Lord Ravensthorpe stood and left the room quite abruptly."

"Did he threaten anyone?"

"No."

"Did he threaten you?"

She shook her head. "He warned me."

"Warned you of what?"

"To be careful."

Gregory's pen paused.

"And did you find that warning credible?"

"I found it insulting at the time," Isabella admitted.

He studied her for a long moment. "Insulting? Why was that?"

After a moment's consideration, Isabella decided there was no reason to hide any of the conversation; it was likely that Banbury and others had already relayed what they'd overheard.

"I told Lord Ravensthorpe that I am not a gullible schoolgirl who can be easily manipulated," she said, raising her chin a fraction. "He took offence at my words. Before we could speak any further, Lord Banbury joined us, and the conversation grew even more tense as Ravensthorpe appeared to accuse our host of deception."

"And how did this conversation end, Miss Hartwell?"

"I informed Lord Ravensthorpe that I didn't require his protection and was insulted by the suggestion that I did. I found his warning melodramatic and patronising."

The inspector scribbled away as she spoke. Then he looked up and asked quite pointedly, "I have been told that you retired early for the night. Where did you go?"

"To my room," Isabella answered as calmly as possible.

"Directly?"

"Yes."

"You did not encounter Lord Ravensthorpe again?"

"No."

This was true. She hadn't seen him and only noticed raised voices. Her pulse quickened. Should she mention this? If she kept it to herself and someone else reported hearing the same, she would seem dishonest. And why shouldn't she explain what she'd heard in the corridor the previous evening? Certainly, she couldn't imagine it would implicate her in any way.

"I overheard something," she replied.

Gregory's gaze sharpened.

Isabella explained, "There were raised voices as I passed the east corridor. I could not make out the words. I also heard what sounded like a chair being overturned."

"At what hour was this?"

"I cannot be certain, though I believe I left the drawing room shortly after ten o'clock."

"Did you investigate the noises?"

She hesitated. "I considered it. I did not."

"Why not?"

"It would have been improper. The east corridor is where the single men are staying."

"Improper," he repeated. "Indeed." It was unclear from his tone whether his response was sincere.

Gregory wrote again. "Did you recognise the voices?"

"I thought that one was Lord Ravensthorpe, but I could not be certain." Isabella considered the shadow she'd seen under her door. Was there any reason to mention it? She told herself it had been a maid making her rounds. Still, she wished she had thought to glance at the clock.

Silence settled between them.

At last, Gregory closed his notebook. "Thank you, Miss Hartwell."

"That is all?"

"For now. However, Miss Hartwell, I repeat, do not leave the grounds under any circumstances."

Isabella left the library with her mind racing. Did the inspector believe she was a credible suspect? She was tempted to go straight to her room, but worried that doing so would make her look as if she had something to hide. Instead, she decided to return to the other guests and hold her head high.

As she re-entered the breakfast room, she became acutely aware of the shift in atmosphere. Conversations faltered as she took her seat again. Lady Brinkley's fan halted mid-motion. Baron Rice avoided her gaze. Even the vicar appeared to scrutinise his teacup with unusual intensity.

Only the dowager smiled at her as she sat. Placing her hand on Isabella's arm, she said in a firm, clearly audible voice, "You are very brave, my dear. I am sure the police will quickly determine that the murderer was perhaps a vagrant who gained entry to the house, or a thief who was interrupted while committing his crime."

No one was foolish enough to disagree with her, at least openly. Nevertheless, Isabella sensed an uneasy atmosphere in the room as her fellow guests wondered what exactly she knew. It seemed that everyone present sensed the tension; a fork clattered against porcelain somewhere down the table, and several people jumped in alarm.

A footman appeared beside her with fresh coffee. Isabella made eye contact with him and recognised him as the poor lad who had to serve Ravensthorpe the previous evening. The footman set her cup down carefully. Their eyes met, and he gave her a brief smile. Isabella felt unexpectedly grateful for the small act of kindness.

One change Isabella observed was Lady Banbury's reappearance. Her complexion was pale but composed. If she had been weeping, there was no visible trace of it now. Her gaze flickered to Isabella and then away too quickly.

CHAPTER 7

I nspector Gregory had not ordered them all to remain together, and the company soon began to drift apart. Unsure what to do next, Isabella remained seated with her coffee.

It was the dowager who first noticed the carriage drawing up outside.

"That will be the police surgeon," she announced authoritatively, craning slightly towards the window without rising from her seat. "They must formally certify the death before anything else may proceed."

Several guests turned towards the gravel drive, where a modest black carriage had pulled up. A man stepped down, his hat low, carrying a medical bag.

"A surgeon?" Lady Brinkley whispered. "Must he examine him?"

"Indeed," the dowager replied, with something dangerously close to enthusiasm. "He must determine the cause and approximate time of death. After that, the coroner will be informed. There may be an inquest."

"A jury?" Baron Rice demanded.

"If the matter proves sufficiently interesting," the dowager said serenely.

Isabella stared out of the window. The word interesting had never seemed so ill-chosen.

"How on earth do you know all this, Lady Pembroke?" the vicar inquired in amazement.

"I have been central to solving a significant number of murder investigations over the past few years. Have I not, Isabella dear?" Isabella was too distracted to do much but nod her head.

As they watched, a footman approached the police surgeon to lead him to Ravensthorpe's room. The murmurs grew louder.

"What happens now?" Mrs James asked.

"They will examine him where he lies," the dowager replied. "Afterwards, the body will be removed to somewhere cold. It cannot remain in the house for too long."

The words affected Isabella more deeply than she had expected. He was now merely a body that needed to be removed from the house and no longer a living man. Despite how challenging Ravensthorpe had been in their few interactions, the thought of this made Isabella unbearably sad.

She rose before she quite knew why and drifted towards the hallway, joining a small cluster of guests who gathered there under the guise of stretching their legs. No one admitted to morbid curiosity, yet they lingered and watched.

Upstairs, doors opened and closed. Isabella heard the murmur of male voices and the heavy tread of boots. She couldn't help herself and crept upstairs, hoping no one would notice her.

The layout of the east corridor was such that one could hide in an alcove and still command a view into Ravensthorpe's room, or it would have been possible if the door had not been closed. Isabella waited, and eventually her patience was rewarded when the door opened. Two new constables carried the body out of the room, moving solemnly and deliberately, while the police surgeon followed closely behind. Ravensthorpe lay beneath a dark woollen blanket, his face covered. Inspector Gregory remained in the room.

Isabella shrank herself into the alcove as far as possible. The policemen were too preoccupied with carrying the body to notice her. She watched as they carried it down the staircase and heard them moving through the front hall.

Then, Isabella crept down the stairs and rejoined the dowager. Before she could speak, footsteps sounded again above, and Inspector Gregory descended the staircase, his face thoughtful. In his hand, he held something folded.

Conversations were cut short mid-sentence. "My lord," he said to Banbury, who had just emerged from his study, "may I address your guests?"

Banbury nodded stiffly. "Of course."

Inspector Gregory stood on the first step. His gaze swept over the crowd. "I realise that you are not all gathered here, but for those of you who are, please be aware that during our examination of Lord Ravensthorpe's bedchamber," he said evenly, "an item was recovered."

He extended his hand. On it rested a square of linen. Isabella felt the blood leave her face before she even saw it clearly. She recognised it instantly: fine white linen, with neat embroidery in one corner, I.H. She had carried it the previous evening. She remembered reaching for it during dinner and realising it was gone. She must have left it in the drawing room, on the arm of the settee perhaps, or near the hearth.

Inspector Gregory's eyes met hers. "Miss Hartwell," he said calmly, "would you care to explain how this handkerchief came to be in Lord Ravensthorpe's chamber? I assume the initials I.H. stand for Isabella Hartwell."

A murmur rippled through the assembled crowd. All eyes turned towards her. If there had been suspicious glances earlier, now the other guests appeared prepared to condemn her outright.

"It is mine," Isabella acknowledged, her voice steadier than she felt.

The dowager's hand rested lightly on her arm and gently squeezed it in support. "I had it with me in the drawing room last night," Isabella continued. "I do not know how it came to be upstairs."

Gregory regarded her, his face a mask of inscrutability.

"It was found on the floor near the bed," he said. "Partially concealed by the edge of the coverlet."

"I did not enter Lord Ravensthorpe's chamber last night," Isabella said carefully.

"No one is claiming that you did. Not at present," Gregory replied. "For now, we are merely gathering information."

Baron Rice cleared his throat. "Surely this proves nothing. Anyone may carry a handkerchief. It may have been misplaced." Isabella was surprised that he came to her defence.

"Indeed," the dowager said crisply. "I misplace at least three handkerchiefs a week. Perhaps Lord Ravensthorpe found it in the drawing room and took it as a keepsake."

A nervous laugh ran through the group.

Gregory folded the linen once more. "Perhaps. Nevertheless," he said, "it remains relevant."

He turned to Isabella once more. "You stated earlier that you heard raised voices near the east corridor after ten o'clock," he said.

"Yes."

"And that you did not investigate."

"That is correct."

"Very well." He slipped the handkerchief into his coat pocket. "For the time being, Miss Hartwell, I must ask that you remain available for further questioning."

The words were polite, yet the meaning was clear.

Isabella sensed the weight of every gaze in the room. Sympathy had disappeared. Curiosity sharpened into something colder. Her mind raced. She had left the handkerchief downstairs. She was certain of it. Yet doubt crept in at the edges of her memory. Had she dropped it on the stairs? Had she returned briefly for something? Had someone...?

Of one thing there was no doubt: she hadn't entered Ravensthorpe's room. Perhaps he had taken the handkerchief from the drawing room, or perhaps someone else had left it by his body, whether by accident or on purpose.

The dowager leaned closer. "We will clear up this misunderstanding, my dear. Do not worry. We proved Jeremy's innocence against far greater odds in Brighton, and we will do so again here."

Isabella flashed her a grateful smile; at least someone was on her side.

When she looked up again, the atmosphere in the hall had shifted. Conversations resumed in low, urgent murmurs. Lady Brinkley whispered behind her fan. Mrs James did not bother to lower her voice. Baron Rice, who had so recently defended her, now found the pattern in the carpet utterly fascinating. Lord Banbury was glaring at her. Lady Banbury stood to his right. Now, her expression shuttered as their eyes met.

Whatever credible doubt about her had existed that morning now hardened into something brittle. Even the servants seemed to sense it. Across the room, the footman who had smiled at her earlier stood by the sideboard, his expression composed, hands neatly clasped behind his back. For a fleeting moment, his gaze lifted and met hers, but this time he did not smile.

Isabella drew herself up and threw her shoulders back with purpose. If that handkerchief had been placed in Ravensthorpe's chamber, someone in this house meant to ruin her. Isabella intended to discover who before they succeeded.

Chapter 8

Isabella stood still for a few moments, contemplating her next move. Around her, the other guests had already begun talking again. Now that suspicion had settled so conveniently upon her, they were free to enjoy the investigation as entertainment.

"Why, it is as if I were in the middle of a Sherlock Holmes novel," she heard one lady say to another.

"This is definitely much more exciting than the house party I attended last month," the other replied. "Then, the only bit of suspense was whether their cook would burn the roast two days in a row!"

"You might consider how lacking in substance your lives must be if this is the most interesting thing that has happened to you recently!" Isabella was jolted out of her musings by the dowager's sharp comment. The two women this was aimed at stared in shock at her words.

"Let us retire to a more congenial spot, Isabella dear," the dowager continued. She led Isabella upstairs to her bedchamber. "Our rooms are the only places where we can be certain of even a modicum of privacy," she explained.

Isabella took a seat in one of the two armchairs, while the dowager sat in the other.

"Do not let those harpies ruffle your feathers," the older woman advised. "Not ten minutes ago, they were concerned that the finger of blame would be pointed at them or their husbands." She smiled. "It still may. It goes without saying that we cannot and will not leave the successful conclusion of this investigation to that so-called detective inspector. Now, what is our plan of action?"

Isabella pressed her fingertips together, steadying her thoughts as she considered the question. What mattered first was the handkerchief. It was the only thing linking her to the murder. Where had she left it, and how had it ended up in Ravensthorpe's chamber?

"It must be the handkerchief," she said. "That is the only thing tying me to the murder. If I can determine how it left my possession, I may be able to identify who placed it there."

The dowager inclined her head approvingly. "Excellent. We begin with logistics, not melodrama."

"I had it with me in the drawing room," Isabella continued slowly, casting her mind back to the previous evening. "I remember using it before dinner. I believe I retrieved it while talking to you and Lady Mary. After that..." She closed her eyes briefly, reconstructing the evening. "I cannot recall returning it to my reticule."

"Then you left it behind," the dowager replied decisively.

"I must have left it there, perhaps on the arm of the settee. Or did I carry it with me as we moved to talk with Lady Brinkley?" Isabella asked, second-guessing her memory. "Do you remember seeing me using it?"

The dowager considered the question for a moment. "I do remember you taking it out of your reticule when that birdbrain aunt of Banbury's was twittering on. Let me consider whether you still had it when we moved." The woman thought for a moment. "No, I do not believe you did. You must have dropped it somewhere between the settee and the fireplace."

"That must be the case," Isabella agreed.

"Very good," the dowager said briskly. "Clearly, someone then picked it up, and somehow it was transferred to Ravensthorpe's room. But how? That should be our next point of inquiry. Let us go and observe the drawing room."

The dowager rose and moved towards the door. "We shall not accuse anyone. We shall observe. There is always far more information in what people do not say."

Isabella rose and followed her into the corridor. It would have been the easiest thing to hide in her chamber and let her indignation fester into helplessness. Instead, she drew a deep breath and went downstairs. She resigned herself to being the focus of everyone's attention, at least until she could prove her innocence.

The drawing room door was open. The chairs had been pushed back into place, the fire replenished with fresh coal, the decanters refilled, and the room had been thoroughly tidied. And, at least, for the moment, it was empty.

"Let us reenact your movements," murmured the dowager beside her.

Isabella crossed to the settee where the dowager and Lady Mary had sat the night before. She stood there, as though recalling some trivial detail of the conversation. Only after a moment did she lower her gaze to the cushions. They were perfectly plumped, and their seams were straight.

"If it fell here," Isabella said quietly, "it was most likely found by a servant. But when was the room cleaned? That is a question to ask the housekeeper."

A gentle rustle behind them signalled the arrival of a maid to light the fire. The girl stopped suddenly at the sight of them.

"I beg your pardon, m'lady, miss. I thought the room was empty."

"It nearly is," Isabella said gently. "You may continue."

The maid bobbed a curtsey and moved towards the mantel, though her ears were clearly straining to hear their conversation. It was likely that word of Isabella's supposed guilt had already reached the servants' hall.

"Was this room cleared before the household retired last night?" Isabella asked, as though inquiring about the weather.

"Yes, miss," the maid replied. "The staff went through it when you all went in for your dinner, and again when you went to your beds."

Isabella felt great sympathy for the servants who had to stay awake until all the guests had retired for the night, only to rise early.

"By whom was it cleaned?"

The girl hesitated only briefly. "The maids clean during dinner, and then the footmen stay up late to collect glasses so we can get to our beds. And Mr Myers oversees them."

"The butler," Isabella clarified.

"Yes, miss."

"And who cleared the glasses from this side?" Isabella gestured towards the settee and hearth.

"That would have been one of the footmen."

"Thank you," Isabella said, dismissing the girl with a nod. "Please leave us. We will only be a few more minutes."

When the maid had gone, the dowager looked at her keenly. "What are you thinking?" she asked.

Isabella moved slowly towards the tall window where Ravensthorpe had sat in shadow the previous evening. "Is it possible that one of the maids picked up the handkerchief? Perhaps the maid who went into Ravensthorpe's room this morning dropped it in her haste when she saw the body."

Isabella turned back towards the door.

"Let us not appear to skulk," the dowager advised. "We shall rejoin the others. If you are to be the principal suspect, you must do so with composure and your head held high."

They stepped into the corridor just as a figure approached from the opposite direction, carrying a polished tray. He stopped just short of colliding with them. Like most footmen in grand houses, he was tall and handsome. Isabella recognised him as the footman who had smiled sympathetically at her earlier.

The man's expression was as composed as ever; his posture remained straight, and his eyes were lowered in professional deference.

"M'lady. Miss," he said smoothly, inclining his head.

Isabella responded to the gesture with composed calm. "I am sorry. I didn't catch your name when you served me this morning."

For a brief moment, his gaze lifted and met hers. Polite. Neutral. Untroubled.

"Hargreaves," he replied. The man nodded again and moved past them.

Isabella watched him walk away.

"He was serving during dinner. But was he the footman who waited up to clear the glasses in the room?" she said quietly. "The housekeeper is the next person we should speak to," she decided.

By chance, a maid was passing by at that moment. Isabella asked for directions to the housekeeper's room, and the girl shyly offered to show her the way.

The housekeeper, Mrs Patrick, was a no-nonsense woman who had started at Banbury Hall as a young scullery maid. She had lived through good times and bad with the family, but she'd never experienced a murder inquiry. The servant gossip mill was as efficient as in any other grand house, so Mrs Patrick had already heard about the suspicion directed at Isabella. When she saw the two guests enter her office, she sighed inwardly; this couldn't bode well.

She stood to welcome Isabella and the dowager and offered them seats.

"Lady Pembroke, Miss Hartwell, how can I help you this morning?"

The dowager looked the woman up and down. Very little happened in a house like Banbury Hall without the knowledge of the housekeeper or butler. The question was: what did this woman know, and how might she be persuaded to cooperate with their investigation?

Although the dowager's usual attitude towards servants was dismissive at best and condescending more often than not, she decided that this situation called for a softness that did not come naturally to her.

"Mrs Patrick, is it not?" the dowager began. Luckily, the woman had mentioned her name when she showed the dowager to her bedchamber on their first day. The housekeeper nodded. "Excellent. First, let me say how well-run I find Banbury Hall. I am the first to notice a badly organised staff."

Like most housekeepers, Mrs Patrick was adept at quickly sizing up guests. It took no more than her brief first interaction with the dowager countess to realise she was a woman who did not suffer fools gladly and would be quick to criticise. She was the type of visitor who ran her finger along mantelpieces, searching for dust. This shift in her manner warned Mrs Patrick that the conversation was about to become awkward.

She was proven correct as the dowager continued, "We are in need of your assistance. If you would be so kind as to spare us some time."

Isabella could tell from the tension around the housekeeper's mouth that the woman would be willing to help, but only to a certain extent. They needed this woman's full cooperation; if the servants could not be persuaded to assist, then Isabella had little hope of proving her innocence.

Any servant contradicting her timeline in any way could ruin her credibility.

"Mrs Patrick," Isabella began carefully, "I imagine that word of what the police discovered in Lord Ravensthorpe's bedchamber has reached the servants' hall by now."

The housekeeper said nothing, but a slight incline of her head suggested that news had already reached the staff.

"I am entirely innocent," Isabella said in a clear tone that held no apology.

"Of course, Miss Hartwell," Mrs Patrick replied evenly.

The dowager stepped in. "Whatever opinions you and your staff may hold on the matter, they are irrelevant to this conversation. Miss Hartwell and I require information, nothing more, so that the police may have the facts before them."

Mrs Patrick pursed her lips and simply nodded.

"Excellent," said the dowager. "Then, we need to find out which maids cleaned the drawing room while the guests were dining, and which footmen cleared the glasses at the end of the evening."

With a barely perceptible sigh before answering, Mrs Patrick replied, "The maids were Agatha Wilson and Tilly Coates, and the footmen Jimmy Hargreaves and Andy Carter."

After tersely answering a few more questions, the housekeeper rose and said more curtly now, "If there is nothing else, I do have to go through tonight's menu with her ladyship."

CHAPTER 9

Despite the dowager's early encouragement not to be cowed, Isabella determined she was unable to face luncheon in the dining room. The thought of all eyes on her and the continuation of the awkward silence, or worse, unsubtle accusations, was more than she could bear at that moment. She knew she couldn't avoid the other guests for long, but she decided she needed some space from them for the time being.

As she and the dowager left the servant hall after their conversation with Mrs Patrick, she voiced these feelings.

In a voice kinder than she used with most people, the dowager responded, "I am sympathetic, Isabella dear. I really am. Nonetheless, you should know that avoiding their company will not prevent the gossip; if anything, it will make it worse. Your absence will be perceived as guilt."

Isabella sighed; she knew the dowager was right, yet she couldn't bring herself to walk into the lion's den just yet.

Correctly interpreting the sigh, the dowager said, "I will be by your side. Etiquette be damned, I will sit next to you and fend off all attacks."

At that, Isabella smiled; she knew she had the fiercest bulldog by her side in the petite septuagenarian, and for that, she was profoundly grateful.

"Let us compromise," Isabella said. "I will take you up on the offer for dinner tonight, and we will face them together. But can we eat in one of our rooms for now?"

The dowager smiled indulgently and consented to the plan. The two women then returned to Isabella's room and rang the bell for a maid to come. They then set about documenting what Mrs Patrick had told them.

When the dowager investigated with Tabitha and Wolf, they used notecards pinned to a corkboard to capture clues. This innovation, which was started by Tabitha, proved to be a very effective way to document and categorise information. Although the old woman would never credit Tabitha, the dowager did recognise how useful the system had been throughout the many murder inquiries the group had worked on together over the past two years.

Now, she wondered if there was a way to replicate this system. Clearly, they didn't have access to a corkboard. Nevertheless, they could make notecards using the writing paper in their rooms and at least approximate the technique. The dowager made this suggestion, and Isabella rose and began cutting the writing paper into manageable pieces. Next, they settled down to review what they knew so far.

They agreed that Mrs Patrick had been careful in her answers. Careful, but not evasive.

"We must distinguish possibility from conjecture," Isabella suggested, her pencil poised.

"By all means," the dowager replied. "Let us untangle this web. I must say, this is a case worthy of The Investigative Countess."

Isabella looked up, curiosity writ large across her face.

With a gleam in her eye, the dowager explained, "When it first became evident that Tabitha and Wolf were attempting to bypass my assistance in their investigations, however unbelievable that might be, I determined that the wise course was to branch out on my own. I then had my own cards made up."

She then reached into her reticule, produced a silver carrying case, and handed Isabella a calling card inscribed with the words: *The Investigative Countess, Rapier-Sharp Logic paired with Great Insight and Boldness. A Private Inquiry Agent.*

Isabella couldn't help but smile. While she had the greatest fondness and respect for the dowager, she knew the woman gleefully tormented her erstwhile daughter-in-law on a regular basis. Although Tabitha acknowledged how much their relationship had improved over the years, the dowager still seemed to take a positive delight in tweaking the younger woman's nose. If it were true that Tabitha and Wolf sometimes avoided including the dowager, this was likely at least one of the reasons.

As she took the card, Isabella said, "I consider myself very fortunate to have such rapier-sharp logic at my disposal." Her words were teasing, but she was sincerely grateful to have the dowager by her side, both as a friend and as an investigative partner. She couldn't imagine how much more difficult the current circumstances would be if she faced them alone.

Then Isabella began to write on a notecard: *Drawing room. Cleared twice. First, during dinner, by the maids. Second, after the guests withdrew, by the footmen.*

"Now, let us map this to what the housekeeper told us," the dowager suggested.

"Two footmen were on late duty, Carter and Hargreaves, under Mr Myers's oversight," Isabella observed as she wrote.

The dowager made a faint sound. "Now, all we have to do is determine which is which. I must say, I find it astonishing that tall and handsome are still the primary qualifications for a footman these days. It makes them nearly impossible to tell apart. Personally, I consider competence, honesty, and loyalty to be more valuable qualities."

Moving on from the footmen, Isabella continued, "The two maids who cleaned the room during dinner were Agatha Wilson and Tilly Coates." She paused. "I recall that Agatha was the maid who discovered Ravensthorpe's body. If I dropped the handkerchief before dinner, it would have been found during the first clearing. The most obvious answer is that Agatha picked it up, perhaps intending to return it the next morning. In the panic of discovering the body, she then dropped it in Ravensthorpe's bedchamber."

"Then let us summon this Agatha and put this matter to rest," the dowager exclaimed with the authority of a general issuing commands to a battalion.

As she uttered these words, there was a knock on the door. It was a maid responding to their earlier tug on the bell cord. She was no more than sixteen years old and a sturdy, ruddy-faced young woman. Isabella was certain this was Agatha; she remembered the girl crying in the housekeeper's arms that morning outside the scene of the crime. How fortunate!

After inviting the maid into the room, Isabella began by requesting that food be sent up. The girl nodded and curtsied, expecting to be dismissed.

Instead, Isabella said in a gentle, kindly voice, "You are the maid who discovered Lord Ravensthorpe's body this morning, are you not?"

Looking like a fox run to ground, the girl nodded mutely.

"Is your name Agatha?" Isabella continued in the same soft tone.

Again, the girl nodded.

"That must have been dreadful to discover, Agatha," Isabella said kindly. "You are very brave to be back at work so soon. Lord and Lady Banbury are fortunate to have such a maid in their employ."

Isabella's words appeared to soothe the maid's unease at being addressed so directly, and her eyes lost some of their startled expression.

Realising she needed to ask her question sooner rather than later, Isabella began, "I lost a handkerchief before dinner last night. Mrs Patrick mentioned that you were one of the two maids who tidied the drawing room during our meal. Did you come across it by any chance?"

Agatha's face was filled with terror. "I didn't steal it, miss. I promise. I was going to return it to Polly, your lady's maid."

"I do not doubt that, Agatha," Isabella assured her.

"I put it down on the kitchen table when I came back to the servants' hall. We were so busy that I forgot about it. Later, when I looked, it was gone. I'm so sorry, miss. I should have told Polly, but then I had the shock this morning, and it went clean out of my head."

Isabella and the dowager exchanged looks at this explanation; why would someone take the handkerchief if not to implicate her in the murder? Even as she thought this, Isabella second-guessed herself; perhaps another maid had merely seen it on the table and taken it for herself. Isabella realised that for a young servant girl, the pretty, delicate, lacy handkerchief would be finer than anything else she owned. Even so, it gave them a starting point. Whoever had taken the handkerchief had been in the servants' hall at some point the previous evening.

Then, she considered how many servants a house as large as Banbury Hall might have. And that didn't include all the maids and valets accompanying the large group of guests. She imagined the kitchen table at the centre of the servants' hall. The number of people who might have passed by it, even in a short period, was large.

"Agatha, because you are a brave girl, I need to ask you to be so again." Isabella smiled encouragingly at the maid. "I need you to tell Inspector Gregory what you have just told me."

Seeing the girl's expression turn fearful, she added, "I promise you that you are not in trouble. You were quite right to pick up the handkerchief with the intention of returning it to my maid. However, you may not realise this, but it somehow made its way into Lord Ravensthorpe's bedchamber and is now being considered evidence that I might have had something to do with his death. So, you can see how important it is that the inspector be told the truth."

Although her fear seemed unabated, Agatha nodded obediently. "Yes, miss."

"Will you come with me now to find him? I promise you that I will stay by your side and ensure that nothing happens to you."

Agatha's expression suggested that she placed little faith in those above stairs looking out for her, yet the girl knew she had little choice but to comply.

Isabella suspected the dowager planned to accompany them to find Inspector Gregory. Still, she'd experienced the woman's glee at putting policemen in their place on enough occasions to know this should be avoided if possible. There was a time and a place for the dowager's imperiousness, but this was not one of them.

"Lady Pembroke, Agatha and I should speak with Inspector Gregory immediately, if possible. I will join you here afterwards to continue our note-taking over food."

She could see the dowager preparing to assert herself, then holding back. Had it been Tabitha and Wolf, the woman would almost certainly have interpreted these words as an attempt to exclude her from an investigation. However, Isabella had earned herself a certain amount of grace, at least for the time being, and instead the older woman indicated her acceptance of Isabella's words.

Isabella was relieved to have averted that skirmish. Agatha's account must reach Gregory soon and without interference.

Before the dowager could say anything that might change the maid's mind, Isabella gently guided the girl downstairs to find the inspector.

CHAPTER 10

Inspector Gregory received them in the library. When Isabella entered with Agatha at her side, the man looked up without rising. Social etiquette no longer seemed to extend to Isabella. The slightest lift of his brows betrayed surprise at her unbidden arrival.

The room looked as if it had been hastily rearranged. The writing desk stood in the centre of the carpet, with a straight-backed chair set opposite it. Perhaps this was considered a more imposing arrangement for questioning. One constable stood by the window, while the other lingered near the door. An open notebook lay before the inspector, his pen resting along its spine.

"Miss Hartwell," Inspector Gregory said warily. "You wish to speak with me?"

"Yes, Inspector," Isabella ignored the tone of the question and replied in an open manner, "This is Agatha Wilson, a maid at Banbury Hall. She has information about the handkerchief found in Lord Ravensthorpe's chamber."

Gregory's gaze shifted to the girl. Agatha's hands were clenched in the folds of her apron. She did not lift her eyes.

"Agatha Wilson," he repeated, glancing down at his notes. "I questioned you earlier."

"Yes, sir," the girl whispered. "I'm sorry, sir. I was all at sixes and sevens and forgot about it altogether."

Gregory sighed and gestured towards the chair opposite the desk. "Sit."

Agatha perched on the edge of the chair, as uncomfortable before her betters as she was in the situation itself.

Gregory briefly turned his attention to Isabella. "Miss Hartwell, you may remain; however, I must insist that you allow the girl to answer for herself."

Isabella inclined her head and moved slightly aside, positioning herself out of Agatha's line of sight.

Gregory folded his hands on the desk. "Miss Wilson, let us begin at the beginning. State your duties from last evening."

Agatha swallowed. "I was assigned to the drawing room, sir, during dinner. Me and Tilly Coates."

"At what hour did you enter the drawing room?"

"Shortly after the dinner bell, sir."

"And what was the state of the room?"

"Glasses and cups about, sir. Cushions disturbed. The fire low. The usual"

"You then tidied the room?"

"Yes, sir. It's what we do every evening while the master and mistress eat."

"Describe what that entailed."

"Entailed, sir?" Agatha stuttered.

"What did you do in the drawing room last night?" the inspector said, rephrasing his question.

Agatha glanced nervously back towards Isabella, then caught herself and fixed her eyes on the desk. "Straightening chairs, sir. Clearing glasses and the like. Brushing crumbs. Setting the room to rights."

Gregory nodded once. "And what happened while you were tidying?"

Agatha's fingers tightened on her apron. "I found Miss Hartwell's handkerchief on the floor."

"Describe this item."

"A white handkerchief, sir. Fine linen. With lace at the edge. Initials in one corner."

"And what were those initials?"

"I.H., sir."

Gregory's pen started to move. "And you are certain of this?" he asked. When Agatha nodded, he pressed on, "Where exactly did you find this handkerchief?"

"Near the hearth rug, sir. Just by the leg of the settee."

"Folded or unfolded?"

"Unfolded, sir. As if it had slipped from someone's hand."

"And you are certain of its location?"

"Yes, sir."

"Was anyone else present at that moment?"

"No, sir. Tilly was at the far end, near the pianoforte."

Gregory's pen paused. "Did Miss Coates observe you retrieve the handkerchief?"

"Not that I know of, sir."

"Did you inform her of it?"

"No, sir."

"Why not?" The inspector's voice had a sharp, accusatory tone. In response, the maid flinched.

"I was going to give it to Polly, sir. Miss Hartwell's maid. I promise I was," Agatha said after a brief hesitation.

Gregory studied her silently for a moment. "So, you removed the item from the drawing room and pocketed it?"

"Yes, sir."

"At what hour?"

"I don't know precisely, sir. It was before the ladies returned from dinner for their tea and coffee."

Gregory nodded again. "What did you then do with the handkerchief?"

"I put it down in the servants' hall, sir."

"Be exact. Where in the hall?"

"On the kitchen table, by a pile of plates. I didn't want to forget to give it to Polly, so I placed it where I would see it later when she came by."

"Was anything beneath it?"

"No, sir."

Gregory leaned back slightly. He regarded the young maid carefully. "Who was present in the servants' hall at that time?" he pressed.

Agatha's breathing quickened. "Cook, sir. And one of the scullery maids. I think. I'm not sure. But there were lots of people coming and going. Maids getting ready to go to their mistress's rooms to help them after dinner. Valets. Footmen coming and going with items for dinner, and the like."

"And you didn't see anyone take the handkerchief?"

"Not that I can say, sir."

Gregory allowed the silence to stretch.

"Not that you can say," he repeated.

"No, sir."

"Very well. What did you do after placing the handkerchief upon the table?"

"I went to fetch fresh coals for the drawing room fire, sir."

"And when you returned?"

"I forgot that I'd put it there, we were that busy. Much later, just before I was ready to go up to bed for the night, I remembered it, went to the table and saw that it was gone."

"Did you ask after it?"

"No, sir."

"Why not?"

Agatha's face flushed. "I thought perhaps Polly had come by, seen it, and taken it back to Miss Hartwell. I didn't think... I didn't think it would signify."

"And so, you did not inform the housekeeper."

"No, sir."

"Did you check with Miss Hartwell's maid?"

"I meant to. But I didn't see her that night, and the next morning, well, by the time I would have expected to see her, I'd been in Lord Ravensthorpe's room, and... well..." At this, the girl's eyes began to well with tears.

"Indeed, we need not go into that again," Gregory said, sparing the girl the distress of reliving her morning discovery and himself the annoyance of a sobbing female. His pen scratched steadily across the page.

"Miss Wilson, earlier, I questioned you about finding Lord Ravensthorpe's body this morning. Yet you failed to mention this handkerchief?"

Now, Agatha fought but failed to hold back the tears. "Yes, sir. I had quite forgotten it. Until Miss Hartwell spoke of it just now and told me it had been found in the room. And before that, I had no reason to think it mattered to you." There was defiance in the maid's tone, and Isabella respected it. Gregory, for all his fairness, was pressing harder than seemed necessary.

Gregory tapped his notebook with his pen. "Did you not hear that the article was found partially concealed beneath the coverlet in Lord Ravensthorpe's bedchamber? I find it hard to believe this news hasn't yet reached the servants' hall."

Agatha's face turned pale. "No, sir. I did not know that. Mrs Patrick allowed me to return to my room and lie down after the shock I had this morning. I went as soon as I'd finished talking to you. I only returned to my duties in time to be summoned by Miss Hartwell."

"And you are sure that you did not enter Lord Ravensthorpe's chamber yesterday evening?"

"I'm sure. Another maid turned down the rooms last night."

"And you are certain you didn't place or drop the handkerchief in that room this morning before you discovered... well, before you saw the body?"

"No, sir. I swear it."

Gregory regarded her for a long moment.

"I do not require your oath," he said quietly. "I require the truth."

Agatha nodded, trembling. Briefly, she glanced back towards the door, as if longing for an escape. As she did so, Isabella saw the fear on the young girl's face; as if finding the body wasn't enough, now she had been plunged even deeper into the heart of the murder investigation.

Gregory then addressed Isabella.

"Miss Hartwell, you have heard this account before, I would imagine."

"Yes, Inspector."

"You did not witness Miss Wilson finding the handkerchief."

"No."

"Yet you are certain that your maid didn't retrieve it?"

Isabella considered the question. She'd missed the opportunity to pose this question to Polly prior to escorting Agatha to speak with the inspector, and now she regretted this oversight.

"I am not certain, inspector," she admitted. "However, unlike Agatha, my maid has been in and out of the servants' hall all morning. I imagine she has heard about the handkerchief found at the scene, and I am sure she would have said something if it were in her possession. That said, I will confirm this as soon as I return to my room."

Gregory inclined his head once, though whether in acknowledgement of her explanation or in questioning it, Isabella had no way of knowing; the man was definitely difficult to read.

The inspector refocused his attention on Agatha. "Miss Wilson," he said finally, "is there anything else relevant you need to share with me? If you are withholding anything, now is the time to reconsider."

Agatha shook her head vehemently. "No, sir."

He watched her for a moment longer before indicating that she might leave. Then he addressed the constable at the door.

"See that Miss Tilly Coates is brought to me."

The constable left without saying a word. Agatha stood unsteadily. Isabella stepped aside to let her pass, offering her a brief, grateful smile.

"The handkerchief moved," Gregory mused. "First, from the drawing room to the servants' hall. Then, from the servants' hall to Lord Ravensthorpe's bedchamber. That movement may or may not be accidental, Miss Hartwell." As he said this, he fixed her with a purposeful stare.

Isabella said nothing in response, waiting to see where the inspector would lead this line of thought.

Gregory stared at her directly. "While this testimony suggests you did not personally carry the article upstairs, it doesn't establish who did."

Isabella held his gaze. "I understand," she replied. Then, worried about how her observation might be received, yet certain she needed to say it anyway, she added, "Though one might surmise that whoever did is the person who killed Lord Ravensthorpe."

In a noncommittal tone, he replied, "Possibly. Possibly. I have learned not to make too many assumptions in the early stages of an investigation, Miss Hartwell."

Then, as if to confirm this assertion, he added, "I would still ask you not to leave the grounds at any point, at least for the time being."

"I will not." If she was disappointed by his reluctance to grant her absolution, Isabella did her best to conceal it. Her previous opinion of Gregory, that he was a fair man, held, at least for now, and she did not doubt he would take Agatha's testimony seriously.

Gregory's eyes narrowed slightly, though not unkindly. "I will make Lord and Lady Banbury aware of this latest revelation; I can imagine that it has been quite uncomfortable for you, being confined here after my remarks this morning." Then he stood, signalling dismissal.

"Thank you, Inspector Gregory," Isabella said with genuine appreciation for the man's understanding.

As Isabella left the library, she allowed herself only the briefest sense of vindication. Progress had been made, but Gregory had not cleared her, and he would not prove her innocence for her. If someone took the handkerchief and left it at the murder scene, then that person deliberately moved evidence to implicate her. She meant to prove it.

CHAPTER 11

Inspector Gregory had forbidden her to leave the grounds, but he had said nothing about remaining indoors. After the stale air of Banbury Hall, heavy with suspicion and speculation, Isabella wanted only to be outside. The day was bright, with the gardens in full spring bloom, and she suddenly found she had no appetite for food

Without bothering to retrieve her cloak, Isabella slipped out of the front door and descended the shallow stone steps. She was mindful of the other guests' watching eyes and kept to the side of the house, following the gravel path until it curved behind a cluster of yew and box trees.

Isabella remembered the bluebells carpeting the small copse, but the air was colder than she expected, so she stayed in the sun rather than venture into the shade of the woods.

Beyond the clipped hedging, the land opened into a gentle meadow slope. Buttercups shone in the sunlight. Hawthorn hedges along the boundary fence were laden with blossoms; their scent was faint yet sweet. It was all quite idyllic and restful for the mind, or would have been if it weren't for the murder inquiry.

Isabella walked towards the yellow carpet of buttercups in the distance. Despite her best efforts, the beauty and tranquillity surrounding her did nothing to ease the whirling of her thoughts. Someone must have taken her handkerchief upstairs and deliberately placed it near the bed. Was it the murderer? That thought settled like a stone in her stomach.

She hadn't gone far from the formal gardens before voices reached her on the gentle breeze. It sounded like a man and a woman arguing; these weren't gardeners at work. Isabella instinctively slowed her pace. Even from this distance, she could hear the tension in their conversation.

The voices seemed to come from beyond a low rise near the hawthorn hedge. Isabella hesitated, then moved more quietly, glad that the grass beneath her muffled her footsteps.

"...should never have let him know," a woman's voice said sharply.

Isabella was certain the voice belonged to Lady Banbury. She froze and listened carefully.

There was a brief pause, then a voice she was equally sure belonged to Lord Banbury responded in a lower, strained tone. "He already knew."

"You told him more than you should have."

"I told him no more than he could have discovered for himself. He insisted on understanding what the loan was for." Lord Banbury did not shout, but spoke in a tightly restrained voice that hinted at barely contained fury.

Isabella moved behind the wide trunk of a sycamore and stayed still.

Lady Banbury spoke again, more urgently. "If he had revealed all he knew, it would have ruined us."

Isabella's pulse quickened.

"Lower your voice," Banbury muttered. "We came out here to avoid being overheard, but that does not give you licence to squawk like a fishwife."

"Do not command me," his wife replied. "You have been reckless. Reckless and foolish. Inviting him here, of all places. Was it to humiliate me?"

"I invited him because he left me no choice. I did not invite him to discuss the estate in the drawing room before a dozen witnesses," Banbury snapped. "He chose that moment. I am not sure I even believe he was the drunken sot he appeared to be last night. I think the entire thing was a charade, staged for the love of melodrama."

There was a faint crunch of a shoe on gravel, as if one of them had turned quickly. Isabella froze, worried she was about to be discovered.

"You should have found a way to stop him earlier," Lady Banbury said.

The words hit Isabella like a physical blow. Stop him. The meadow buzzed with bees. Birdsong filled the air. The incongruity of the setting made the phrase sound even darker.

Banbury's reply came low and furious. "And how, precisely, was I to do that?"

"You could have persuaded him."

"I tried."

"You might have paid him some of what was owed."

"With what?" Banbury's laugh was short and bitter. "You know the accounts as well as I do. Besides, I do not think he cared about the money; he enjoyed the leverage the debt gave him far too much."

A cold ripple of understanding washed over Isabella. The estate. This was precisely what Ravensthorpe had tried to warn her about. Had he threatened to expose the estate's true condition, even beyond what he said to her the previous evening?

Lady Banbury's voice, when it came again, was different. Less angry, more wounded. "You should never have turned to him for assistance."

"Is that so? I consider it the very least the man owed me, owed us, given everything!"

"Are you suggesting this is my fault in some way?" she demanded. "I was not the one who made poor investments and reckless decisions about the estate."

"Perhaps if your father had kept his promise, those decisions might have paid off," Banbury shot back. "I kept my end of the bargain and married you after Ravensthorpe deflowered you and then refused to do the gentlemanly thing."

There was a stunned silence.

Isabella sensed the air shift, as if something more menacing had entered the exchange.

"What do you mean by that?" Lady Banbury asked, her voice dropping almost to a whisper that Isabella needed to strain to hear.

"I mean," Banbury said carefully, "the man was a cad, yet you insisted on his remaining in our orbit."

"You are being unfair. That was a long time ago, and Ravensthorpe had his reasons. You know he did. Before his brother's death, he had no expectations." Lady Banbury's voice wavered slightly as she uttered Ravensthorpe's name.

"Am I being unfair?" Banbury's tone sharpened. "He acted as if he still had a claim on your attention, which you indulged and even encouraged for far too long. Until suddenly, you wanted nothing more to do with him, by which time it was too late; I owed him too much."

Isabella's mind raced. A debt. A former attachment. A spurned lover.

Lady Banbury replied, but a brittleness crept back into her voice. "He could be cruel and selfish, but at least *his* love for me was genuine," she said.

"And now he is dead," Banbury said abruptly.

Lady Banbury spoke again, still softly but no less urgently. "If Gregory discovers what Ravensthorpe intended to reveal..."

"He will not," Banbury interrupted.

"How can you be so certain?"

"Because I have handled the matter."

Isabella exhaled sharply. *Handled the matter.* What did that mean?

"Do not look at me like that," Lady Banbury said in a petulant tone.

"Like what?"

"As though I wished this."

"You wished him out of the way, did you not?"

The phrase hung in the air.

"I did not mean..." she stopped herself. "You know I did not mean it like this."

Lord Banbury didn't reply immediately. Finally, he said, "Whatever your intention, we must now face the consequences."

"Do not lecture me about consequences," she retorted. "If the truth about the estate had come out, what then? Bankruptcy? Public humiliation? The loss of everything?"

"And you believe this is better?" he demanded.

There was a lengthy pause. "I believe," Lady Banbury said slowly, "that what is done is done."

The finality in her tone made Isabella's heart pound.

Banbury drew a sharp breath. "If anyone hears you speaking in that manner, there could be even more dire consequences yet!"

"Which is why we are having this conversation in a field," she replied tartly.

Isabella did not wait to hear any more. A sudden realisation of how close she was to the couple overwhelmed her. If either of them stepped around the hedge...

She retreated cautiously, keeping the sycamore trunk between herself and the hawthorn. Only after there was a distance between her and the Banburys did she turn around completely and walk away.

Her thoughts were in turmoil. The Banburys had argued about the estate, Ravensthorpe's threats, and ultimately about wishing him "out of the way." Yet none of it was a confession. Every phrase could be interpreted in more than one way. Even wishing him out of the way might mean wishing him gone from their lives.

And yet.

The Banburys had motive, that was plain enough. Debt, humiliation, exposure, old resentments. Still, motive was not a confession, and every phrase she had heard admitted of another reading, however sinister it might have sounded. Suddenly, even with the sunlight on her skin, Isabella felt a shiver run down her spine.

If they had reason to silence Ravensthorpe, then her handkerchief in his chamber might have served the couple very well indeed. Could the violence in Ravensthorpe's bedchamber the night before have been something other than sudden madness? Perhaps it was born of something much deeper, darker, and more premeditated.

Yet would the Banburys really invite suspicion into their own house? Then again, a house party, with an eclectic crowd gathered under one roof, might provide the perfect cover for murder.

Isabella had gone outside to clear her mind, but she was returning indoors with her thoughts in even greater turmoil than before.

CHAPTER 12

As she returned from the meadow, Isabella found herself at the door to the servants' hall. Through the window, she observed the cook kneading bread with steady, practised motions, her forearms dusted with flour. The large range glowed behind her; copper pots hung in neat ranks.

Isabella paused. Even in America, one did not barge into the staff's inner sanctum without reason, and certainly not in a house that was not one's own. Yet the alternative was to ask Lady Banbury's permission to question her servants in some upstairs parlour, under her watchful eye. In light of what Isabella recently overheard in the meadow, this was not a feasible option.

Yet she needed to find out who might have taken the handkerchief; someone must have noticed something. Isabella realised she needed to be decisive and act. She took a deep breath, squared her shoulders, and pushed the door open.

All conversation suddenly faltered. The rhythmic thud of dough against wood slowed, then stopped. A scullery maid froze, a stack of plates in her hands. The footman, who had earlier introduced himself as Hargreaves, had been polishing a tray at the long central table and now straightened, the soft leather cloth still in his hand.

Isabella couldn't remember the last time she felt so conspicuous.

Fortunately, Mrs Patrick was standing near the range, quietly discussing household matters with a maid. The housekeeper recovered herself more quickly than the others and stepped forward.

"Miss Hartwell," she said smoothly, "is there anything I can assist you with?" The words were courteous. The woman's meaning was not.

Isabella could not let herself be cowed. The only way through was to use the authority that came with being above stairs.

"I hope so," she replied, attempting to project composure and command of the situation. "I fear I am intruding, but I have a small matter I hoped to clarify. It concerns last evening."

A flicker crossed Mrs Patrick's face at that phrase, though she showed no outward sign of resistance. "If this again concerns the unfortunate events in Lord Ravensthorpe's chamber, Inspector Gregory has already spoken to the staff at length," she said.

"I am aware of that," Isabella said kindly but firmly. "I do not wish to impede his work. I merely seek to understand the house's usual routine. I find that sometimes clarity lies in the ordinary details of life." She paused, unsure how much she wanted to explain herself, but then realised she might have to say at least something more.

In a lower voice, she continued, "As I said earlier, given that my handkerchief was found in Lord Ravensthorpe's room, the shadow of suspicion hangs over me. I feel I must do whatever I can to help clear my name."

That answer, though perhaps not fully explanatory, seemed adequate, and Mrs Patrick inclined her head. "Very well, miss. What would you know now?"

"You told me earlier that the drawing room is cleared during dinner," she began. "By the maids."

"Yes, miss. As I mentioned before, two maids handle the cleaning while the family and guests dine, and two footmen finish up after the master and his guests have retired for the night." This was said rather pointedly.

"And the bedchambers?" Isabella asked. "Are they attended to before dinner?" She felt embarrassed to realise she rarely paid attention to this, simply accepting it as a task someone took care of sometime before she retired for the night, wherever she was staying.

Mrs Patrick nodded. "Turned down in the late afternoon. Fires laid. Water refreshed. Curtains drawn. There is rarely cause for a maid to return unless summoned."

Isabella absorbed this information.

"Then after dinner," she said, as if merely thinking aloud, "who would have reason to be on the upper floors?"

"One of the footmen remains on late duty until past midnight as needed," Mrs Patrick replied. "To answer bells and escort any gentleman who has taken too much wine. Last evening, that would have been Carter."

The footman at the table resumed polishing the tray, though his strokes slowed. Perhaps he was the footman on duty that night and wondered whether he was about to be drawn into the conversation.

"And the gentlemen's valets?" Isabella continued.

"They attend to their own masters, of course. If a gentleman calls for assistance, his valet would answer."

Isabella nodded thoughtfully. "But otherwise, no one has any reason to wander around upstairs?"

Mrs Patrick's mouth tensed before she responded. "This is not an inn, Miss Hartwell. Our staff do not wander about."

"I did not mean to imply they did," Isabella said quickly. "I am merely trying to understand how an object might move from one part of the house to another without attracting notice."

Silence settled briefly over the kitchen.

"A house under mine and Mr Myers's care is not lawless," Mrs Patrick said in a voice that suggested resentment at any such suggestion. "Duties are assigned and performed efficiently. We accept nothing else, and the staff knows it."

"I have no doubt of that," Isabella assured her. "Which is precisely why I am puzzled."

She allowed her gaze to drift, not accusingly but curiously, towards the footman. "Earlier, you said that Carter was the footman on duty late last night, correct?" she asked, though she knew the answer.

"Indeed," Mrs Patrick confirmed, a little impatient at repeating herself. "Hargreaves was on duty downstairs, and Carter had the late watch."

At his name, the footman's hand paused for a brief instant before resuming his task.

Isabella continued as though she noticed nothing. "And if a gentleman required coal or assistance with his fire after the rooms had been turned down?"

"The scuttles are filled before dinner," Mrs Patrick replied. "There would be no need. However, if a bell were rung, the footman on duty would answer."

"And none of the staff reported any unusual bell calls?" she asked, turning slightly towards the footman as she said this.

Mrs Patrick hesitated slightly. "Not to me."

The footman set down the tray he had been polishing. "If I may, miss," he said, keeping his eyes respectfully lowered, "Lord Ravensthorpe was not known for retiring early. It would not have been unusual for him to move about after the others. He sometimes called for more brandy."

"Indeed," Isabella said evenly. "And did he last night?"

"Not that I was aware of," the footman replied.

There was nothing insolent in his tone. Even so, a tightness remained in the man's posture and expression, as if he were bracing himself. For the moment, Isabella let the matter rest.

"I appreciate your patience," she said to Mrs Patrick. "I will not trouble you further. I only wished to understand the servants' movements last evening more clearly."

"The order of this house is quite firm, Miss Hartwell," Mrs Patrick replied, not unkindly.

"Of that I have no doubt," Isabella said.

As she turned to leave, she paused at the threshold before turning back and, almost as an afterthought, said, "One more question, if I may. Agatha told me she found my handkerchief in the drawing room last night and planned to return it to my maid, Polly. She left it on the table at one point, and when she returned, it was gone. Did you see anyone pick it up?"

Mrs Patrick's brow furrowed. "Agatha's a good, honest girl. If she said she meant to return it, I'm sure she did." Turning to the servants in the room, she asked, "Did anyone see a handkerchief on the table last night?"

A chorus of negatives followed, with heads shaking around the room.

Isabella inclined her head. "Thank you for your time, Mrs Patrick."

She couldn't ask directly whether Lord or Lady Banbury had been seen in the kitchen; no housekeeper worth her salt would speak of her employer's movements.

She left the servants' hall, the door swinging shut behind her. The sounds from the kitchen resumed almost immediately: the thud of dough, the murmur of low voices, the scrape of metal against wood.

Isabella realised that the dowager was likely speculating about her whereabouts and needed to be updated about everything that had occurred since Isabella left with Agatha to speak to Inspector Gregory.

As she climbed the staircase to her room, Isabella considered the questions before her. She now knew of at least two people with strong motives to want Ravensthorpe dead, but it seemed unlikely that either of the Banburys had personally taken her handkerchief directly from the servants' hall. If neither of the Banburys had touched it, then someone below stairs must have, despite their silence when Mrs Patrick asked the question.

Could a servant have picked up the handkerchief for the most innocent of reasons, only for it to end up in Lord or Lady Banbury's possession later that evening?

Then she considered the voices she heard when she went to bed. On reflection, she was confident that one of them belonged to Lord Ravensthorpe. She recalled thinking that Lady Banbury might have gone to reason with him. Was that the case? And if so, was that when he had been killed?

Again, this didn't seem like a question she could ask Lady Banbury directly. Instead, Isabella tried to recall whether their hostess had been in the drawing room when she claimed a headache and retired early. She knew the woman had left during dinner, but did she return?

She hoped the dowager might remember if Lady Banbury returned to the drawing room after leaving the dinner table. Then Isabella would be closer to determining whether their hostess had been arguing with Ravensthorpe that night.

CHAPTER 13

"Where on earth have you been?" the dowager demanded. "If I were more of a worrier and you were less competent, I might have been concerned that a misfortune had befallen you. As it is, the food has been sitting here so long that I felt compelled to finish almost all of the rather delicious game pie, for fear it would spoil."

Isabella reassured her friend that she was quite well and not at all hungry.

"Then I hope you at least have some interesting information to share to justify such a long absence." As the old woman said this, she picked at the last piece of the game pie.

After taking a moment to consider her news and the best order in which to relay it, Isabella told the dowager everything she'd learned. As she did so, she wrote up notecards.

The dowager was not usually one to keep her tongue, even when it would be wiser or more prudent to do so. Nonetheless, she remained silent during Isabella's explanation, so captivated that she even forgot the wedge of cheese still on her plate.

When Isabella finished, the dowager sat back in her chair. "Well, I never!" she exclaimed. "You have been busy. I might even excuse your tardiness and your leaving me to sup alone."

Isabella had been worried the dowager would take offence at being left out of the afternoon's activities. Fortunately, it seemed she was to be spared a tongue-lashing.

Between the interview with Inspector Gregory, the overheard exchange in the meadow, and the conversation in the servants' hall, the dowager seemed unsure which titbit to focus on first.

Finally, she chose the piece of information she considered the most salacious. "So, either one of the Banburys or both killed him! Over love and money, it sounds like."

Isabella was less certain. She had not come away from overhearing Lord and Lady Banbury's conversation with anything like the dowager's confidence about its implications.

Cautiously, she replied, "There is no doubt they both have motive. Yet I didn't hear a clear confession of murder."

"Tell me again exactly what they spoke of," the dowager said sceptically.

"Lord Banbury said, 'You wished him out of the way', and Lady Banbury replied, 'I did not mean it like this.'"

"There you go, then!" To the dowager, it seemed this was proof enough. Isabella was not so easily persuaded.

"If I had to name what I heard," Isabella said, choosing her words carefully, "I would say they both sounded relieved to have one problem behind them, only to realise it had been replaced by an even worse one. It sounded as if the Banburys both had complicated relationships with Ravensthorpe. More importantly, it appears he enjoyed the leverage he had over Lord Banbury and was perhaps less interested in revealing what he knew about the estate's finances than in using that knowledge to taunt our host."

The dowager's expression remained sceptical.

Isabella could see that the woman's doubt would not be assuaged for now, so she decided to change the subject from motive to opportunity.

"I have been trying to recall whether Lady Banbury was still in the drawing room when I left early last night," Isabella mused. "However, I simply cannot remember definitively either way. I recall you sitting with a group of older women; if I am not mistaken, Lady Rice and Lady Mary were among them. But where was Lady Banbury? Did she ever return after she left during dinner?"

The dowager gazed into the distance, casting her mind back. "Did she even come into the drawing room from dinner?" she mused. "Now that I think about it, I remember a maid coming in with tea and looking around for her mistress." Then, with greater certainty, she said, "Yes, yes! I do recall now what happened. The maid was looking for permission to serve, and when she could not see Lady Banbury, she turned to Lady Mary."

"That is extremely helpful, Julia!" Isabella said excitedly. "Did Lady Banbury return before you all retired?"

Again, the dowager considered what she remembered for a few moments. "Yes. I remember looking up and seeing her talking to that wan-looking woman who keeps boasting that she's the granddaughter of a duke."

"What time would you guess that was?"

"Actually, I know exactly when that occurred because I glanced at the clock on the mantelpiece at the same time and wondered how much longer the dreary evening might last. It was quarter past ten when Lady Banbury returned. Although she merely came back to apologise and say she was going to bed, she left less than five minutes later. Frankly, I am unsure why she bothered. Rather impolite for a hostess, if you ask me.

The timing aligned with what Isabella remembered. "I stayed in the drawing room after dinner for no more than twenty minutes before excusing myself a little after ten o'clock. It took me no more than two or three minutes to walk upstairs and down the corridor, and it was then that I heard the altercation I believe was taking place in Ravensthorpe's room. It must have been Lady Banbury arguing with him."

Given that she had already concluded as much at the time, this was hardly a revelation to Isabella. Nonetheless, she pressed the thought further now. "The question is: was Ravensthorpe alive when she left him? Or did she return to the drawing room in the hope of establishing her whereabouts?"

Then she realised something quite obvious: "I assume that Lady Banbury returned wearing the same dress; she wouldn't have had time to change if she was back by quarter past. Yet how could she have stabbed a man and not ended up with any blood on her?"

"Certainly, if she had returned to the drawing room looking like Lady Macbeth, someone would have noticed," the dowager agreed, somewhat disappointedly, Isabella thought.

Reflecting on what she witnessed of the murder scene, Isabella considered how much blood there truly would have been. "I remember that the wound was quite clean. I don't know much about such things, but based on what I recall, I would say that Ravensthorpe was stabbed once, very cleanly. I don't think this was an act of passion or that he put up a fight. I saw no sign of a struggle. So, perhaps it would have been possible to commit the deed without much blood splattering."

Then, she reflected on what she had just said and added, "He must have been asleep or unconscious when whoever killed him drove a blade into him with such precision and force. And let us not forget that no weapon has been found, so it must have been removed as well. I simply cannot believe Lady Banbury has the strength or nerve to do that. Certainly not during the argument I overheard."

Continuing with the logical progression of her thoughts, she asked, "Is it possible that she returned later when she believed Ravensthorpe would have fallen into a stupor and brought the murder weapon with her?"

That possibility unsettled Isabella more than she liked to admit, and it raised another question: what were Inspector Gregory and his men doing to find the murder weapon? She wished she could ask, but doubted the inspector would welcome any more interference from her.

Turning away from the murder itself, Isabella voiced the question she kept returning to: who had dropped the handkerchief in Ravensthorpe's room? "If Agatha is telling the truth and the handkerchief was taken from the kitchen table, was it dropped by accident or on purpose? According to Mrs Patrick, no staff member should have been in Ravensthorpe's room yesterday evening so late. In fact, the bed was turned down, and the room prepared long before dinner, when I still had my handkerchief with me."

Then she paused and reflected on everything she'd said and written down so far. "Let us suppose for a moment that Lady Banbury argued with Ravensthorpe but didn't kill him. That means someone else visited his room later, and perhaps that person dropped the handkerchief."

No sooner had she spoken these words than there was a knock at the door. Isabella assumed it was a servant come to collect the luncheon tray. What she didn't expect was to find Lady Banbury standing in the doorway. Isabella was so surprised that she stood there mutely for a moment.

The awkward silence was broken when Lady Banbury said, "Might I have a word with you in private, Miss Hartwell?"

Her tone was sharp, making Isabella immediately suspicious. Did Lady Banbury realise that Isabella had overheard her conversation with her husband? She stepped back and invited Lady Banbury into the room.

"Oh, I did not realise you were not alone," her hostess said, noticing the dowager sitting by the fireplace. "Perhaps it would be best if I returned later."

"Anything you wish to say to me, you may say in front of Lady Pembroke," Isabella assured her. If the conversation was as uncomfortable as she suspected it might be, she would welcome the dowager's support.

"Very well then," Lady Banbury said, moving further into the room.

Isabella took a seat and invited her visitor to join her. For a moment, it seemed as if Lady Banbury would insist on remaining standing, but then she sat, perched on the edge of the chair.

"It has come to my attention that you have been questioning my servants," the woman said in a strained voice that seemed caught between embarrassment and irritation. "In fact, it appears you did so earlier, and again a short while ago."

Isabella did not reply. There was nothing to say. It was obvious that the housekeeper had gone straight to her mistress to describe the encounter.

"I am not sure how things are done in America," Lady Banbury said stiffly, "but in Britain, it is not customary for a guest to enter the servants' hall uninvited and without prior approval from the mistress of the house. It is certainly not the done thing for a guest to interrogate the staff."

Despite the harshness of her words, there was no doubt that Lady Banbury was deeply uncomfortable speaking them. Given the woman's usual, almost preternatural serenity, it was no surprise she found herself ill-equipped for such a conversation.

Before Isabella could respond, the dowager interrupted. "Of course, it is not customary for one guest to be murdered, and another accused of being the killer."

She made no effort to soften her acerbic tone. At her words, the marchioness shrank in on herself. Isabella almost felt sorry for her; the woman had more than met her match in the dowager countess.

"Well, yes, that is true," Lady Banbury replied, almost apologetically. "However, in the future, if you have anything you wish to discuss with a member of my staff, please ask me first. Though I cannot imagine why you feel the need to interview any of them. You can be certain that Inspector Gregory has it all in hand."

The statement was clearly rhetorical, and Isabella did not reply. This was just as well, because she didn't want to share her thoughts and worries with someone still one of her primary suspects.

Instead, she apologised with all due politeness and assured her hostess it would not happen again.

"Well, then, let us speak no more of the matter," Lady Banbury said with evident relief, rising. "I will leave you. I hope that we will see you both at dinner."

When the door had closed behind her, the dowager hardly waited long enough for the woman to be out of earshot before declaring, "I cannot imagine a clearer expression of guilt. The lady doth protest too much, methinks."

Isabella was more circumspect. She was not prepared to mistake discomfort for guilt. What was clear was that she would have to be far more careful about whom she questioned.

CHAPTER 14

Isabella knew she couldn't avoid the other guests forever, so she braced herself to go down to dinner. As she dressed, she considered how she might learn more from the servants now that she'd been effectively forbidden from speaking to them directly.

"You look quite lovely, miss," Polly said in her broad Irish accent, lately tinged with some Brooklyn intonation. She paused, a little embarrassed to say what was on her mind.

Isabella knew her maid well enough to see that she was holding something back. "Whatever it is, Polly, you may speak freely."

"I wasn't gossiping, you know," the maid said, "but I couldn't help overhearing the other servants talking about your handkerchief being found and you seeming guilty, and the like. I wasn't sure what to say. I know you're innocent, but it felt as if I'd be gossiping about you if I said anything."

"It is not your job to defend me, Polly. I appreciate your confidence in my innocence, though," Isabella assured her.

With a little smile of gratitude at these words, Polly continued, "Earlier, the servants said you missed luncheon and that you must be ashamed to face everyone. So, I just wanted to tell you not to mind any of them.

You have nothing to hide or be ashamed of. If that's not too forward of me."

Now, Isabella turned to look her maid straight in the eye. "That isn't too forward at all, Polly. I am grateful for all the support I can muster at this point."

Isabella realised she had forgotten to ask whether her maid had retrieved the handkerchief the night before. She confirmed, as expected, that Polly had never received it. After all, how would it have ended up in Ravensthorpe's room under those circumstances?

This conversation made her think of something. "As the staff have been talking about me, did they mention my visit to the servants' hall earlier this afternoon?"

"Aye, they mentioned it," Polly admitted. "The scullery maid, Nancy, feels sorry for you, but the footman, Hargreaves, was all up in arms about it. He said you're trying to shift the blame from yourself to a servant. He was quite offended by the questions you asked, so he was."

Isabella wasn't particularly surprised to learn this and simply shrugged in response. "Polly," she said instead, "I have a favour to ask you. Before you agree, you should know that I will understand if you do not want to help and won't hold it against you in any way."

"Miss, you know I will do whatever I can for you. My job is to serve you," her maid reassured her.

"But that is just it. What I am going to ask is not your job. It is a favour, and you may refuse." Isabella paused, still unsure of the wisdom of making the request. Finally, deciding there were few other options, she said tentatively, "I did not get all the answers I needed from the servants. Lady Banbury has now forbidden me from questioning them further."

"And so, you want me to see what I can learn?" Polly guessed.

"I dislike asking this of you," Isabella admitted. "And to be honest, it is not exactly spying that I mean. If you start asking questions, the assumption will be that it's on my behalf, and that won't be helpful. However, if you could perhaps keep your ears open and report back to me anything you find concerning, I would be very grateful. Though again, you can refuse this request," she hastened to add.

Polly smiled. "Of course, I will help you in any way I can, miss. Would it be useful if I shared my impressions of some of the servants so far?"

"It would. It certainly would. I know that someone took that handkerchief, and that person was likely in Lord Ravensthorpe's room last night. While they might not be the murderer, their unwillingness to come forward is highly suspicious."

While Polly fixed Isabella's hair, she ran through the servants she'd interacted with since their arrival. For the most part, she had nothing negative to say about them. In the course of her duties, Polly encountered nearly every servant in the house and found the Banbury Hall staff courteous, helpful, and efficient. In particular, she agreed with Isabella's assessment that Agatha was an honest and trustworthy girl.

"And what of the two footmen on duty last night? Carter and Hargreaves, I believe, are their names."

"Well, that Carter is a bit too full of himself, if you ask me. Most of the girls are wild about him. He's a good-looking lad, I'll grant you that, though too pretty for me." Isabella smiled at her words.

Polly continued. "Hargreaves is less vain and nicer, all in all. He doesn't get as much attention from the maids, but that's just because he's quieter and doesn't flirt with them. He grew up on the estate. His father began as a footman and rose to the position of butler before retiring some years ago. There's no doubt he's very protective of the family."

Then she added, "He's especially particular about her ladyship. Not in an impertinent way. More as if he thinks it's his duty that nothing should ever trouble or embarrass her. He said it was a disgrace that Banbury Hall should be turned into a place of suspicion. He was quite put out."

"And, from what you gathered, neither footman saw nor heard anything unusual last night?" Isabella pressed.

"Not that I was told. Though..." Polly paused. "Hargreaves wasn't meant to be on duty upstairs late. Cook mentioned that he came down to the kitchen just before eleven, saying he'd heard a bell, which is why he'd been upstairs when it was supposed to be Carter on duty. She was just finishing up for the night and told him she hadn't heard anything, then left him to it."

She nodded, though her thoughts were racing ahead. Mrs Patrick had been clear: no unusual bells were reported. If Hargreaves had mentioned one to the housekeeper, she would have remembered. The household took pride in its order. Yet, the detail remained lodged in her mind all the same.

"Did Hargreaves seem flustered by my questioning earlier?" Isabella asked.

"Not flustered, exactly," Polly replied. "More... offended. As if he didn't care to be questioned, particularly by you. He said a gentleman's house ought not to be turned upside down over idle talk."

"A gentleman's house," Isabella repeated softly.

"Aye. He's that protective of them, miss. Of the family, I mean. Because he grew up here, he has a sense it's his own, in a way."

Isabella rose from her dressing table and smoothed the pale silk of her gown. It was a soft shade of blue that complemented her complexion and gave her an air of composure she did not fully feel. The fabric shimmered as she moved.

She slipped her gloves on, flexing her fingers to ensure they fit properly. The timing, as described by Polly, bothered her more than she wanted to admit; Hargreaves claimed to hear a bell just before eleven. Perhaps Ravensthorpe rang to summon a servant. If so, had someone else responded to it? Just because the cook told Hargreaves he'd been mistaken didn't mean another servant hadn't answered it.

"Polly," Isabella said, turning away from the mirror, "remember, you must not ask questions. I don't want to put you in an awkward position with the household staff."

The maid gave her a small, determined nod. "I understand, miss. I'll just listen."

"That is all I ask."

A distant chime echoed faintly, signalling that dinner would soon be served.

Isabella drew a steadying breath. "You were right earlier," she said. "I cannot hide in my room like a guilty schoolgirl."

"You've nothing to be ashamed of," Polly repeated firmly.

"Whether or not I feel shame, the spotlight of suspicion still shines on me," Isabella said, with a faint smile to soften the words.

She moved towards the door. For a moment, her hand rested on the handle. Downstairs, the measured civility of dinner awaited, the clink of crystal and the murmur of restrained conversation. Yet beneath the politeness demanded by etiquette, many watchful eyes would be upon her.

"Very well," she murmured. "If they wish to observe me, I shall give them something worth observing."

The corridor outside was quiet, illuminated by the warm glow of wall sconces that softened the edges of the long runner beneath her feet. As she descended the staircase, each step felt purposeful. She kept her chin raised and her pace unhurried. If anyone expected to see a woman bowed by accusation, they would be disappointed.

At the entrance to the drawing room, Isabella paused just long enough to compose her expression into graceful serenity. Voices drifted through the partially open door. Perhaps it was her imagination, or did the laughter sound a little too bright, and was the conversation pitched just slightly too high? It seemed as if they were an audience eagerly awaiting a spectacle.

She pushed the door open and stepped inside. The conversation faltered for a moment before resuming.

Isabella was not fooled. They had been waiting for her. She inclined her head in greeting, every inch the composed guest.

She would not give them the satisfaction of seeing her falter.

CHAPTER 15

Isabella scanned the room, hoping to spot the dowager already present, but the woman was nowhere in sight. Gritting her teeth, Isabella told herself she would have to manage alone for now. While calling herself a pariah of New York society might be an exaggeration, she was undeniably regarded as an oddity because of her passion for engineering and her father's willingness to indulge it. Given this, she was accustomed to entering a room and seeing raised eyebrows and ladies whispering about her behind their fans.

Though at least back home, people tried to hide their gossiping. The group gathered at the house party didn't bother with such a charade. Did the British upper classes not pride themselves on good manners? These people plainly thought that an American, suspected of murdering one of their own, deserved no such courtesy. Instead, all conversation came to a halt, and every pair of eyes became fixed on her. Several embarrassed faces confirmed that she had been the main topic of conversation.

From the stiffness of their expressions, Isabella suspected that many of her fellow guests believed she ought to have appeared sooner, if only to satisfy their scrutiny. Instead, she had stayed out of sight, an absence which, in their minds, could only confirm her guilt.

Just as Isabella was contemplating whether to ignore the ghost at the feast and confront the room directly, she heard a noise behind her.

"Rarely have I seen so many agape mouths at once," the dowager said acerbically. "One would think none of you ever experienced a whisper of scandal before."

As grateful as Isabella was for the support, even she wondered whether this statement was a little too pointed.

However, it seemed the dowager was just getting started. Moving to Isabella's side, she began calling out various members of the aristocracy who caught her eye. "Why, Mrs Madison, I see you at the back, looking particularly appalled that my dear friend, Miss Hartwell, has dared to show her face. I should think your household's prior difficulties, saved from scandal only by a whisker, would make you less eager to pass judgement."

The dowager paused. "I could go on, of course. Or perhaps it is wiser if we all recall the chapters of our histories we prefer not to reopen, and show Miss Hartwell here some grace."

One by one, conversations resumed; at first too brightly, then with studied normalcy.

The room had only just regained its brittle civility when the doors at the far end opened once more. Lord Banbury was the first to enter. If he overheard the dowager's remarks, he showed no sign. His face remained calm, almost solemn, as he paused just inside the doorway, seemingly taking in the gathering. Behind him, a servant lingered nearby, waiting for orders.

"My friends," he said, in a tone carefully pitched between apology and authority, "I must beg your indulgence for a slight change to our arrangements this evening."

The murmur, which had tentatively resumed, fell silent again.

"Given the unfortunate circumstances in which we find ourselves," he continued, "it seemed only proper to extend my hospitality to Inspector Gregory while he remains in this house, and he has accepted my invitation to dine with us."

For a fraction of a second, the silence was absolute. Then came the faintest sounds: a teaspoon striking porcelain a shade too sharply, the soft rustle of silk as someone shifted in her seat, a gentleman's cough that tried to pass as indifference.

Isabella felt a ripple of disquiet move through the room. Whether it was because the inspector's presence might inhibit the gossip and conjecture they'd hoped to indulge in, or the staggering breach of etiquette in having a mere policeman share their dinner table, she couldn't be sure. Still, no one openly objected.

The dowager, at Isabella's side, inclined her head ever so slightly. "How very... interesting," she murmured under her breath. Of course, Isabella knew the dowager well enough by now to realise that, under normal circumstances, she would have been amongst the first to protest such a breach of social standards.

Across the room, Lady Banbury stood beside the mantelpiece, one hand resting lightly on its carved edge. She had not spoken during her husband's announcement, nor had she changed her expression in any noticeable way. However, Isabella observed that her fingers tightened slightly against the polished wood.

Just for a moment. Then the door opened once more.

Inspector Gregory entered with the air of a man used to walking into rooms where his presence was unwelcome. Clearly, he was aware of how true that must be among such a crowd. He was dressed in evening wear, though from the fit, Isabella wondered whether it had been borrowed, possibly even from their host.

"My lord," he said, bowing to Lord Banbury. "You are most generous and obliging."

"Nonsense," Banbury replied. "We are indebted to you for your diligence and discretion in this matter." What did he mean by 'discretion'? Isabella wondered.

She watched Gregory's gaze sweep across the room. It lingered on nothing and no one for long, yet seemed to miss nothing. A thought occurred to her: had he asked to be included tonight to observe the guests in their natural environment?

When his gaze met hers, it lingered. It didn't appear accusatory, though she wouldn't have called it friendly. Instead, the inspector seemed to be calmly observing her.

She returned his look steadily. If Gregory was surprised to find her standing composedly beneath the scrutiny of the entire company, he did not show it.

At the inspector's entrance, several guests shifted, as if suddenly uncertain about the propriety of their earlier whispers. A gentleman near the window made a show of asking after the weather. Lady Brinkley examined her gloves with sudden concentration. No one appeared comfortable with the addition to their party. Though that might have been the intention.

Isabella allowed her attention to drift until it landed on Lady Banbury. The marchioness had now moved, crossing the room to greet the inspector with impeccable courtesy. There was nothing in her manner to suggest agitation. She extended her hand, and Inspector Gregory bowed over it.

"I echo my husband's words; we are grateful for your efforts, Inspector," Isabella heard her say. "I trust you have found our household at your disposal."

"Your cooperation has been most helpful, my lady," Gregory replied.

As polite and almost bland as this interaction was, Isabella noticed the faint tension in Lady Banbury's posture. It was not the tremor of grief; any show of that had ended as quickly as it had begun when Ravensthorpe's body was first discovered. Nor was it the restless agitation of fear. It appeared more self-contained, more tightly coiled.

Isabella considered the woman's demeanour. If she once harboured a dangerous attachment to Ravensthorpe, the argument in the meadow might be easily explained. A former liaison had become inconvenient. Perhaps a threat had been uttered in anger. But the woman she had just observed did not seem like someone mourning a former lover, nor even like someone freshly parted from one. She appeared to be a woman quietly assessing the room in a rather calculated manner, ready to act if necessary.

The dowager's voice cut through her thoughts. "Is it not fascinating," she murmured gleefully, without turning her head, "to observe their shock at the inspector's presence among them? It is possible that one of them even has more reason than the others to feel discomfort at being so closely observed." As she said this, the dowager lazily inspected the room.

There was no doubt that Inspector Gregory's presence sharpened every exchange. Conversations resumed, but now they were careful.

Measured. As if the speakers worried that each word might later be recalled and weighed.

Lord Banbury approached his wife and said something quietly. Isabella could not hear the words, but she saw Lady Banbury incline her head, her expression serene. When his hand brushed her elbow, she stepped forward a fraction sooner than necessary, as if eager to withdraw from the contact.

The movement was subtle, almost unnoticeable. Yet, Isabella did not miss it. Maybe it was nothing more than the strain of hosting a house full of guests while a murder inquiry was conducted right under their noses? Certainly, from what Isabella overheard earlier, the Banburys had more than enough reason to be anxious.

When a bell chimed faintly from somewhere deep within the house, Hargreaves's head lifted at once, and once again he made brief eye contact with his mistress, who gave the slightest of nods. He then announced dinner.

As Isabella followed the others into the dining room, she suspected this meal would yield more than just polite conversation.

Chapter 16

It would take more than a gruesome murder to disrupt the running of a grand house like Banbury Hall. The table had been set with all the precision and grandeur one might expect. The silver gleamed beneath the chandelier's glow; the crystal caught the candlelight, splintering it into colourful shards that danced across the highly polished wood of the table. Isabella's gaze flicked over the place settings, taking in the arrangement and pondering their possible strategic intent.

As expected, Lord Banbury took the head of the table nearest the door, and Lady Banbury presided at the opposite end. Isabella once again found her name placed at Lord Banbury's right hand. To his left sat the dowager, who had taken her seat as if expecting nothing less. Perhaps more telling was that Inspector Gregory sat on Lady Banbury's left.

Was this all quite deliberate? If Lord Banbury aimed to demonstrate impartiality, seating the accused beside him was certainly one way to do so. If Lady Banbury aimed to show composure, dining beside the man investigating the murder in her house was yet another ploy.

Isabella took her seat. From her position at the table, she had a clear view of Lady Banbury and, beyond her, of Inspector Gregory. The inspector's presence had not lost its novelty. Several guests cast him sidelong glances, as though unsure whether they were required to include him in their polite dinner conversation or could pretend he was invisible.

The first course was served with meticulous efficiency. Hargreaves stood among the footmen assigned to Isabella's side of the table. He moved with steady precision, placing dishes and replenishing the wine with an economy of motion that suggested long practice. The footman she assumed was Carter stood on the opposite side, equally polished and efficient.

After their earlier exchange in the kitchen, Isabella was keenly aware of Hargreaves. He poured her wine, and his hand remained steady. If he resented her earlier questions in the servants' hall, he showed no sign of it now.

The dinner conversation started cautiously, each guest careful of their words. Lady Brinkley commented on the weather, and her neighbour replied with measured politeness. The dowager, for once, let the small talk develop without interference.

Inspector Gregory said little. He responded when spoken to, his voice steady, neither acknowledging his lower social rank nor claiming his legal power. If he felt the weight of aristocratic disdain pressing upon him, he bore it without visible discomfort.

Isabella noticed that several guests, having exhausted the topic of the heavy rains that spring, began circling her with polite enquiries that barely concealed their true intent.

"Miss Hartwell," Mrs Madison ventured from halfway down the table, "you must find our English countryside very different from New York's."

"I find it charming," Isabella replied evenly, adding archly, "Though less forgiving of newcomers."

A faint, embarrassed titter rippled along the table. Mrs Madison lowered her eyes.

The second course was served.

Midway through the fish course, as glasses were being refilled, Inspector Gregory cleared his throat. The sound was not loud, but it carried.

"If I may, my lord," he said, addressing Lord Banbury with courteous gravity, "I believe it is prudent to correct a misconception that has, regrettably, circulated and may have taken hold."

Every fork paused. Isabella found the eager anticipation on her fellow diners' faces comical.

Lord Banbury inclined his head. "By all means, Inspector," he said.

Gregory's eyes moved deliberately along the table. "Earlier today," he continued, "a member of the household staff confirmed that Miss Hartwell's handkerchief was dropped in the drawing room before dinner last evening. It was retrieved by this servant and, for reasons we are still investigating, later found in Lord Ravensthorpe's chamber. I am aware that when the item was initially found, suspicion may have fallen on Miss Hartwell. However, further testimony establishes that the handkerchief's presence in the deceased's room cannot serve as evidence that Miss Hartwell entered that chamber during the relevant window of time."

Aware that many eyes immediately turned towards her, Isabella didn't allow herself to react.

The effect on the rest of the room was more pronounced; Lady Brinkley's fork resumed its movement with unnecessary deliberation. Mrs Madison blinked rapidly, as if recalibrating her internal narrative. A gentleman at the far end coughed.

No one spoke. Whether it was guilt over their earlier treatment of her or disappointment at the loss of a source of gossip, Isabella could not have said.

Across the table, Lady Banbury briefly lowered her gaze. When she lifted it again, her expression was serene.

Lord Banbury offered a tight smile in Isabella's direction. "There, you see," he said. "I trust that puts one unfortunate matter to rest."

The dowager lifted her glass and addressed the table. "How gratifying," she observed, "to have justice delivered alongside our fish mousse."

A few strained smiles greeted her comment.

Inspector Gregory folded his hands lightly on the table. "Which obliges us," he added, "to consider who else may have placed the handkerchief in Lord Ravensthorpe's room. Our witness's testimony is considered reliable."

There was no accusation in his tone; no suspect implied. The statement was factual. Yet it landed like a heavy stone dropped into still water.

If Isabella had previously been the most convenient suspect, she was no longer so. The discomfort in the room grew worse.

When it became clear that Inspector Gregory would say no more on the subject, at least for the time being, the conversation resumed, if hesitantly. There was now an even more careful weighing of words. The guests were suddenly aware that even the most seemingly harmless conversation might be misconstrued.

Isabella allowed herself a measured breath. At the opposite end of the table, Lady Banbury engaged the inspector in a quiet conversation. Her features remained calm, and her gestures were controlled. At one moment, she inclined her head towards him and graced him with a smile of complete serenity.

Yet Isabella could not forget the tightening of her fingers on the mantelpiece, nor the slight withdrawal from her husband's touch. Beneath the show of calm, the marchioness appeared to be recalibrating.

After the final course had been served and cleared, Lady Banbury rose. "Shall we adjourn to the drawing room?" she suggested.

The ladies withdrew first, as propriety required.

Isabella rose with the others. As she moved past Hargreaves, she sensed him at her shoulder. He stepped aside immediately, letting her pass. His expression was neutral. Given what Polly had told her of his loyalty to the family, it would not surprise her if he still preferred that the guilt lie anywhere but within Banbury Hall. In fact, the same was likely true of most of the servants.

In the drawing room, Isabella seated herself beside the dowager on the settee.

"Well," the older woman murmured, fanning herself rather too melodramatically, "that was illuminating."

"In more ways than one," Isabella replied softly.

"You have been publicly absolved," the dowager continued. "A development I find deeply satisfying."

"As do I."

"And yet," the dowager added, "you look less relieved than I had expected."

Isabella stared into the fire. "If I did not place that handkerchief in

Lord Ravensthorpe's chamber," she said softly, "then someone else did so."

"Quite so."

"And that someone likely wished me to bear the consequences."

The dowager's fan fell still. "Some of us arrived at that conclusion before the soup course," she observed dryly.

"When the inspector finished speaking, did you notice anyone at the table reacting unexpectedly?" Isabella asked.

"What would you regard as unexpected? The general reaction seemed to be one of shock, with just a hint of disappointment at having to find a new source of gossip and entertainment. Though I will admit to espying more than one look of concern that they might now be the target of suspicion. It was quite delicious to witness."

Across the room, Lady Banbury stood near the pianoforte, conversing with Mrs Madison. Her posture was graceful and composed.

As the gentlemen re-entered the drawing room a short while later, the murmur of conversation grew louder. Isabella felt the situation had become more tense, and possibly more dangerous.

She was no longer the accused, meaning the real murderer had lost their shield and would fear exposure. Fear bred desperation. And desperation led to mistakes.

CHAPTER 17

The next morning, as Isabella went down to breakfast, she marvelled that it was only twenty-four hours since Ravensthorpe's body had been found. Somehow, in that short time, she had gone from being the primary suspect to being exonerated. Now she questioned what remained for her to do. Her attempts to find the actual murderer were to prove her innocence, but that no longer seemed necessary. Still, she couldn't simply walk away. She had come too far and learned too much just to abandon her investigative efforts.

Now that Inspector Gregory did not believe that her handkerchief linked her to the murder, the question was whether she might share her findings and suspicions with him. After all, there seemed little doubt that he was a reasonable, fair man. As Isabella pondered this, she poured herself a cup of coffee and took a seat next to Lady Rice.

THE FIRST THING SHE NOTICED THAT MORNING WAS THAT everyone sitting around the table was eager to make eye contact with her. More than that, she found herself greeted with many friendly smiles and morning salutations. After Inspector Gregory announced her presumed innocence the previous evening, the other guests initially seemed unsure how to revise their judgment of her, and the conversation remained awkward.

Now, after a night to sleep on it, everyone had concluded that Isabella was worthy of redemption, and people seemed to be falling over themselves to ingratiate themselves with her.

"Oh, Miss Hartwell," Lady Rice gushed. "It was such a relief to hear the inspector clear your name last night. Of course," she confided in a low voice, "Lord Rice and I never doubted your innocence. Though, some people were less than Christian in both word and deed." As she said this, Lady Rice cast a knowing look in Lady Brinkley's direction.

Even more unsettling than this entirely disingenuous conversation was that the young man, whom Isabella was now certain was Lady Banbury's brother, made a point of taking the empty seat on Isabella's other side. If nothing else, being a suspect in a murder inquiry had made moot whether she'd been invited to Banbury Hall to be married off. However, now that she'd been absolved of any guilt, it seemed that at least some people now considered her fair game again.

Isabella guessed that Mr Shrewsbury, for that was his name, was about her age, maybe slightly younger. From what she had learned during her stay so far, he was a permanent resident of Banbury Hall, living primarily on his brother-in-law's largesse. Given what she now knew about the state of the estate's finances, Isabella wondered how much of Mr Shrewsbury's sudden interest in her was driven by fear that his gravy train might be running dry.

Although she had no interest in encouraging his suit, or indeed anyone's, it occurred to Isabella that Mr Shrewsbury might help her understand her sister's marriage more clearly.

"I am so relieved that your name was finally cleared," the young man gushed. "Of course, it was always incomprehensible to me that you were guilty; everything about you suggests an almost angelic innocence."

Under normal circumstances, Isabella might have been tempted to make a tart retort to such absurd and insincere flattery; now she forced herself to smile sweetly and thank the man.

"It is quite a relief," she confided. "Now, I can enjoy my time at Banbury Hall and appreciate the full beauty of the estate."

Isabella hoped that this final line would provide sufficient encouragement for Mr Shrewsbury.

Fortunately, although the young man was slow to do many things, including finding himself gainful employment, he was never slow to recognise a potentially advantageous opportunity.

"It would be my honour to show you some of the most delightful spots on the estate, Miss Hartwell. If you would permit me," he said with exaggerated gallantry.

Isabella nearly laughed aloud; this was expressed with such affectation that she wouldn't have been surprised if a deep, almost knightly bow had accompanied it.

Glancing out the window, Isabella could see it was going to be another beautiful spring day. Perhaps a walk around the grounds would help clear her head and organise her thoughts.

"That would be lovely, Mr Shrewsbury," Isabella said. "Shall we say eleven o'clock? I will meet you in the vestibule."

Looking like the cat who got the cream, Shrewsbury assured her of his eagerness for their outing as he stood and excused himself; it seemed his goal for breakfast had been achieved.

Isabella finished her coffee and toast as quickly as possible; there was only so much insincerity she could tolerate so early in the morning. She then withdrew to her bedchamber. She knew it was far too early for the dowager to be up and about, and decided her own company was preferable at this point.

In her room, she found Polly tidying up.

"I hope the welcome you received this morning was an improvement on yesterday, miss," her maid said with a kind smile.

"Too great an improvement," Isabella admitted. "They are now falling over themselves to prove they never believed such a scurrilous accusation in the first place." She then regarded the day dress she was wearing; it wouldn't do for a brisk walk on the grounds. She shared this thought with Polly, who busied herself choosing more suitable attire and footwear.

As she worked, Polly chatted away. Sometimes, Isabella found her maid a little too talkative, but this morning her nattering was almost soothing.

For a few minutes, Polly regaled her mistress with some below-stairs gossip about the scullery maid and the boot boy. Then, lowering her voice as if there were people nearby who might overhear, Polly said, "Actually, I almost forgot that I do have something to tell you, miss. Though it might be nothing at all."

"One never knows when a seemingly innocuous piece of information might be important," Isabella replied, turning slightly in her chair.

Polly hesitated. "Well, Cook told me that Lady Banbury takes a warm cup of milk most nights, for her sleep, you understand. Cook says it settles her nerves."

"That seems sensible enough," Isabella said.

"Aye. Her ladyship is not one for late nights, as a rule; apparently, she often wakes in the night and can't get back to sleep, so she likes to try to fall asleep on the early side. So, the milk is usually sent up at half past ten, because her ladyship is particular about it being fresh from the scullery."

Isabella considered Lady Banbury slipping out of the drawing room early; maybe there was nothing nefarious about her departure after all. "Who usually takes her this milk?"

Polly smoothed an imaginary crease from the counterpane. "Usually, young Carter, if he's on the late shift. But on the night of the murder, Hargreaves offered to take it up himself, saying he was already going that way."

"Did he now?" Isabella's tone was mild, though her fingers stilled on the arm of her chair.

"So Cook said. She thought it odd enough to remark on. Hargreaves told her he was already going up to check something and would take the tray with him."

"To check something?" Isabella repeated.

"That was how Cook put it."

"And what time was this?"

"Half ten. Perhaps a minute or two after."

Isabella's mind raced swiftly. "And where is Lady Banbury's chamber?"

In a rather gossipy tone that Isabella knew she should have discouraged, Polly said, "Well, it seems that not only do Lord and Lady Banbury not share a bedchamber, but they also don't even adjoin."

There was nothing unusual in an upper-class couple keeping separate bedchambers. More unusual was that their rooms were not even adjacent. It was interesting that the Banburys eschewed even this custom.

Polly continued, "Her bedchamber is at the opposite end of the upper corridor, just before you reach the east corridor."

Isabella's gaze lifted. So, to reach Lady Banbury's room from the servants' staircase, did someone have to pass the alcove that led towards Ravensthorpe's suite? It seemed that Polly wasn't sufficiently familiar with the layout of Banbury Hall to answer that question. Isabella filed away the thought to investigate it further.

Polly shrugged. "It may mean nothing at all, miss."

"Yes," Isabella agreed softly. "It may."

Polly lingered for a moment longer, then curtsied and withdrew, leaving Isabella alone with the quiet crackle of the fire. She stood and moved to the window, but the glass reflected only her own thoughtful face.

Half past ten.

Hargreaves claimed to have heard a bell just before eleven. He claimed that was why he'd been upstairs so long. Mrs Patrick had denied hearing one. The matter was left there.

Instead, had he been upstairs at half past ten, delivering Lady Banbury's milk, and not come down at all until just before eleven? Of course, there was nothing particularly suspicious in that, in itself. Still, if his main night duties that night were to answer any bells, why would Hargreaves not have immediately returned to the servants' hall after delivering the milk? What was he doing for the better part of half an hour?

If a servant were seen near the guest chambers at an hour when he ought not to be, what explanation would serve him best? That he had been summoned. That he had responded dutifully to a bell. That he had found nothing amiss.

Unless the bell had not summoned him at all, but served afterwards as a convenient explanation. If he had seen Lady Banbury where she ought not to have been, or guessed more than was safe, a loyal servant might choose silence over truth. That did not make him a murderer. But it might make him dangerous to question.

Isabella walked slowly back to the hearth.

If Hargreaves had delivered the milk at half past ten, how long had he lingered upstairs?

Her thoughts shifted again, more cautiously. Lady Banbury's chamber was separate from her husband's. Not adjoining. Not even adjacent. This offered privacy. And privacy presented opportunity. But opportunity for what? She wished she knew for certain whether the argument she'd heard coming from Ravensthorpe's room had been with Lady Banbury. And if so, had the lady herself confessed as much to Inspector Gregory?

Isabella reconsidered the timing of the evening of the murder: she was sure she had heard the clock strike ten o'clock when she left the drawing room, so that she couldn't have heard the argument any later than five past ten. The dowager had said that Lady Banbury returned to the drawing room at a quarter past the hour, only to leave again almost immediately. Certainly, there would have been more than enough time to reach her bedchamber before her milk was delivered. But what if that wasn't what had happened? What if she had returned to Ravensthorpe's room and murdered him?

Did Hargreaves find his mistress in her room when he delivered the milk? More importantly, considering the man's loyalty to the family, would he tell the truth if he hadn't?

The facts were still too slight, too circumstantial. Yet they niggled at the edge of her mind.

She decided that the best option was to put the investigation out of her mind, at least for now. Isabella hoped her walk with Mr Shrewsbury would clear the cobwebs and allow her to reconsider everything she'd learned with a fresh perspective.

CHAPTER 18

Isabella met Mr Shrewsbury in the vestibule at precisely eleven, her expression composed and her mind ready for the respite from the investigation she expected the man's nonsensical flirting to provide.

He was already there, leaning with studied nonchalance against a marble column, as if he believed the pose showed him to better advantage. As she approached, he straightened and offered a bow that was barely short of theatrical.

"Miss Hartwell, I have been counting the minutes."

"Was that the most productive way to spend the hour and a half since breakfast?" Isabella replied lightly. Not waiting for whatever absurdity Shrewsbury was likely to reply with, she gestured towards the front door and asked, "Shall we?"

Mr Shrewsbury offered his arm. Isabella took it, realising she had little choice, and together they stepped out onto the gravel sweep in front of the house.

The promise of the morning had settled into a glorious spring day: the sky was a brilliant blue, with puffy white clouds drifting across it, and the sun felt warm on Isabella's skin. Despite being unable to avoid Shrewsbury's company, Isabella was looking forward to the walk.

For a while, their progress was marked only by Mr Shrewsbury's florid commentary on the estate's landscaping.

He discoursed on the lake as if it were his grandfather who had built it: "Artificial, of course, though most visitors are convinced otherwise".

The man had much to say about the folly visible through a cluster of beech trees: "A tribute to the old marquess's classical enthusiasms," he said, before admitting, "Although I confess I have never found it particularly charming."

Isabella listened with half an ear, nodding occasionally, while the other half of her mind sifted through the details Polly had supplied. She'd intended to use the walk to clear her mind, but she couldn't help dwelling on everything she'd learned so far. It didn't help that her companion was a dull speaker, yet strangely vainglorious when describing the features of an estate on which he was, in truth, little more than a hanger-on.

They reached the bend in the path where the house was partly obscured behind a sweep of ivy-covered wall when Mr Shrewsbury paused to point out a distant stretch of woodland.

"The east copse," he said. "It was once considerably larger. Banbury sold part of it three years ago. A temporary need, you understand."

"Temporary," Isabella echoed, though she was not looking at the trees.

"Yes. A most inconvenient downturn in agricultural returns coincided with certain... investments." He coughed. "My brother-in-law is an optimist."

"An admirable trait," Isabella said.

"Occasionally ruinous," he replied, and for the first time that morning, his tone carried a sharper edge than mere vanity. "A man can survive many things, Miss Hartwell, but not always the loss of the roof over his head." It was unclear whether he was speaking on Lord Banbury's behalf or his own. He shook his head sadly. "I tried to advise him, but he refused to listen."

Shrewsbury didn't specify what professional experience he possessed that might persuade Lord Banbury to heed his advice.

While Isabella was tempted to ask about this, she ultimately was unsure how far to press the issue. The pair carried on walking for a few minutes.

Then, with curiosity getting the better of her, Isabella decided to challenge the man's words. "You speak as though you have some first-hand knowledge of these matters," she said.

Shrewsbury laughed hollowly. "My dear Miss Hartwell, one cannot reside in a house for this long without becoming aware of its cracks." He flicked an imaginary speck of dust from his sleeve with his free hand. "Though one may prefer not to discuss them."

"Of course."

They passed through an iron gate into the kitchen gardens, where tidy rows of young vegetables lined the beds. A gardener tipped his cap as they neared.

"It must be a considerable burden," Isabella ventured in a casual tone, "to maintain such a property."

"You cannot imagine," Shrewsbury replied quickly. "The taxes alone... well." He paused and chuckled softly. "I do not wish to bore you."

"On the contrary, I find the practical realities of estate management far more interesting than many subjects considered suitable for polite conversation," she assured him.

He looked at her with genuine curiosity. "Do you indeed? How unusual," he said.

"I do," Isabella repeated.

"Well, let me just say," Shrewsbury continued, "that one learns, living in another man's house, that economies have a way of reaching farther than people expect. I expect this has not been the case while we have guests, but I have noticed a decided decline in the quality of the meat we have been eating recently."

Isabella wondered why a cash-strapped estate was hosting such a large party, but she assumed it was an attempt to keep up appearances. Certainly, she didn't ask the question.

They arrived at a low stone bench overlooking a shallow valley where sheep grazed peacefully, creating a picture-perfect pastoral idyll. Shrewsbury nodded towards it. "Shall we rest a moment?"

"If you like."

They sat silently for a few moments, with only the faint bleating of lambs and the gentle whistle of the breeze breaking the quiet.

Shrewsbury tapped the end of his cane against the ground. While Isabella was enjoying the man's silence, she also sensed that he was struggling to find the right words. She waited patiently.

Isabella expected to be subjected to yet more disingenuous courtship, so she was surprised when Shrewsbury blurted out, "Ravensthorpe was not a man inclined to moderation."

"Was he not?" she replied carefully, unsure where this conversation was leading, but curious to follow her companion's line of thought.

"No. When he wished to wound, he preferred to draw blood."

The very specific phrasing caused her to glance sharply at the man next to her, though his gaze stayed fixed on the valley below.

"You refer to his manner rather than literally, I assume?" she asked.

"To his tongue," Shrewsbury said. "And occasionally to his pen."

"His pen?"

Shrewsbury hesitated before shrugging. "You must understand, Miss Hartwell, that Ravensthorpe took pride in knowing others' private affairs. It amused him. And in Banbury's case, it pleased him especially to have something over him."

"And he possessed such knowledge of Banbury Hall?" While she had her own reasons for believing this to be true, Isabella was curious to hear Shrewsbury's viewpoint.

Shrewsbury's jaw tightened almost imperceptibly. "He possessed too much knowledge of too many things."

Isabella kept her tone mild. "Including your brother-in-law's investments?"

He exhaled through his nose. "You are remarkably direct," he said.

"I have been told that we Americans often are."

The man turned to face her directly at last. "Very well. Yes. Ravensthorpe was aware of certain... difficulties."

"And he intended to act upon that awareness?"

Shrewsbury's cane stopped tapping. "He intended to make an example," he said. "He said as much."

The words settled heavily in the stillness of the morning.

Isabella did not move. "You heard this yourself?"

"I heard part of it on the night of his death," he admitted. "I had retired early, just before ten. I left the dining room and did not return to the drawing room. You would not have seen me go. My room is in the east corridor," he explained.

Her pulse quickened, though her expression remained unchanged. "And you heard this shortly after ten?"

"Yes, I recall the clock striking as I ascended."

"And you are certain it was Ravensthorpe's voice?"

"I am," he confirmed. "His voice was raised. Heated." He frowned slightly. "It was the kind of conversation where one forgets to be careful about who might hear."

"And the other voice?" Isabella asked cautiously.

Shrewsbury's mouth curved faintly. "You wish to know whether it was my sister or her husband?"

"I wish to understand what you heard."

He looked back towards the house, though it was no longer visible from where they sat.

"I did not see her," he said at last. "I heard only a low female voice. It may have been her. It may not. Though I think it is likely. They had quarrelled before."

"About the estate?"

"Among other things." He shifted slightly on the bench. "Ravensthorpe accused Banbury of deception, implying that certain obligations were being concealed."

"Concealed from whom?"

"From creditors. From friends. From family." His gaze flicked to her and away again. "From prospective alliances."

The implication was not lost on Isabella.

"And what did Ravensthorpe threaten?" she asked quietly.

Shrewsbury's voice dropped. "That he would not continue to play along with such a charade."

"Did he specify what he might say?"

"That Banbury Hall was not solvent. That..." He broke off.

"That what?"

"That the estate might not survive another season without drastic measures."

Isabella folded her gloved hands in her lap.

"And after this exchange?" she asked.

"I heard this as I was walking down the corridor," Shrewsbury said slowly. "By the time I was outside of Ravensthorpe's room, the voices had subsided. I assumed the matter was concluded."

Isabella wasn't sure why Shrewsbury was suddenly confiding in her. However, the more pressing question was whether he had told Inspector Gregory. She asked as much.

Shrewsbury hesitated before replying. "I did not. There is no doubt in my mind that my sister is innocent of Ravensthorpe's murder."

"How can you be so sure?"

"Because she has loved him since she was a child. There was a time when they were inseparable, and their betrothal seemed merely a formality. While she surprised us all by marrying Banbury, there is no doubt in my mind that she never stopped loving Ravensthorpe."

Isabella found it difficult to reconcile Shrewsbury's tale of innocent young love with the harsh words she had overheard Lord Banbury hurl at his wife the day before: *I kept my end of the bargain and married you after Ravensthorpe deflowered you and then refused to do the gentlemanly thing.*

"And anyway," Shrewsbury said, as if it were an afterthought, "I saw Ravensthorpe after the argument, so I know it was not my sister who stabbed him in the heat of their fight."

Isabella's breath stilled. "When did you see him?"

"I left my room to use the facilities. A single sconce burnt outside Ravensthorpe's door, and by its light, I saw him outside his chamber, returning inside," Shrewsbury continued. "He was alone. I assumed that he had also visited the W.C."

"And this was after the argument?"

"Yes."

"After ten?"

"Yes. It was shortly before half past ten, I believe."

"Was he injured?"

Shrewsbury gave her a startled look. "Injured? No. He appeared... agitated. But whole."

Isabella's mind recalibrated in an instant. If Ravensthorpe were alive, upright, and uninjured after the argument, the quarrel she had heard did not culminate in immediate violence.

"Did Ravensthorpe see you?"

"He glanced up. We exchanged no words."

"Was he still there when you entered your chamber?"

"I did not look back."

A silence stretched between them.

"Miss Hartwell," Shrewsbury said suddenly, his tone changed, "I tell you this because my sister had nothing to do with Ravensthorpe's death. That is why I said nothing to that police inspector. I saw no need to cast a shadow over her unnecessarily."

There was one thing that Isabella didn't understand. "Why are you telling me this?"

For a moment, she thought he wouldn't answer. Then he replied, "I saw you in the corridor, Miss Hartwell, that night. You paused not far from Ravensthorpe's door. It was clear you had heard something. I assume you would prefer not to embroil yourself further. There seems no reason to trouble the inspector with what was, after all, merely raised voices."

Isabella felt the faintest prickle at the back of her neck. Mr Shrewsbury's vanity had concealed something sharper beneath it. Was this the real reason he had invited her on the walk?

Shrewsbury's expression hardened. "I considered speaking with Ravensthorpe the following day about what I had heard, but then reconsidered. If the man was upset by the conversation, well, he should have been. After all, he intended to ruin us."

"Us?" she repeated softly.

"My sister," he corrected. "Banbury. The household."

Isabella considered pressing this point but decided not to challenge Shrewsbury, at least for the time being.

As if shaking off the dark turn the conversation had taken, Shrewsbury rose and again offered his arm. "But let us talk of more pleasant subjects, Miss Hartwell. Tell me about America. I have long been considering setting sail for its shores. I hear that a man can make his fortune more easily there than anywhere else. Perhaps you might even be my guide."

These words were spoken with such playfulness that Isabella felt no need to worry that Shrewsbury intended to go beyond flirtation. Smiling, she took his arm and amused him with tales of life in New York.

Isabella was not particularly tall and disliked taking the arm of men much taller than she was, so that she felt half-dragged, rather than escorted. Luckily, while Mr Shrewsbury could not have been called short, he was not so tall as to make the arrangement awkward.

CHAPTER 19

Despite the earlier dullness of the conversation, Shrewsbury proved to be amusing enough company, and Isabella found herself enjoying the walk more than she'd expected, especially once the spectre of an unwelcome courtship had been lifted.

When they finally returned to the house for luncheon, he bowed over her hand in a very gallant, though less theatrical, manner than before, and begged that they might repeat the outing during her stay at Banbury Hall. As he did so, she caught the scent of verbena, good soap, and hair pomade. It was not unpleasant, merely the clean, careful scent of a man who paid close attention to his appearance.

"Certainly, Mr Shrewsbury. You have demonstrated yourself to be an excellent guide to the estate, and I would very much enjoy learning more." Isabella was surprised by how genuine these words were. Her lingering trepidation when Shrewsbury spoke about the estate's finances and Ravensthorpe now sat alongside her unexpected pleasure in his company.

By the time she had discarded her outerwear and made her way to the dining room, a large crowd had gathered there. It appeared this was to be a rather casual meal, with an abundant cold collation laid out on the buffet table and guests helping themselves before sitting wherever they chose.

Noticing the dowager with an empty seat beside her, Isabella seized the chance to claim the spot for herself.

"Where have you been?" the dowager asked. "Your colour is high, and your hair looks shockingly windswept. Having been resurrected from your earlier position of disgrace, it behoves you not to become the subject of mealtime gossip again, merely by virtue of your coiffure."

Isabella smiled. "Noted. Certainly, I do not want to give Lady Brinkley any new reason to cast aspersions upon me. However, there was a good reason: Mr Shrewsbury, Lady Banbury's brother, took me on a tour of the grounds," she said.

"Did he indeed? Shrewsbury? Is that the boy who looks almost as wan and delicate as she does?"

"The very same. It was quite an interesting outing, and I have some things to share with you. However, they need to be discussed in private." Isabella spoke in a low voice, aware of the people all around them.

The dowager looked suitably intrigued. "Very well, my dear. Though, as I am often forced to remind Tabitha and Jeremy, I am an elderly woman and might expire at any moment. Do not dither too long before revealing all."

Isabella had heard the dowager threaten others with her supposedly imminent death many times, using it as an excuse for her excessive impatience. She smiled and assured her that they could return upstairs to speak as soon as they had eaten.

Once everyone was seated, Lady Banbury tapped lightly on her glass to attract their attention.

"Friends," she announced. "Lord Banbury and I are well aware that you joined us at Banbury Hall for a week of rest and enjoyment. Instead, you have found yourselves in circumstances of the most distressing kind. Though we are all still shocked by Lord Ravensthorpe's death, I thought we might distract ourselves somewhat with an afternoon of archery followed by tea at the folly."

"How reassuring. Apparently, the remedy for violent death is archery and cucumber sandwiches," the dowager observed in an acerbic, but luckily low, voice.

Even so, Isabella wondered whether the marchioness had overheard, because the woman added, "I realise that this might seem quite callous given recent events. However, I think it would benefit us all to get some fresh air and have a change of scenery. I hope you will agree that sitting inside for the next few days waiting for this killer to be caught will not bring Ravensthorpe back, nor make the investigation move along any quicker."

From the looks on everyone's faces, no one was inclined to disagree with her.

The gathering was busy enjoying their raised game pie and other delicacies when Inspector Gregory entered the room. Every conversation ceased, and forks were held mid-air as every face turned in anticipation; even the servants seemed to stiffen. Perhaps the murderer had been detained, and they could all return to enjoying the house party without the fear of being killed in their beds or being arrested at any moment.

Gregory inclined his head in acknowledgement of the assembled company, then moved to a position slightly apart from the table yet within full view of every guest.

"My lord," he said, addressing Banbury, "I thank you for permitting me to speak to your guests."

Banbury gave a brief nod. "If you must. I trust you will not sour our appetites." This might have been said in jest, but the inspector didn't smile. Instead, Gregory clasped his hands behind his back.

He began in a measured tone, filled with quiet authority. "Ladies and gentlemen, although I regret the need for further disturbance, certain developments in my inquiry require me to clarify several matters of timing."

A murmur rippled faintly across the table before fading away.

Gregory continued, "I have questioned all of you and the staff, and a timeline has emerged. It has been established that Lord Ravensthorpe was alive shortly before half past ten on the evening of his death."

How did he know this? Isabella wondered. Unless Shrewsbury had changed his mind and spoken to the inspector, it followed that someone else had seen Ravensthorpe outside his room that night.

Lady Banbury's hand tightened slightly around her napkin. Shrewsbury remained still, though his gaze grew sharper. He didn't look in Isabella's direction, but suddenly, she wondered if he suspected her of talking about their conversation to the inspector.

Gregory's eyes passed over them without pause. "A servant has confirmed this time," he continued.

Hargreaves, standing along the wall with the other servants, kept his expression impassive. Only those watching closely might have noticed that his jaw had tightened. Given what she knew about the footman's movements that night, it was possible he was the person to have seen Lord Ravensthorpe.

"It follows," Gregory said evenly, "that the fatal injury was inflicted sometime after half past ten, which I understand is around the time at which many of you began to retire for the night."

Mrs Davenant let out a small, involuntary gasp.

Baron Rice's voice cut across the table. "Are you suggesting that one of us could have killed Lord Ravensthorpe? Jolly bad form, Inspector, jolly bad form."

Isabella noted that Lord Rice had not taken umbrage when she was a suspect. Apparently, she was not considered "one of us."

"I am suggesting nothing beyond what the evidence supports," Gregory replied calmly. "Only that, given what I now know, the field of potential suspects has widened."

A flicker of surprise crossed more than one face.

Then, Lady Banbury spoke, her voice tight but controlled. "You have spoken with all the servants, I presume."

"I have."

"And you are satisfied with their accounts?"

Gregory did not answer at once, then said rather obliquely, "They have given me accounts." He shifted his weight slightly. "I would ask that each of you consider your movements after ten thirty. If any of you have information that has not been shared before, please seek me out in the library. By that I mean not merely where you were, but whether you observed anyone else on the upper floor."

His eyes briefly rested on Isabella. She met his gaze unflinchingly.

Lord Banbury bristled. "You cannot expect us to recall every trivial detail," he said. "After so much claret, Inspector, I cannot be expected to recall minutiae."

"I would ask everyone to do what they can, my lord," Gregory replied. "It is often the trivial details that prove decisive."

Shrewsbury spoke again, his tone smooth. "You suggest, then, that someone encountered Ravensthorpe before his death?"

"I suggest that it is possible."

Lady Banbury's composure began to fray. "Inspector, this is intolerable. I was certain you would have identified the killer by now. Instead, we are being asked to tattle on each other, even as we may break bread with a cold-blooded murderer."

A brittle silence followed. Isabella wondered at Lady Banbury's outburst. After all, no one had ever seriously suggested that the killer was an intruder, so it was always likely that it was someone in the house, whether family, guest, or servant.

Inspector Gregory allowed her words to stand for a moment before continuing. "There is one further matter." Several guests shifted uneasily.

"I have been informed that Lord Ravensthorpe held confidential and sensitive information on various individuals under this roof."

Banbury half rose from his chair, but then thought better of admitting anything in public. Lady Banbury went very still.

Shrewsbury's fingers briefly tightened around the stem of his glass.

"I have no interest in the financial or personal arrangements of anyone here beyond their relevance to motive," Gregory continued. "But I will assume that if any person present feared imminent public exposure, that fear may have influenced their subsequent actions."

Mrs Davenant's fork clattered onto her plate.

Banbury's voice was low and dangerous. "What are you accusing us of?"

"I am accusing no one of anything," Gregory said. "I am merely presenting the facts as I know them currently."

Who had spoken with him, and what had they admitted? Isabella wondered. Certainly, it seemed the man was keeping the details close to his chest.

The inspector slightly turned his head towards the servants. "I will also note that the service staircase provides access to the east corridor without using the main staircase."

Isabella's heart skipped a beat. Several guests looked genuinely startled.

Lady Banbury's brows drew together. "The service staircase? Surely…"

"Surely what?" Gregory asked mildly.

"Surely no one would use it except the servants."

"That is its intended purpose," Gregory agreed. "But it is not inaccessible to everyone else. Until proven otherwise, I am assuming that anyone in this household, including but not limited to the staff, might have used that staircase to access Lord Ravensthorpe's room."

A faint tremor went through the room. Now that Isabella was no longer the convenient suspect, the murder seemed to have lost much of its titillating charm for the assembled guests.

Gregory folded his hands once more behind his back. "I will not detain you any longer. Once again, I request that no one leave the estate until my inquiries are complete. If any of you recall even the slightest detail about movements in the east corridor between half past ten and eleven, I urge you to inform me immediately."

He inclined his head to Banbury. "My lord."

Banbury did not return the gesture. Inspector Gregory turned and left as quietly as he had entered, closing the door behind him.

For a moment, no one spoke. Then Mrs Davenant whispered, "A service staircase. As if I would deign to use a service staircase." It appeared she was more appalled by that thought than by the possibility of being accused of murder.

Shrewsbury chuckled softly, though there was no humour in it. "One would think we were characters in a transpontine melodrama."

Banbury's gaze snapped toward him. "This is not amusing."

"I did not say that it was."

Lady Banbury pushed her plate aside. "I cannot bear this," she murmured.

Isabella watched the interplay closely. Shrewsbury looked entertained rather than alarmed. Banbury radiated fury. Lady Banbury looked less fearful than anxious.

Mrs Davenant leaned towards Isabella. "Miss Hartwell, you went upstairs early, did you not?"

Isabella turned her head slowly. "I retired shortly after ten."

"Did you see anyone?"

Isabella paused briefly before answering. "I did not." And that was true. She had heard voices but seen no one. Well, no one except the faint shadow that slid past her door.

Mrs Davenant's eyes widened slightly, as though she sensed something more beneath the words.

At the head of the table, Banbury rose abruptly. "This farce must end," he declared. "My wife and I will not be subjected to further insinuations."

Lady Banbury stood as well, though her expression was distant.

Shrewsbury rose with languid composure. "Inspector Gregory appears determined. We would do well to cooperate," he said, with a slight raising of one eyebrow.

Banbury shot him an irritated look. "Easy for you to say."

Shrewsbury's smile was faint. "Is it?"

"Well, you have little to lose."

The exchange mattered more than the words themselves. From the look their host gave his brother-in-law, Isabella inferred that there was little affection between Lord Banbury and Mr Shrewsbury.

Isabella sensed the atmosphere shift once more. Guests rose from the table in small groups. Conversations picked up again, but in softer, more nervous tones.

As she stood to leave, Shrewsbury stepped into her path.

"Well," he murmured, his tone almost conversational, "our inspector enjoys a dramatic flourish."

"Is that what you believe he was doing?" Isabella replied evenly. "Speaking for effect?"

"Of course, I hope our earlier conversation remains between us. As I said, there is no reason to share it with the inspector." Shrewsbury's gaze searched her face, as though seeking confirmation.

Isabella gave a slight smile and offered him nothing.

Chapter 20

"Well, my dear, now we must speak without delay," the dowager insisted as she watched Shrewsbury leave the room. "I cannot wait a moment longer to know what that was about."

Although this was said in a low voice, Isabella was cognisant that groups of people were still milling around.

"Let us go for a walk," she suggested. "The grounds are delightful, and it is a beautiful day." Because she was well aware of the dowager's views on uncalled-for perambulation by the upper classes, she added, "If we keep disappearing to my room together at odd hours, we may cause speculation amongst the other guests. Whereas a leisurely stroll after a meal will go unremarked."

The dowager narrowed her eyes somewhat as she interrogated Isabella's logic.

Finally, she replied, "Very well then. However, I insist that you return to your room and re-pin your hair. If you do not start off this walk fit to be seen, I can only imagine how you will return."

Isabella smiled and assured the dowager she would return to her room and have her maid see to her hair, and suggested they meet in the vestibule within the quarter hour.

It didn't take Polly long to make Isabella presentable again, and almost exactly fifteen minutes later, she went downstairs to find the dowager waiting for her impatiently.

"I would ask what took you so long," the old woman said irritably, "but given your appearance earlier, that seems an unnecessary expenditure of breath."

This was one of those times when Isabella appreciated how much self-control it must take for Tabitha not to roll her eyes and sigh deeply on a regular basis.

Instead of pointing out that she was not late or mentioning that she only returned to her room at the dowager's behest, Isabella smiled and said, "Then let us waste no more time and take a turn around the rose garden."

She offered the dowager her arm, and the two women left the house. The dowager was using her silver-topped cane, but even so, Isabella was careful not to walk too fast. She remembered seeing the garden on her return from her walk with Shrewsbury that morning and set off toward it.

Once they were far enough from the house to be sure of not being overheard, the dowager asked, "So what did you learn from that pasty-faced youth?"

While that wasn't how Isabella would characterise Shrewsbury's pale complexion, this was not the time for such a debate. She told the dowager all she had learned on her morning walk with the man.

"So, that ornamental parasite is concerned that his time as a pensioner upon his brother-in-law's generosity may be in jeopardy, is he?" the dowager said, with a touch too much delight in the man's predicament.

Isabella pondered her words for a few moments. How would she characterise Shrewsbury's response to the threat he claimed Ravensthorpe had presented?

Choosing her words carefully, she replied, "He appears genuinely attached to the estate and all it represents." Before the dowager could interrupt, she added, "Including, though I do not think limited to, his own self-preservation. He certainly seems genuinely fond of and concerned for his sister."

Something she hadn't considered earlier, when Shrewsbury was talking, but now popped into her mind was a particular discrepancy between what she'd overheard the Banburys discussing and what the brother had reported.

Now, she said slowly, phrasing her words carefully, "He said it was a surprise when his sister married Banbury because it had always been assumed she and Ravensthorpe would wed."

"I cannot imagine that ever having happened," the dowager observed. "Back then, Ravensthorpe was a second son whose father was disinclined to support his son's life of leisure. From what I remember, he was rather a wastrel in those days, and the earl insisted he do something productive with his life and join the military." She chuckled. "While the church might have been the more usual path, Ravensthorpe's father, the Earl of Grantly, seems to have been sufficiently clear-eyed about his son's character to recognise the wisdom of steering him away from it."

"If that was the case," Isabella guessed, "Ravensthorpe would have been unable to support a wife, I assume."

"Certainly, one would imagine so," the dowager agreed. "I do not know the marchioness's father well; he is, after all, a mere industrialist." It seemed to have conveniently slipped the woman's mind that the same could be said of Isabella's father. However, it was an inopportune time to point this out.

The dowager continued, "The man was as determined to buy his daughter a title as if he were an American." She chuckled at her own joke. "I only knew about this because he had been sniffing around Jonathan for a while. Luckily, my son had no need of the dowry Pater Shrewsbury was offering for his daughter and was not sufficiently tempted by his waif of a daughter."

Isabella considered the dowager's words in light of the argument she'd overheard. "From what I overheard, it seemed as if Lord Banbury rescued the woman after Ravensthorpe deflowered her, then refused to marry her."

"If that is true, then I am sure he was paid a pretty penny to do so," the dowager observed wryly.

"Perhaps that was what he'd been assured of, but from the insults Banbury was throwing at his wife yesterday, it sounded as if Mr Shrewsbury may not have made good on whatever dowry he was promised. Are these things not normally worked out and set in stone ahead of time?"

She didn't have much understanding of how such matters were conducted in America, much less Britain. But, given how many of these marriages were essentially business arrangements, Isabella assumed that both parties ensured appropriate legalities were in place.

The dowager shrugged. "Certainly, that is the norm. However, the comment about deflowering suggests a degree of haste might have been necessary." Then she stopped and turned to face Isabella. "Perhaps Lady Banbury even found herself enceinte, and Banbury was persuaded to take his payment for saving her on faith."

It took Isabella a moment to realise what the dowager was implying. "You believe she might have been pregnant? Yet, there is no child."

"A woman may conceive and yet never bring a child to term. Tabitha knows that only too well," the dowager said with just a tinge of regret in her tone.

This all begged another question: "If old Mr Shrewsbury was or is a wealthy industrialist, why is his son destitute?"

"Ah!" the dowager replied. "Fortunes are lost all the time, are they not? Perhaps that was even why Banbury did not receive what he was promised; the cupboards may have been barer than it appeared."

Her words made sense, and they would certainly explain much about the current situation the Banburys and their long-term houseguest seemed to find themselves in.

Now, Isabella turned to the most recent piece of evidence that Shrewsbury had revealed and that Inspector Gregory had confirmed. "There seems little doubt now that Ravensthorpe was not killed during the argument I heard around ten o'clock. While that doesn't rule out Lady Banbury, it does make her no more likely than anyone else who was upstairs after half past ten."

"I would not be so quick to discount either Lord or Lady Banbury," the dowager advised. "They seem to have the most to gain by Ravensthorpe's death and, as the master and mistress of the house, certainly the most opportunity to manipulate the servants into supporting their chosen narrative."

"You think one of the servants is lying?"

"I think it is highly likely. I know firsthand what lengths a loyal servant will go to in order to protect their master or mistress. Did I ever tell you the story of when my butler, Manning, was arrested for murder? He was entirely innocent, but refused to defend himself solely because he believed that, if he confessed, I might be saved the scandal of a long, drawn-out and very public trial."

Isabella did not know this story and made a mental note to ask Tabitha what really happened. It wasn't that she thought the dowager had made it up out of whole cloth; rather, it seemed somewhat implausible that the imperious woman commanded such loyalty from her staff.

She was still considering this when a movement on the gravel path ahead caught her eye.

Lady Banbury approached from the direction of the rose walk, accompanied only by a maid lagging several paces behind. The marchioness moved slowly and appeared somewhat aimless in her wandering. At one point, she raised a gloved hand to her midsection as if she were experiencing some pain or discomfort. Even from a distance, there was a hint of strain in her composure.

The dowager saw her as well. "Well," she murmured, lowering her voice, "speak of the devil and she shall appear."

As the two groups drew nearer, Lady Banbury attempted a smile that was wholly unconvincing.

"Lady Pembroke, Miss Hartwell," she said. "I hope I am not intruding upon your walk."

"Not in the least," the dowager replied. "Though you do not look as if fresh air agrees with you."

If the remark stung, Lady Banbury showed no more than a slight tightening at the corners of her mouth. "I am quite well. Merely a little overtired."

Isabella did not believe her. The woman's complexion, always pale, now bore a curious waxen pallor, and shadows beneath her eyes could not be entirely hidden by powder. As she stood there, a gust carried a strong floral scent. Lady Banbury's expression shifted instantly. She turned her face away sharply and pressed her fingertips to her lips.

The maid took a step forward. "My lady?"

Lady Banbury recovered almost instantly. "It is nothing, Bowen."

Nothing. Yet there had been a moment, no more than a second, when she had looked distinctly as though she might be sick.

The dowager's eyes flicked once to Isabella's. That was enough. The older woman had seen it too.

"You should not remain standing if you are indisposed," Isabella said quietly. "I believe there is a bench just beyond the yew hedge."

"That is very kind, but I shall return to the house," Lady Banbury said gently but firmly. "If you will excuse me."

She inclined her head and moved on, more quickly now, the maid hurrying after her.

For a few moments, neither Isabella nor the dowager spoke. Then the latter said, in a voice stripped of its recent flippancy, "Well."

"Yes," Isabella replied.

"You observed it."

"I did."

The dowager tapped her cane once on the path. "Then I think the Banbury marriage becomes more intriguing by the minute."

Isabella watched the retreating figure of Lady Banbury, her thoughts shifting suddenly and involuntarily. Ravensthorpe's threats. Banbury's bitterness. The old scandal. And now this.

If they were correct and Lady Banbury was with child, what if it was not her husband's? Certainly, the distance between their bedchambers did not suggest much intimacy between the couple. Could Ravensthorpe have wielded more than just financial leverage? Did he possess the power to ruin not only the estate's financial status but also Lady Banbury's reputation?

"We must speak to her," Isabella said at last.

The dowager lifted one eyebrow. "Directly?"

"As directly as she will permit."

"And if she refuses?"

"Then," Isabella replied, already thinking ahead, "we shall have to employ a more devious strategy."

These words were music to the dowager's ears, and she was so eager to return to the house that she almost skipped all the way back.

CHAPTER 21

After she and the dowager parted to rid themselves of their outer garments, Isabella reflected on the new information they believed they'd just surmised: Lady Banbury was possibly with child. Of course, it was still possible that the baby was Lord Banbury's, and yet, it would explain so much if it wasn't. One question she kept returning to was whether Lord Banbury knew.

Isabella cast her mind back to the conversation she'd overheard between the couple. She tried to remember the precise wording of a particular line that Lord Banbury had hurled at his wife: *He acted as if he still had a claim on your attention, which you indulged and even encouraged for far too long. Until suddenly, you wanted nothing more to do with him, by which time it was too late.*

There was so much that might sit behind such words. What did it mean that she encouraged Ravensthorpe? Was that nothing more than a polite euphemism for having carried on an affair? And then, the last line. Why did she suddenly want nothing further to do with the man? More importantly, what did it mean that it was "too late"?

The truth was that the conversation could be interpreted in many ways, from the merely banal idea that Lady Banbury merely kept an old friend close and then fell out with him, to a more scandalous interpretation involving a pregnancy.

Given what Ravensthorpe knew about the estate's finances, perhaps his personal entanglements with the Banburys had nothing to do with his murder. And yet, something Tabitha recently shared with Isabella was that Wolf had once told her that people usually commit murder driven by four core human emotions, and that her experience confirmed this. The most common motives were thwarted love, money, power, or revenge. Certainly, the Banburys had motives that seemed to cover three of these four easily.

Isabella was deep in thought as she ascended the staircase. Walking along the corridor, she was just about to reach the junction with the east corridor when a door opened, and the maid she'd seen with Lady Banbury exited and headed in the opposite direction.

She had nothing to lose, Isabella thought, and went to knock on the door. Of course, she could not be certain it was Lady Banbury's room, nor that the marchioness was inside. However, recalling how unwell the woman had looked not long before, it seemed a reasonable assumption.

After a few moments, Lady Banbury opened the door, appearing surprised, perhaps even slightly shocked, to find Isabella standing there.

"Oh! Miss Hartwell, can I assist you in some way?" the woman asked in confusion.

"Actually, might I speak with you for a few moments on a rather delicate matter?"

From the look on her face, Isabella guessed that Lady Banbury would have very much liked to decline the request, but in the end, good manners and a hostess's sense of social duty prevailed.

"Please, do come in," Lady Banbury said, standing aside.

Her bedchamber was decorated in the same simple yet tastefully elegant style as the rest of the house. However, this room had distinctly feminine touches. The colour scheme blended pale pinks and mint green. It could have been quite garish, but instead it was delicate and charming.

Lady Banbury hesitated briefly before offering Isabella a chair, almost as if she hoped her unwelcome guest would say what she needed and then leave immediately. When it became clear that Isabella couldn't be dealt with so swiftly, a comfortable armchair by the fire was offered, and Lady Banbury took its matching partner on the other side.

Resting her hands in her lap, she looked at Isabella expectantly. "How may I help you, Miss Hartwell?"

"Actually, it is I who wonders if I might help you. I believe you may have found yourself in a very difficult position." Isabella answered.

Lady Banbury's expression changed so quickly that Isabella immediately realised she had come close to the truth. It was not outright outrage, but initial alarm followed by caution.

"I do not understand you," the marchioness said, though her expression suggested that might not be entirely true.

Isabella kept her voice quiet and steady. "I do not come to pry into your private affairs for gossip's sake, but because I believe you are frightened, Lady Banbury."

For a moment, Lady Banbury remained still. Then she let out a faint, brittle laugh. "You are very direct, Miss Hartwell."

"So I am often told."

"And do American ladies generally walk into their hostess's bedchamber and announce such things?"

"I have never followed the rules for what a lady on either side of the Atlantic should do," Isabella confessed. "And when I see a perilous situation, I feel the need to act."

At that, something flickered across Lady Banbury's face. Not relief. Not quite. Something more complex, as though she had spent so long suppressing her feelings that she no longer knew how else to act.

"I assure you," she said carefully, "there is no danger to me now."

The last word hung in the air: *now.*

Isabella allowed the silence to sit between them for a few moments. Lady Banbury's hands remained clasped tightly in her lap, her knuckles almost white. Her breathing was uneven, and her eyes unnaturally wide. The woman looked like a fox cornered by hounds.

"At luncheon," Isabella said finally, "Inspector Gregory said that Lord Ravensthorpe possessed sensitive information about people in this house. He also made it clear that such knowledge might have given someone a motive to silence him."

Lady Banbury looked away towards the fire. "I was there. I heard the same," she replied in an almost sarcastic tone. "It would not surprise me; Ravensthorpe delighted in learning the secrets of others and then holding them over their heads."

For the first time, Isabella wondered who had provided Inspector Gregory with this information and who else, besides the Banburys, he might have been referring to.

Realising that worrying about that detail wouldn't help her now, Isabella refocused on the conversation before her. "Indeed. From what I overheard yesterday morning in the meadow, it seems Lord Ravensthorpe knew a very great deal about the estate's finances and was attempting to use this as leverage against your husband."

The marchioness's head swung sharply back. "You overheard us?"

There it was. No denial. No doubt about what conversation Isabella meant.

"I didn't mean to," Isabella admitted. "I had gone out for air. I heard raised voices and stayed long enough to understand that Lord Ravensthorpe had been using what he knew to exert pressure."

Lady Banbury abruptly rose, then immediately seemed to regret the movement. One hand shot to the back of the chair beside her, gripping it as if the room had shifted. For a moment, she closed her eyes. When she opened them again, they were steady, though the effort of maintaining her composure was plainly visible.

"You should not have listened," she said.

"No," Isabella agreed. "I should not. But I did. And having done so, I cannot pretend ignorance."

Lady Banbury remained standing. Isabella had the impression that the woman was unsure whether to dismiss her or confide in her, and that the struggle between those options was draining.

"Lord Ravensthorpe knew things that were not his to know," the marchioness said at last. "That much I can admit. He had a deplorable habit of prying into matters that did not concern him, and once he had obtained some morsel of knowledge, he could never be content merely to possess it. He had to use it."

"In what way?"

Lady Banbury's mouth tightened. "In every way. To unsettle. To humiliate. To remind others that he held some advantage over them."

"Including over your husband?"

"Yes."

The answer arrived too swiftly to be anything other than the truth.

Isabella watched her intently. "And over you?"

This time, Lady Banbury did not answer immediately. She turned away and moved to a small table near the window, where a cut-glass decanter and two tumblers sat. She poured water into one, though her hand trembled enough to cause a little to splash onto the polished wood. She took a sip, but only a small one, as if swallowing required more effort than she had anticipated.

When she spoke again, her voice was lower. "Lord Ravensthorpe and I were old friends."

That was a considerable understatement of fact, and both of them knew it.

Isabella considered how to put what she needed to say somewhat delicately. Finally, she concluded there was no way to do so.

Instead, she said as gently as possible, "You know I heard your conversation, and so it will not come as a surprise to realise I understand that you and Lord Ravensthorpe were once more than friends. Much more than friends."

She paused, momentarily hesitant to push the conversation into more delicate territory. Then, with a sigh, she added, "And perhaps, that friendship had reignited of late."

Although she might have been expected to be angry or upset, Lady Banbury merely appeared sad. She offered a faint smile. "You are relentless, Miss Hartwell."

"I am trying to determine whether the pressure he exerted on you was merely financial."

At the word merely, something in Lady Banbury's composure snapped.

"Do you think financial ruin is a trifling thing?" she asked, with sudden heat. "Do you think the loss of one's home, one's name, one's standing, and every obligation attached to them is some abstract inconvenience? Banbury Hall encompasses generations of people, responsibilities, and expectations. It is every servant under this roof. Every tenant. Every acre. Every promise made and inherited."

Isabella allowed the outburst to run its course. It revealed more than the words alone.

"No," she said. "I do not think it is trifling. But I think you fear something beyond that."

Lady Banbury turned fully and looked at her. "You have no idea what you are talking about."

"Then tell me."

The marchioness gave a brief, humourless laugh. "You make it sound so simple."

"Sometimes it is easier to speak plainly to someone who is not already entangled," she offered.

Lady Banbury set the glass down too firmly. The clink echoed sharply in the silent room.

"Very well," she said. "If you insist on your plainness, I will offer some of mine. Yes, I met Lord Ravensthorpe privately. More than once. Is that what you wished to hear?"

Isabella kept her expression neutral as she asked, "He requested these meetings?"

"Insisted upon is a better word. He claimed he had not offered for me when we were younger because he had no prospects. But now that his circumstances had changed, losing me was his biggest regret. With the debt he held over Banbury's head, he left me very little room to refuse him."

Isabella wondered why Lord Banbury had gone to Ravensthorpe for a loan in the first place. He knew about the man's history with his wife.

As if she could read Isabella's mind, Lady Banbury said, "My husband is a fool. Certainly, he was regarding Ravensthorpe. Word of his financial distress reached Ravensthorpe, who approached him as a man throwing a drowning soul a lifebelt. Banbury never stopped to consider why my one-time love might choose to save him."

"And why do you believe he made the offer?" Isabella had little doubt why Lady Banbury had almost said as much, but she wanted to hear it stated plainly.

Lady Banbury sank back into her chair as though defeated. "He already knew far too much about Banbury's affairs. About the debts, and the loans, and what had been pledged against what. To secure the loan,

Banbury had to disclose even more. Ravensthorpe insisted on scrutinising the estate finances in minute detail. He took a perverse satisfaction in that knowledge."

So far, the story had been straightforward enough to understand, sordid, ugly, but simple. Ravensthorpe had persuaded Lord Banbury to accept his money and had then used it as leverage to force Lady Banbury into his bed. Yet, Isabella didn't believe that was where the story ended. If nothing else, the suspicion she and the dowager had formed that morning suggested there was more to it.

"And was that the extent of his pressure on you and your husband?" Isabella asked carefully.

"There were consequences beyond debt," Lady Banbury said. "If he had spoken openly, it would not only have ruined the estate."

Isabella felt a strange tightening in her chest. Suddenly, she was filled with nothing but pity for Lady Banbury and almost believed that, if she had murdered Ravensthorpe, perhaps she had just cause.

"He had no right," the marchioness said with sudden bitterness. "No right to speak as though he governed my future. No right to decide what must be exposed and what concealed. He behaved as though he was entitled to destroy everyone around him if he so chose."

"Was he at all willing to relent?"

Lady Banbury gave the faintest shake of her head. "I had hoped so, but no."

Isabella sat back. She could now see the vague outline of it all, though not the full shape. Yet none of it answered the main question.

"Lady Banbury," Isabella asked carefully, "did you kill him?"

The words were blunt and landed heavily. For the first time since Isabella had entered, Lady Banbury looked at her without a veil between them. The shock on her face was genuine. So was the hurt. But beneath it lurked something darker, something Isabella could not quite name.

"No," she said. "I did not kill Lord Ravensthorpe."

It was a straightforward answer. Not tearful, not indignant. Yet Isabella was unsure whether it satisfied her more or less than any elaborate denial might have done.

Lady Banbury rose once more, this time more slowly. "I think," she said, "that you have had all that I can give you."

It was dismissal; polite and calm, yet one, nonetheless.

Isabella also stood. "You have given me more than I expected."

"Then I advise you to be satisfied with that, Miss Hartwell."

At the door, Isabella paused. "If Lord Ravensthorpe was capable of such blackmail against you, then who else might he have threatened in the same manner?"

Lady Banbury's hand tightened on the back of the chair. "Indeed," she said. "That is what I have been asking myself."

And with that, she approached the door and opened it, clearly signalling that the conversation was over.

CHAPTER 22

Isabella had learned, or at least confirmed, valuable information during her conversation with Lady Banbury. However, what did it really tell her that she didn't know before? After overhearing the Banburys' argument, it was clear there was a personal entanglement between Ravensthorpe and the marchioness. That had been verified, yet it didn't really help move the murder investigation forward. More importantly, Isabella had been excused before she could verify the theory that Lady Banbury was with child.

None of this was enough to share with Inspector Gregory. At the moment, it was little more than idle gossip. Yes, her conversation with Lady Banbury implied that Ravensthorpe had brandished his financial help as a weapon to coerce the love affair, or at least that was the claim. It gave either of the Banburys' motives more teeth, but was it enough?

Her conflicting feelings about what she'd learned must have shown on her face, because when she entered her bedchamber, Polly looked up with an inquisitive expression.

"Is everything alright, miss?" the maid asked. "You look all at sixes and sevens."

After closing the door behind her, Isabella went and sat in one of the armchairs in front of the fire, considering the question.

"I just had a conversation with Lady Banbury that, on the one hand, was illuminating, but on the other hand didn't really advance my understanding of who might have killed Lord Ravensthorpe," she admitted.

Polly left the pile of laundry she was folding and moved to a position where she could look at her mistress more clearly. "I thought that policeman said you were off the hook now. Aren't you?"

With a sigh, Isabella admitted she was no longer the primary suspect. "Yet I feel I cannot simply let this be. If I have learned anything from my time with Lord and Lady Pembroke, it is that those of us in the upper classes often have access to information the police might struggle to obtain. I believe Inspector Gregory to be both fair and competent, yet as a guest in the house, I see and hear things he might not."

Polly decided to speak her mind. "That might be miss, but isn't it best to leave well enough alone? You've only a few more days here, after all."

It was a valid question, and Isabella thought it over for a moment. "Of course, that assumes we will be allowed to leave as scheduled if the killer hasn't been found by then. Yet another reason for me to do all I can to help."

"Then, what can I do, miss?" Polly asked.

"You have already done a lot just by keeping your eyes and ears open, Polly," Isabella assured her maid. "I assume there is no more information about what the footman, Hargreaves, might have been doing during the time between when he went to take the marchioness her hot milk and when he returned to the kitchen, claiming he had heard a bell."

Polly shook her head. "Nothing more than I told you before, miss. Not outright. Only that he's been very put out ever since the murder, and that he doesn't like hearing her ladyship's name mentioned in connection with any of it."

Isabella fell silent for a moment. The fire gave a soft crackle behind the grate. Outside, somewhere in the corridor, a door slammed shut.

"It is that very point that troubles me," she said at last. "Everyone in the house seems to have settled on one of two conclusions. Either Lord and Lady Banbury are to blame for everything, or they are innocent victims compelled to host a killer. While I am unsure of the marchioness's guilt, it does seem as if Hargreaves has unaccounted-for time on the night of the murder, and I wonder why. I just don't know how I might discover why."

Polly answered this in her practical way. "If you want the truth, miss, there's only so much more you'll get by asking questions upstairs. Below stairs is where people talk. Not always directly, but they do talk. And if Hargreaves knows more than he ought, it's more likely to come out there than if you put the question to him face to face. Particularly you, miss, if you don't mind me saying. He seems especially distrustful of you."

Isabella looked up sharply. "Do you think he would speak to you?"

The maid gave a slight shrug. "Not if I marched up and asked him what he was doing on the night of the murder. He'd shut up like a trap at once. But if I happened to fall into conversation with him and let him think I was curious rather than suspicious, he might say more than he intended. I've found that, as a rule, he likes to talk, particularly to the girls."

It was exactly the sort of servant-world intelligence Isabella could never have managed herself. Still, she felt a qualm. "I do not like asking you to put yourself in an awkward position for my sake."

Polly smiled. "I shouldn't be putting myself in an awkward position, miss. Just having a little chat."

"With a handsome footman."

That made Polly colour slightly, which in turn confirmed Isabella's suspicion that the girl understood perfectly well what sort of conversation this would have to be.

"Handsome men are often the easiest to draw out," Polly said, trying for dignity and not quite achieving it. "They are used to being sought out."

Despite everything, Isabella chuckled. "There is a good deal of truth to that."

Polly came and perched on the edge of the other chair. "If I were to go down to the servants' hall now, or perhaps to the back passage by the laundry room, I daresay I might chance to meet him. He's on afternoon duty today, I know that much. I could ask after the unpleasantness in the house, or say I was sorry he'd got caught up in it. Men often begin by saying very little. Then, if one offers a sympathetic ear, they soon say more."

"And what precisely would you try to discover?"

Polly frowned, considering. "First, whether he truly heard a bell or only said so to explain being upstairs for as long as he was. Second, whether he was doing something for her ladyship that he didn't want repeated. Third..." she paused. "Third, whether there's anyone in the house whose name puts him on his guard more than the others."

Isabella leaned back in her chair and thought. It was a good plan. A dangerous one, in its small way, because it required delicacy and left much to chance. Yet if Hargreaves had lied, first to protect Lady Banbury, he might say something revealing now if he believed he was speaking to someone sympathetic rather than someone interrogating him.

"I do not want you to press too hard," Isabella warned. "If he doesn't trust me, he may grow suspicious if you start asking questions too directly. If he grows wary, retreat. I would rather know little than have him warned that we are looking in his direction, or worse."

"I understand."

"Do not, under any circumstances, let him think you are acting on my instructions."

Polly looked faintly amused. "Miss, if I know one thing, it is how not to let a man think he is being managed."

Isabella smiled. Polly was younger than Isabella, yet Isabella suspected she was far more worldly in many respects.

The two women spent the next few minutes finalising the details. Polly would not go directly to the servants' hall, where questions might seem too pointed. Instead, she would first carry some linens down, which were entirely in keeping with her duties. The back passages near the pantry and laundry room formed a crossroads through which most of the indoor staff passed at some point in the afternoon. If Hargreaves were about, he would almost certainly pass that way soon enough.

"And if he does not open up to you?" Isabella asked.

"Then I shall find another way. There is always another way below stairs."

When Polly had gone, Isabella found that waiting was harder than she had expected. She rose, crossed to the window, sat again, then picked up the novel from her bedside table and found she could not read so much as a sentence. Her mind went round and round the same points. Lady

Banbury's fear. Ravensthorpe's pressure. The quiet certainty with which he had wielded knowledge and help as a weapon. And now Hargreaves, who might prove to be either a simple servant with an overdeveloped sense of loyalty or the keeper of a much more dangerous truth.

Just as she was sure she could stand the suspense no longer, she heard the faint tap of hurried footsteps in the corridor. Polly appeared in the doorway a moment later, her expression bright with the particular excitement of one who had succeeded in a delicate mission.

"Well?" Isabella asked at once.

Polly glanced over her shoulder, then closed the door. "I did not get everything I wanted, miss, but I got something."

"Sit down and tell me everything."

Polly obeyed.

"I took the laundry down as planned. Mrs Finch in the laundry room kept me longer than I liked, talking about suet puddings, and I thought the chance had gone. Then, just as I was coming back along the passage by the pantry, I met Hargreaves carrying a tray of glasses."

"Alone?"

"Yes. He was coming from clearing the dining room after luncheon. I said hello, and he stopped. He's a vain one and can't resist the idea that a girl has taken a fancy to him." This was said with a knowing look that made Isabella smile.

The maid continued, "He asked me about my stay in the house. I admitted that it had become an uncomfortable place to work, and that it seemed to me that some people upstairs were making much too free with servants' names."

"What did he say?"

"At first, not much. Only that servants were paid to endure discomfort and keep their thoughts to themselves. So, I laughed a little and said it might be easier if some of us were not being questioned as if we had driven the knife in ourselves."

Isabella nodded. That was well judged. Polly was a pretty young woman, and she imagined her maid tossing her auburn hair, her blue eyes twinkling.

"Then he asked whether I had been questioned. I told him not by the police yet, though Mrs Patrick had asked whether I knew anything about the handkerchief. I said it was at least a mercy that her ladyship had been spared the worst of it, as she seems so delicate."

Polly paused. "That did it."

"In what way?" By this point, Isabella was riveted by her maid's account.

"He looked at me real hard like, and asked what I meant by delicate. I said only that any woman would be upset after such a shock, and that Lady Banbury had looked fit to faint more than once. Then he said, very sharply, that if the house had any decency left, her ladyship would be left in peace and not stared at like a curiosity."

"Strongly put," Isabella murmured.

"Yes, miss. Far more strongly than I think the comment deserved. I said I meant no harm and only hoped she had someone attending to her, because gentlemen were all very well in a crisis, but not much use with a lady's private distresses."

That last phrase was well chosen, and Isabella turned and looked at Polly with open admiration.

"What then?"

Polly's lips twitched. "Then he coloured, just a little. Not enough to notice, unless one was looking for it. And he said that her ladyship's comfort and good name had been taken care of, and that there was no need for the rest of the house to make tales of every little thing."

"Did he say by whom it had been seen to?"

"No. But I said, 'It was you who took up her milk that night, was it not?' He looked vexed and replied that if he had, there was nothing strange about it. Someone must attend to the mistress of the house."

Isabella felt her pulse quicken. "That is not an answer."

"No, miss. Then, I said I had only asked because people were talking about the bell he claimed to have heard, and how unfortunate it was that it had placed him on the floor at just such a time."

"And?"

Polly drew a breath. "He said, 'There was no bell worth the name, only enough to explain why I was gone. I'd no wish to have the whole house discussing why I was delayed.' Then he seemed to realise what he had said and went very stiff indeed."

For a moment, Isabella said nothing. There it was. Not a full confession. Not even a full explanation. But enough.

"He said that exactly?"

"Those were not all his words, miss, but near enough."

Isabella set the book she'd been trying to read aside and leaned forward. "The bell was nothing more than an excuse after all!"

Polly nodded. "Or not entirely a lie, perhaps. But not the real reason he'd been upstairs at that time."

"And did he say why he was delayed?"

"No. I tried. I said that if her ladyship were indisposed, there was no harm in saying so. He replied that some things were better not made into kitchen talk. Then he told me I would do best to mind my own business."

"Which, in itself, is an answer."

"Yes, miss."

Isabella rose and began to pace slowly in front of the fire.

Lady Banbury had admitted to pressure, fear, and private rendezvous with the deceased. Now Hargreaves had all but confirmed that he lied about the bell because he had been delayed on Lady Banbury's account and wished no one to discuss the reason. That did not prove murder. But it did prove concealment. More importantly, it suggested that Lady Banbury's movements on the night of the murder might have been sufficiently compromising to prompt a servant to fabricate an explanation for his absence to shield her.

Polly, watching her mistress, said, "I do not think he is the sort to kill a man in his bed, miss."

"Perhaps not," Isabella said slowly. "Though I couldn't say with certainty what kind of man might be that sort. Certainly, none of those currently residing under this roof strikes me as that kind of man."

"But he knows something."

"Yes," Isabella agreed.

Isabella stopped pacing. "Hargreaves told you the first part without meaning to," she said. "He lied to protect Lady Banbury. That much is clear now. But that is not the same as saying she killed Ravensthorpe."

"Then what does it say?"

"I am unsure," Isabella acknowledged.

Polly looked at her uncertainly. "What do you do next?"

For a moment, Isabella did not answer. Her thoughts had already raced ahead. If Lady Banbury had been compromised and Hargreaves had lied to spare her, then anyone who knew that fact had a ready-made screen behind which to hide. Someone clever enough might let the whole house believe that shame, debt, and old love were explanation enough for the murder.

At last, Isabella said, "Next, I find out who else knew she had something to hide."

CHAPTER 23

No sooner had Isabella said this than she noticed the time and realised she needed to change for the afternoon's planned activities. She had no idea what the British wore when they did archery. As no one had expected such an event, she assumed her dark green walking dress, a high-collared cream blouse, a neat hat, and the sturdy boots she'd worn earlier on her walk would suffice.

After making her way downstairs, she was directed outside and around to the back of the house, where the targets had been set out on the lawn. There were already quite a few of the other guests gathered, and Isabella was relieved to see that her assumptions about attire were correct.

The lawn sloped gently away from the house towards a belt of trees, and at one end, two circular straw butts had been set up, each bearing a bright target on its face. A table had been brought out and covered with bows, quivers, finger tabs, and leather bracers.

While the other guests were making do with whatever outdoor clothes they had brought, Lady Banbury was quite another matter. As if determined to normalise the afternoon as much as possible, she was kitted out for an afternoon of serious club shooting. Her archery costume, in a soft shade of sage green, was not only plainly the work of an excellent dressmaker but also seemed specially made for the sport. The fitted jacket and high collar preserved the elegance expected of her, yet the skirt was cut with a practical simplicity that allowed freer movement than an ordinary day dress. A small hat was pinned securely over her pale hair, and when she took up the bow, the leather bracer at her wrist made it clear that this was not her first appearance on an archery lawn.

Her composure would have been impressive, had it not also looked so effortful. Her face was even paler than usual, and each strained smile seemed to cost her. Given what Isabella and the dowager had guessed, the paleness and strain might have been nothing more than symptoms of her condition. Yet as Isabella watched the marchioness, almost forcing herself to act as a gracious hostess, she wondered.

Lord Banbury, meanwhile, was almost offensively genial, laughing too heartily at remarks that scarcely warranted a smile. It struck Isabella that husband and wife were each, in their own way, performing. The question was: why?

The dowager, who had joined Isabella on the lawn, surveyed the proceedings with undisguised scepticism.

"Well," she murmured, leaning slightly on her cane, "at least if any of these people proves too insufferable, there is a bow conveniently to hand." While she spoke in jest, it was impossible to witness the tableau before them without considering that one amongst them was likely a murderer.

"Please do not say that where the police might hear you," Isabella replied under her breath.

The dowager chuckled. "Why ever not? Do you believe I might become a suspect? Certainly, the good inspector seems to be struggling to pinpoint anyone more plausible."

Their murmured exchange was interrupted by Lady Brinkley's approach, who, like the dowager, didn't seem to have dressed with any intention of participating in the afternoon's activities.

"Miss Hartwell," she said, "do tell me, are you an accomplished archer? One hears the most extraordinary things about American girls, and I imagine this might be something you were raised on. I know that your forebears had to fight on the frontier somehow."

Given that Isabella's grandfather had emigrated from Germany to New York and had never travelled further west than Pennsylvania, she didn't imagine he had spent any time fighting the Cherokee.

However, she checked herself from making such an observation and instead answered, "I fear I shall be a disappointment. I have never held a bow in my life."

Lady Brinkley looked quite shocked to hear this. "Well, Mr Shrewsbury assures me that it is quite simple," she said, adding, "Though I will not be attempting it." Addressing the dowager, she continued, "I am sure you will agree, Lady Pembroke, that such things are for the young rather than for you and me."

While there was little doubt that the dowager hadn't intended to participate, assuming this of her was beyond the pale, particularly when the assumption was that she was too old.

"You may find yourself too frail, but I intend to take part fully in the competition," she replied in a haughty tone. Isabella exercised self-control and did not raise her eyebrows at the remark.

Suddenly, Shrewsbury appeared at Isabella's elbow. He offered a welcome distraction from what Isabella had feared would be a quick escalation of hostilities between the two elderly women. He was dressed very well indeed, in a light country suit that looked both fashionable and suitable for the occasion. His pale beauty, which had first struck Isabella as almost too refined to be pleasing, looked better in the sunlight. Or perhaps it was simply that she had become accustomed to him and was even coming to enjoy his company.

"Miss Hartwell," he said, bowing slightly. "I had hoped to find you among our sportswomen."

"I am no such thing," Isabella told him. "I have just confessed my ignorance to Lady Brinkley."

"Then you are fortunate," he replied smoothly. "I am an excellent archer and a willing tutor. Nothing would give me greater pleasure than to guide you."

The dowager let out a small sound that might have been a snort.

Shrewsbury, to his credit, gave no sign of having heard it. Instead, he turned to the table and selected a bow. "May I?"

Isabella hesitated for only a moment before inclining her head. If she were to make a fool of herself, she might as well do so under the guidance of someone who at least appeared to know what he was about.

He handed her the bow with an air of ceremony. "First, you must stand properly. No amount of good intention can save a poor stance."

As she took the bow, Isabella wondered whether her previous assumption that the man was uninterested in courtship was correct. Alternatively, was it possible that Mr Shrewsbury took a longer view of such an endeavour and felt no need to propose immediately? Given what she knew about the man's financial predicament, it wouldn't be surprising if he saw her fortune as his easiest way out of his dependence on his brother-in-law. In fact, she would almost have been offended if the thought hadn't crossed the impecunious man's mind.

To Isabella's mild surprise, Shrewsbury proved a patient and able teacher. He adjusted the angle at which she held the bow, explained where to place her feet, and showed her how to fit the finger tab without ever making her feel clumsy. There was something unexpectedly deft in the way he moved. He had none of the self-conscious gallantry she had half expected, nor the smirking sense of superiority some men adopted when instructing women in practical matters. If anything, he seemed genuinely interested in the business of making her competent.

"Do not hold your shoulders so stiffly," he advised. "You need to be less self-conscious when holding the bow."

"That is easier said than done when one has all of Banbury Hall watching," Isabella replied. It was true; her archery lesson seemed to be viewed as entertainment by the other guests as they waited for the competition to begin.

Addressing the dowager, Isabella asked with genuine curiosity, "Would you like Mr Shrewsbury to help you as well?"

"I would not," the dowager answered succinctly. What went unsaid was whether she didn't need the help or didn't want it. Time would tell, Isabella thought.

On her first attempt, Isabella loosed the arrow with more determination than skill. It struck the outer ring of the target and ricocheted away.

"Well," said the dowager from behind them, "at least you did not kill anyone. That is more than can be said of someone in this house this week!"

This wasn't said as quietly as it might have been, and the dowager found herself the recipient of quite a few outraged stares and muttered "Shocking!"

The old woman smiled serenely, making it clear she considered their rebukes of no concern.

"Again," Shrewsbury said, as though the interruption had not happened. "Better this time. However, you are being too timid."

"Timidity is not something I am usually accused of," Isabella joked.

"I can well believe that, Miss Hartwell," Shrewsbury replied with a light laugh.

Under his instruction, Isabella tried again. The second arrow landed closer to the centre, though still well short.

"There," he said approvingly. "You learn quickly."

"That is because I am desperate not to bring disgrace upon myself."

"And you will not, I assure you. In archery, as in so much of life, half the battle is believing you are more competent than you perhaps are. Hold yourself with ease and assurance, and your aim will be true." Then, in a mock whisper, the man added, "I have it on good authority that this is true with any weapon, even when wielding a fly-flap."

Isabella chuckled. It felt rather inappropriate to be laughing and enjoying herself so much, barely two days after a man had been brutally murdered in their midst. Yet in this setting, on a lovely, warm spring day, Shrewsbury's dry manner was amusing and helped inject a sense of normality into what was otherwise an awkward afternoon.

Around them, the rest of the party had arranged itself into the sort of groups that any outdoor amusement encouraged. Baron Rice had taken to the sport with blustering seriousness and was attempting to explain the appropriate trajectories of arrows to anyone who came within earshot. Mrs James maintained that she had no talent for games of any kind, while clearly taking the competition extremely seriously. The vicar, to Isabella's mild astonishment, proved an excellent shot.

Lord Banbury moved among his guests with forced bonhomie, praising this shot and that attempt, while keeping a watchful eye on his wife. Lady Banbury had not yet taken up a bow. She stood speaking to Lady Mary and one of the older gentlemen, her gloved hands clasped tightly before her.

"Do not draw with your arm alone," Shrewsbury was saying. "Use your back as well. No, not like that. You will wrench yourself before tea."

"You have a low opinion of my strength."

"Not at all. Only of your technique."

The arrow she sent next hit the red ring.

"There," he said. "Look at that! Another quarter-hour and I shall have you ready to best even Alice Legh herself."

Isabella had no idea who that was, but assumed it was a compliment.

To her great surprise, Isabella found that the ease between them felt very natural. Just that morning, she had found the man a bore. Next, she had tolerated him. At some point, she had begun to enjoy his company more than she'd expected. Now, as he corrected her grip and spoke in a low tone that only she could hear, she found him not merely tolerable but decidedly agreeable. While Isabella was no more inclined to accept a betrothal than she had been, the thought of Shrewsbury attempting to woo her wasn't unpleasant.

"You improve very quickly," he said after her next shot landed respectably close to the centre.

"Perhaps I have an undiscovered talent."

"Perhaps you do," he agreed. Then his tone altered almost imperceptibly. "I am sure you have many talents I have yet to discover." There was little doubt that this was said in a distinctly flirtatious tone.

Shrewsbury watched another arrow fly from her hand before adding, rather a non-sequitur, "Ravensthorpe could not bear to be anything less than the best at everything. If he were alive and participating, he would take this competition far too seriously. The man took everything far too seriously and did not know how to laugh at himself."

The shift in subject was so smooth that Isabella did not answer at once. It took her a moment to realise that Shrewsbury had done what she had hoped, though she had not imagined he would do: slipped a relevant truth into the conversation as smoothly as if it were no more than another piece of instruction.

"Do you speak from personal experience?"

"Ha! Yes, I was not as cowed by his tongue as others were. Perhaps because he had nothing to hold over me personally."

Before Isabella could press him further, Lord Banbury called for the first round to begin, suggesting, with over-bright enthusiasm, that they start with the ladies competing among themselves.

The next hour passed more pleasantly than Isabella expected. While some people took the competition a little too seriously, most seemed to view it as an entertaining enough way to spend what might otherwise have been another boring afternoon spent waiting for Inspector Gregory's conclusions. Isabella even found herself enjoying the discipline of the sport. She found that archery required stillness, precision, and the temporary exclusion of every thought except the next shot. That concentration gave her relief from the incessant whirling of her mind, at least for a short time.

When she next became aware of Shrewsbury, he was standing just behind her left shoulder, not touching her but close enough for her to feel his presence.

"Your hand is too tense," he said quietly. "It looks as if you are trying to throttle the bow."

By now, even the dowager had conceded that Isabella was acquitting herself tolerably well. "I suppose," she said grudgingly, "that if society abandons you entirely, there may still be a future for you in rural entertainments."

"High praise indeed," Isabella murmured.

For her part, the dowager was surprisingly adept with a bow and arrow. Isabella longed to know the story behind such skill and made a point of setting this aside for tea-time conversation.

At last, Lady Banbury herself was persuaded to take a turn. The company fell into a more attentive quiet as she stepped forward. Isabella watched her closely. The marchioness's grace did not fail her, but her movements were strained, as though forcing herself to act through a layer of fatigue. She let one arrow loose cleanly enough, accepted the polite praise that followed, and then, with a smile that looked entirely insincere, declined a second turn.

Shrewsbury, standing beside her, said in a very soft voice, "She should have remained indoors." There was no mockery in his tone now. Only concern.

"For her health?" Isabella asked.

"Yes, and for the sake of her sanity," he answered with a knowing look.

Again, he had offered a truth, but only in the smallest measure. Again, it was impossible to tell what his motive was.

After an hour of archery, a servant appeared at Lord Banbury's elbow and spoke quietly. The marquess then announced that tea had been laid out at the folly for anyone who wished to continue the afternoon there.

There was an immediate stir as everyone decided they were ready for scones and cream. Bows were surrendered, gloves adjusted, hats straightened. The guests broke into small groups and began to drift along the path across the lawn towards the folly, talking more naturally now that the awkward duty of amusement had been discharged.

Shrewsbury offered Isabella her arrow back, the one she had sent closest to the centre, which a footman had retrieved.

"A trophy," he said. "To remind you of your first, but I hope not your last, archery competition."

Isabella smiled. She took the arrow, and their fingers brushed for the briefest moment. Something in Shrewsbury's expression then, a knowing smile, made her think again that he was far better company than she had first supposed. She asked the footman to have the arrow taken to her room.

"May I accompany you to tea, Miss Hartwell?" he asked. "I know a better approach to the folly than the main path. While longer, it offers a more picturesque view, and after all this effort with the bow, you deserve some recompense."

Before she could answer, the dowager called from ahead, "Do not let that young man lead you into a bog, Isabella. I have no intention of explaining such an incident to your aunt."

"I will protect Miss Hartwell with my life," Shrewsbury replied with ironic gallantry.

Chapter 24

The path that Shrewsbury led Isabella along went around a large pond fringed with reeds and early loosestrife foliage. There were several weeping willow trees, their branches dipping gracefully into the water, and the lily pads had begun to spread across the pond, though the flowers were not yet out. It was a very picturesque scene, and Isabella was glad to have this quieter moment, away from the other guests, to enjoy it.

"The folly is over there," Shrewsbury said, pointing to a spot further along the path around the pond.

"I was embarrassed to ask what a folly was when you showed it to me the other day," Isabella confessed. "You had said it was a tribute to the old marquess' classical enthusiasm. Even so, I am still confused about why he would build such a thing."

Shrewsbury laughed. "Do you not have such things in America? A folly is nothing more than an ornamental garden structure, built by people with more money than sense. They are often quite fanciful, though they can be nothing more than pavilions or belvederes."

"Well, people certainly have pavilions, gazebos, and summerhouses in America, but we call them by those names."

"You are a plain-speaking people," Shrewsbury said with a smile. "Perhaps the British are more whimsical."

"And so why has this folly been allowed to fall into such disrepair?" Isabella asked.

Now, Shrewsbury really chuckled. "That is the absurdity, the folly, if you will; it was built like that."

"It was built to look ruined? Why?" Isabella was utterly bemused by the idea.

"I have no idea. This one was built by Banbury's father, who, by all accounts, was an eccentric man."

As they drew closer, Isabella could see that on one side of the folly, there were some majestic oak trees and that the tables for afternoon tea had been set up in their shade.

"Is it entirely for show, or is it possible to go up what there is of the tower?" Isabella asked.

"We can go in if you would like. Since it is not actually ruined, the steps are quite safe," he assured her. "And you do get a wonderful view from the top."

"Then I should like to see it," Isabella said.

A few minutes later, they were at the folly. Isabella surveyed the faux ruins. Up close, it was clear that the stones scattered around the tower had been crafted to look ravaged, while the structure itself looked well-built. She could see everyone else now, gathered under the trees, beginning to eat cake and scones and sipping tea.

Shrewsbury gestured for her to precede him through the narrow-arched opening into the tower. "After you. I would not dream of depriving you of the first look."

Inside, the air was cooler, though, at barely twenty years old, the tower's atmosphere lacked the dampness of truly old stone. The staircase wound tightly upwards, its steps worn a little in the centre, as though by generations of feet, though she assumed this was also fake. Isabella kept one gloved hand lightly against the wall as she climbed.

"You were right," she said over her shoulder. "This is far sturdier than I expected."

"Of course," Shrewsbury shouted up to her. "The old marquess was eccentric, but not a fool. He ensured this would be as sound as any other modern structure."

She laughed softly and continued upward. At the top, the view was, as he had promised, excellent. The pond, with willows trailing into it, lay below them, almost like an oil painting. Beyond the oaks, the tea tables stood in orderly rows in the shade, with white cloths, polished silver, and the bright colours of the ladies' gowns scattered among them.

"It is beautiful," Isabella said.

Shrewsbury, who had stood at her shoulder, looked not at the view but at her. "Yes, this view is beautiful."

The answer was a little too smooth, yet it pleased her more than it should have. There was no great harm in a little gallant flirtation, provided one recognised it for what it was.

From below came the distant murmur of voices and the occasional peal of laughter.

"We ought to go down," Isabella said. "There may be no scones left if we do not hurry. And I have become quite the devotee of your English cream teas."

"Then I would not be the cause of you missing out," Shrewsbury replied. "Though there is another way back. A shorter path from the far side, if you do not object to a less ceremonious descent."

Isabella glanced at him. "That depends on how much danger it poses."

"Very little, I promise. Only a slightly uneven patch of ground. I should never forgive myself if I led you into actual peril instead of towards Victoria sponge."

The path he referred to ran behind the folly, where the grass gave way to a narrow strip of genuinely worn flagstone set into a slight slope. On one side, the ground fell away gently towards the pond, where the bank was studded with primroses and new spring growth.

As they emerged from the tower into the sunlight, Shrewsbury offered his arm.

Isabella did not take it, though she smiled at the gesture. "You need not look so disappointed. I am perfectly capable of walking on my own."

"I had not the slightest doubt of it," he said. "But the path is a little uneven here. It predates the folly by many decades, and there is a loose edge on the third stone. It has been catching people out for years."

He spoke carelessly enough and moved slightly ahead and to the side of Isabella, leaving just enough room for her to pass. Though he was trying to be helpful, his movement pushed Isabella to step where the path narrowed. Almost at once, the stone shifted beneath her. It was not a great lurch, but it was sharp and sudden. One foot slipped forward, the hem of her skirt caught on the broken edge, and for a breathless instant, the world seemed to tilt unpleasantly to one side.

Isabella gave a small, involuntary gasp, and Shrewsbury caught her at once. One hand closed firmly around her forearm; the other shot to her waist with such speed and certainty that by the time she fully realised she was falling, she was already being steadied. By luck, he had positioned himself perfectly to rescue her.

"The folly seems determined to live up to its name," he said lightly.

Isabella took a moment to catch her breath and realised she was now much closer to Shrewsbury than propriety dictated. She could feel the pressure of his hand through the fabric at her waist, warm and steady, and was suddenly, annoyingly aware of her own lack of composure.

"How mortifying," she said, when she had recovered herself enough to speak. "I suppose I must now thank you for saving me from a most ridiculous death."

"I doubt the fall would have been fatal, except perhaps to your dignity," he replied. "I am glad I was able to preserve that. Now you may safely enjoy your scones and cream with your head held high."

That made her laugh and feel better at once. Shrewsbury released his grip on her waist and stepped back just far enough to restore the proper distance between them.

"I beg your pardon," he said. "I ought to have warned you more clearly. In hindsight, 'a loose edge on the stone' perhaps understated the peril."

"But you did warn me. You even offered me your arm. It was I who was foolhardy and failed to pay attention," Isabella said firmly. "And now I must thank you for saving me from myself and from a serious injury."

"I saved you from a slight twist to the ankle at most," he replied graciously.

Isabella looked down at the offending stone. It sat at an odd angle, one corner lower than the others, its edge cracked and half hidden by moss. Now that she saw it properly, she wondered how she had missed it.

Shrewsbury, meanwhile, had crouched slightly and nudged the stone with the side of his boot. It shifted again.

"You see?" he said indignantly. "Perfectly treacherous. I have told Banbury more than once that it ought to be repaired, but it has stayed exactly as it is. I know better than to trust it now."

There was something faintly odd about the way he said it, as though he were suddenly determined to paint the near fall as more dangerous than it had been. Yet there was nothing on his face but mild amusement and concern.

"Well," Isabella said, "I shall certainly know better in future."

Now, Shrewsbury offered his arm again, more quietly, and this time Isabella took it. There seemed little point in insisting on absolute independence after nearly slipping at his feet. Together, they walked the rest of the path towards the tea tables beneath the oaks.

As they approached, the party came gradually into focus. Lady Banbury was already seated, her pale green gown spread elegantly around her chair. Mrs Humsby, with whom Isabella had exchanged barely a word, sat nearby in mauve silk, speaking in a voice that carried farther than she likely intended. Lord Banbury stood near the samovar, overseeing matters with what seemed, again to Isabella, a rather forced brightness. It was as if the marquess were doing all he could to pretend that a murder investigation wasn't waiting for them back at the house.

The dowager, settled in the deepest shade with a plate already in hand, looked up as they approached. Her sharp eyes travelled at once from Isabella's face to Shrewsbury's arm and back again. One eyebrow lifted a mere degree, but it spoke volumes.

"Well," she said as Isabella took her seat, "you seem to have survived your excursion."

"Barely," Shrewsbury said before Isabella could answer. "I was not the guide and protector I should have been and had promised to be." As he said this, he hung his head in what was almost a parody of sheepishness.

The dowager's gaze sharpened. "Really? Miss Hartwell seems to be in one piece. Was there an incident whose scars are not visible?"

"There was a loose stone," Isabella said. "I ignored Mr Shrewsbury's offer of his arm, and then I slipped. Luckily, he caught me before I made a complete fool of myself."

"How fortunate," said the dowager. The words were perfectly civil, yet Isabella recognised the meaning beneath her tone: the old woman had noticed rather more than she was letting on.

Across the table, Lady Banbury had also looked up. Her glance flicked briefly from Isabella to Shrewsbury and then away again, though not before Isabella caught a fleeting expression there, neither quite concern nor quite irritation. If there was any tension, it vanished at once beneath the marchioness's usual serene composure.

Lord Banbury called out with hearty cheerfulness, "Miss Hartwell, Shrewsbury, come, come, you are in danger of missing the best of the sandwiches."

"After our brush with catastrophe, that would be too cruel," Shrewsbury said quietly in Isabella's ear as he drew out a chair for her. "Would you allow me the honour of fetching you a plate?" he asked.

While Isabella's first instinct was to insist that she was more than capable of fetching her own food, she caught herself before saying so. She found that her view of Mr Shrewsbury had shifted, however slightly, that afternoon. Not only was she grateful to him for catching her, but she was also appreciative of the lightness he had brought to the incident. He had been gallant without being patronising. Instead, he had been charming and gracious.

When she had needed a steady hand, he had proved to have one. That, Isabella thought, was worth noting.

CHAPTER 25

Isabella had to admit that the afternoon tea at the folly was a welcome distraction. Shrewsbury remained attentive, but not cloyingly so. He even engaged the dowager in light-hearted banter, which, surprisingly, she didn't seem to mind. The old woman shot her the occasional knowing look, and Isabella suspected they'd be having a heart-to-heart before the day was out. As they made their way back to the house after eating their fill of scones, cakes, and tea sandwiches, Isabella considered, in anticipation of such a conversation, what she would say.

She had been determined that her travels to Britain were about adventure rather than matrimony. It was also undoubtedly the case that Aunt Caro had not had an untitled, down-on-his-luck man in mind for her niece when she first suggested the trip. Those things aside, Isabella couldn't deny Shrewsbury's charm. And while she didn't usually favour the pale, undernourished, poet look that the man perfectly exemplified, Isabella had to admit that he had beautiful eyes and a very sweet smile.

Nevertheless, as much as she was enjoying his flirtation, her heart remained untouched. Isabella was a level-headed, practical young woman and realised that finding a man good company for a few hours was a far cry from considering him a solid candidate with whom to spend the rest of her life. Finally, she decided that, if he were to raise the subject of matrimony, she would tell him they were insufficiently acquainted to discuss such a question, but, if he were interested in furthering their friendship when she returned to London, she would not be averse to the idea.

As she suspected, when Shrewsbury was called away by his sister, the two women entered the house alone, and the dowager said in a low voice, "I will join you in your room after I have dressed for dinner."

The dowager was as good as her word, and just as Polly was putting the finishing touches to Isabella's hair that evening, there was a knock at the door. Polly opened it, and the dowager swept in.

"Well, you look particularly charming this evening, my dear," the dowager said, inspecting Isabella's new, pearl-grey silk evening gown. "Is all this effort for anyone in particular?"

Isabella knew she needed to get this conversation out of the way, so she dismissed Polly before joining the dowager, who had taken one of the armchairs.

"Is there anything you wish to ask me, Julia?" she asked.

"Is there anything you wish to tell me, Isabella?" the dowager asked with a sly smile.

Sighing, Isabella replied, "I do not believe Mr Shrewsbury is wooing me." Seeing the dowager about to interrupt with her own observations, Isabella held up a hand. "I do not deny there is some flirtation. However, I have no reason to believe it goes any further than that."

"And if it does?"

"Then I shall inform him that I have no immediate plans to become betrothed and that, moreover, we do not know each other well enough for that to be a conversation at this point."

"So, that is not a no," the dowager observed.

"I will not be getting betrothed this week or anytime soon," Isabella said with more conviction. "However, I cannot deny that Mr Shrewsbury has turned out to be a surprisingly charming companion. Given everything else that has happened this week, he has been a very pleasant diversion."

"You are young, beautiful, rich, and charming, my dear. I do not begrudge you a harmless flirtation, and I am happy to hear it is nothing more than that," the dowager assured her with a motherly smile.

Isabella was tempted to ask why the other woman was so happy about this news, but she suspected she knew. There was no doubt that, apart from his personal charms, Mr Shrewsbury was an ineligible match. Of course, if she loved him, Isabella wouldn't care about such things. But she didn't.

Hoping to change the subject, she said, "I never told you about my conversation with Lady Banbury earlier."

"No, it seems you have been keeping many things from me!" she said, rather petulantly.

"Rather, this is the first opportunity we have had to speak privately," Isabella said, a little defensively.

"That may well be," the dowager conceded. "However, now that we are alone, tell me everything."

When she had finished relaying the details of that conversation, Isabella added the titbit that Shrewsbury had earlier revealed about Ravensthorpe. "While I am not condoning murder in any shape or form," she said. "It has to be said that Lord Ravensthorpe sounds like an unpleasant man who enjoyed having leverage and power over people and used them to rather horrible effect."

"Indeed. One has to wonder whether our list of possible suspects is long enough. It sounds as if the number of people with reason to want the man dead might be legion."

This observation led Isabella to consider something that had flickered through her mind many times: how much Inspector Gregory had learned, and whether, as she'd mentioned to Polly earlier, she should now seek a meeting with the inspector.

Thinking about the conversation with Polly made Isabella realise the key piece of information she'd failed to share with the dowager: her maid's conversation with Hargreaves. She quickly rectified that oversight.

"The footman admitted all that?" the dowager said in amazement when she had finished. "That maid of yours is a canny little thing. I have always found my maid, Withers, a serviceable gatherer of gossip, but I very much doubt she would be as adept at field operations as your Polly." This was all said in the most admiring of tones.

"He certainly admitted that his story about hearing a bell was nothing more than a cover to explain why he had been upstairs for so long."

"What had he been doing during that time?"

"Therein lies the rub," Isabella admitted. "Hence, the reason I believe I now have to speak with Inspector Gregory. My ability to tease out the details may have reached its natural limits. However, he can take what I have learned and ask questions as directly as necessary. Certainly, Lady Banbury would not dare throw him out on his ear as she did me earlier."

It was hard to argue with her logic, and so the dowager agreed with the plan.

"I will do my best to speak to him this evening and ask for a time to meet," Isabella decided.

With nothing more to discuss, the women went down to the drawing room for pre-dinner drinks. Isabella hoped the inspector would join them again, and was relieved when he walked into the room wearing the same, probably borrowed, evening wear as the previous day.

While she wished to speak with him, Isabella knew that rushing up to the man would be far too conspicuous. Yet again, all eyes turned on the inspector as he entered, no less wary than the evening before. As luck would have it, after casting around the room for where he might receive a more welcoming reception, Gregory's gaze fell on Isabella. She smiled, and he took that as a sufficient invitation to head in her direction.

Isabella and the dowager had been standing together, sipping sherry. Once Inspector Gregory joined them, the other guests seemed inclined to leave the small group alone and return to their conversations.

"Miss Hartwell, your ladyship," the inspector said with a slight bow. "How was your afternoon of archery?" If the policeman had any thoughts on the assembled guests, or, as he saw them, suspects, indulging in such frivolities while a murder investigation was underway, he kept them very much to himself.

"It was my first attempt at the sport, but I believe I acquitted myself adequately," Isabella replied.

"More than adequately, my dear," the dowager added. "I believe that if you practised, you would be quite adept."

Then, because it seemed a natural thing to say at that juncture, Isabella asked, "How was your afternoon, inspector? How is your investigation going?"

Gregory smiled. "Of course, you realise I cannot divulge as much, Miss Hartwell."

"Of course," she said. Then, in a much lower voice, Isabella added, "I would like a word with you in private when you have time."

"Is this about the investigation?" he asked. Isabella nodded slightly.

"Then, let us speak after dinner. I will excuse myself when the ladies leave the room, and perhaps you can feign a headache or something similar. I will meet you in the library." The suggestion was surprisingly conspiratorial for so sober a man, though perhaps the circumstances warranted it.

It seemed the timing of the conversation was fortuitous; no sooner had this arrangement been made than Lord Banbury assailed their group.

"Inspector, I am glad you could join us this evening," their host said graciously.

"A man has to eat," Gregory replied rather gruffly.

And with that, they were summoned to dinner.

Isabella found herself entirely distracted during the meal, considering exactly what she would say to Inspector Gregory and anticipating how he might respond to her information. It seemed that in little more than a day, she had moved from the inspector's prime suspect to his principal informant!

CHAPTER 26

Standing in front of the library door, Isabella felt surprisingly nervous. She was the one who had requested the meeting, after all. What was she so worried about? The truth was, she felt a degree of guilt, both for continuing to investigate after her name had been cleared and for doing so without immediately reporting her findings to the inspector. While she had told herself there wasn't sufficient concrete information to take to him earlier, was that how Gregory would see it?

She wasn't a coward. She could face her fears and take responsibility for her actions, even if it meant the inspector forbade her from continuing to interfere in his investigation. After taking one more deep breath, Isabella knocked lightly on the door and was invited to enter.

"Come, come, Miss Hartwell. And shut the door behind you," Inspector Gregory said in an urgent tone. "I assume that you wish this conversation to remain confidential."

"Indeed, inspector," she agreed, shutting the door and crossing the room to take the seat in front of the desk where he was seated.

Sitting opposite the inspector, Isabella could see how weary he was.

"I doubt this is the easiest investigation for you and your men," she said sympathetically.

"That is an understatement," he agreed. "At least when I'm dealing with hardened criminals, their antagonism and lack of cooperation are out in the open. But with this bunch," he said, gesturing with his thumb towards the dining room, "well, with them, it's all politeness and 'Do join us for sherry in the drawing room', with the lies sitting just close enough to the surface to be sensed."

As he said this, the inspector seemed to realise to whom he was speaking. "Excuse me, Miss Hartwell. I didn't mean to speak ill of your friends."

"Oh, these people are not my friends," she said quickly. "Well, Lady Pembroke is my friend, but for the rest, I have hardly known them any longer than you have. And as an American, I know exactly what you mean about the British stiff upper lip and the pantomime of good manners and etiquette."

Even as she said this, Isabella wondered whether Mrs Astor and the Four Hundred were much better. Perhaps such behaviour was more a function of class than of nationality.

Whether this was true or not, her words seemed to comfort Inspector Gregory, who smiled. "How can I help you, Miss Hartwell?" he asked.

"As you know," she began hesitantly. "I did some investigating on my own to prove my innocence."

"Indeed, you did," the inspector replied in a noncommittal, but not angry, tone. "I would like to believe that my men and I would have reached that conclusion anyway, but I acknowledge that you helped us reach it more quickly."

"That is very kind of you, Inspector." Isabella hesitated; that had been the easy part. Then she continued, "However, I did not stop, even though my innocence was beyond doubt."

The inspector pursed his lips for a moment. "Is that so? Might I ask why not? Do you lack confidence in my competence?" There was a slight edge to his voice now, hard to miss.

"Not at all. Truly. It is rather..." She tried again. "For the past few months, I have found myself involved in quite a few murder investigations."

It seemed this was not what the inspector expected to hear.

"Might I ask how that happened?"

"I have become friends with the Earl of Pembroke and his wife," she explained.

"I assume these Pembrokes are related to your friend, the dowager countess?"

"They are. They have been involved in such investigations for the past two years."

When the inspector raised his eyebrows at this, Isabella added, "In the second investigation I was involved in, the Queen requested their assistance."

"Our queen?" he asked in disbelief.

"Yes. Your queen."

"So, you believe yourself something of an expert now?" There was that edge again.

"I wouldn't say I'm an expert. However, what I have come to see is that, when the upper classes, particularly the aristocracy, are concerned, it is far easier for someone like me, whom they consider, if not an equal, at least on a similar footing, to ask questions than it often is for the police."

Gregory considered her words for a few moments. Finally, he seemed to have made up his mind. "I will grant you that," he admitted. "And so, is that why you have continued to poke around?"

"It is. And although I did learn some things, nothing seemed sufficiently concrete to merit your attention."

"Until now?"

"Yes. Until now." Then Isabella added hurriedly, "And I am fully aware that you may already know everything I am about to tell you, and that even if you do, it is unlikely you will acknowledge it to me."

"Well, let me be the judge of how useful your intelligence is. Now, tell me everything."

And so, she did.

Gregory did not interrupt her at first. He sat very still, both elbows resting on the arms of his chair, as she began with the overheard quarrel in the meadow and then moved on to her private conversation with Lady Banbury. Only when she reached the part about Polly's conversation with Hargreaves did he shift.

"Stop there," he said.

Isabella, who had been speaking more quickly than she realised, broke off immediately.

"You are telling me that your maid deliberately drew the footman into conversation to discover whether his account of the bell was truthful?"

There was no point in pretending otherwise. "Yes."

"And did this seem to you a sensible course of action? Did you consider the danger she might be putting herself in?"

Isabella was chagrined. Of course, she had considered it and had warned Polly. Nonetheless, in hindsight, had it even been wise to let her do as much as she had?

In an uncertain tone, she said, "At the time, such a conversation seemed the only likely way to yield anything useful." She accompanied this with a slight shrug of her shoulders. Even to her own ears, it sounded like a weak excuse.

Gregory looked at her for a long moment. To her relief, he did not seem angry so much as drained.

"The only way to yield anything useful?" he repeated. "To permit your servant to put herself in harm's way?"

Isabella bristled. "There was no coercion. Quite the opposite, in fact; it was her idea. I was very uncertain and needed persuasion. And trust me, inspector, I would never have agreed if she'd been putting herself at any real risk."

"Or any real risk, as far as you could determine," he said dryly.

The rebuke stung because it was deserved. Isabella lowered her gaze for a moment, then forced herself to meet his eyes.

"Be that as it may, Inspector, she did learn something." She then finished telling the story of Polly's conversation with Hargreaves.

Isabella related the encounter as accurately as she could. She repeated Hargreaves's insistence that Lady Banbury ought to be left in peace, that her comfort and good name had been taken care of, and, most importantly, his admission that there had been no bell worth naming, merely something sufficient to explain why he had been away so long.

"Your maid did learn a lot," the inspector admitted when she was done. He exhaled through his nose, then leaned back. "Is there more?"

Isabella indicated that there was. She was careful to relay only what had truly been said and what had plainly been implied. She gave him none of her inferences or suspicions. Lady Banbury admitted that Lord Ravensthorpe had insisted on private meetings. He had known far too much about the estate's finances and had used that knowledge to exert pressure on both husband and wife. There were, she had suggested, consequences beyond debt. Consequences that would have ruined more than the estate if spoken of openly. And yet, when directly asked whether she had killed Ravensthorpe, she had denied it.

Gregory listened without moving.

Finally, Isabella had told him everything. Well, almost everything. She couldn't decide whether to reveal the suspicions that she and the dowager had about Lady Banbury's condition.

"Inspector, there is one more thing," she offered.

"Even more?"

"Well, this might be categorised as speculation. However, the dowager countess and I agree on what we saw. If we are right, it might be very pertinent to the investigation."

"Your caveat is understood," Gregory assured her.

She told him what they had witnessed that morning when they'd met Lady Banbury outside, and what they'd surmised from it.

The inspector rose abruptly and crossed to the fireplace, where he stood with his back to her for a few moments. Isabella had the strong impression that he was not merely considering her account, but fitting it into something already half-formed in his mind.

He turned back towards her. "I've been at this game for more than twenty years, Miss Hartwell. I've seen it all. And I know what it likely means when a married couple sleep on opposite sides of an enormous house. This is not as shocking to me as you might imagine," he said at last.

"I can only imagine," Isabella conceded.

He continued, "When you first spoke of what you had overheard between Lord and Lady Banbury, it seemed almost too perfectly set up for a murder. Almost as if it were in a Penny Dreadful: a compromised married woman, a dead former lover, a husband in debt to him, and now, perhaps, she is carrying the other man's child. The story practically writes itself."

"It does," Isabella agreed.

"And that," Gregory said, turning back towards her, "is exactly what troubles me now."

She frowned. "Because it is too obvious?"

"It certainly seems too easy. If your suspicions are correct, that is even truer."

He resumed his seat and explained. "Lord Banbury strikes me as an intelligent man. While it seems undeniable that he had reason to wish Lord Ravensthorpe dead, was stabbing him in such a gruesome manner the most sensible way to do so? I had already learned from another guest about the estate's financial situation."

When he saw Isabella's surprise at his words, he added, "It seems that Ravensthorpe was not the first person to whom the marquess went with his begging bowl."

"So, you would have learned of his debt to Ravensthorpe eventually," Isabella guessed.

"Eventually. And more than one person was quick to tell me about the marchioness's personal history with Lord Ravensthorpe."

Isabella could see the inspector's point. Certainly, as far as Lord Banbury was concerned, killing the man under his roof in a way that couldn't be construed as anything other than murder seemed somewhat clumsy.

"Furthermore, Miss Hartwell, what you have brought me tonight does not prove that Lady Banbury killed Lord Ravensthorpe. It suggests that she had reason to lie, and that Hargreaves might have reason to lie on her behalf. Those are not the same thing as murder."

He continued, "People will endure a great deal to keep private shame from becoming public scandal. They will lie for it, conceal for it, and perjure themselves for it. But that does not mean they will resort to violence. Sometimes disgrace is merely disgrace."

Isabella thought of Lady Banbury's face when she had been asked outright whether she had killed Ravensthorpe. There had been shock. Hurt, too. But not guilt. Or not of murder, at least.

"Then you believe them both innocent?"

"I did not say that." Gregory's voice was brisk again. "I said only that concealment is not proof of murder. It may yet turn out that her ladyship wished him dead badly enough to contrive it, or at least to resort to it in a moment of insanity."

Gregory steepled his fingers. "Tell me again. You say that Lady Banbury used the phrase 'consequences beyond debt'?"

"She did."

"And Hargreaves spoke of her 'good name'?"

"Yes."

"Then the matter is almost certainly as one would expect." He did not elaborate, but Isabella knew what he meant and agreed.

The inspector considered all she'd said, then spoke. "While I do not claim to be an expert on such matters, my understanding is that, when it comes to the future of the estate, if Banbury claims the child as his at birth, the child would be accepted as his heir."

Isabella had no idea and deferred to his greater knowledge. However, she could see where he was going with his line of thought. "So, even if the child is Ravensthorpe's, and even if Lord Banbury knows or at least suspects as much, for practical purposes, it would have made no difference. Unless he chose to use that knowledge to divorce his wife, there was little her lover could have threatened her with besides gossip."

"I believe that to be the case." He went on. "What interests me more at this moment is not merely that Hargreaves lied, but when and why he lied. If he needed an excuse for the time he had been upstairs, we must ask what he was concealing during that interval. Was he shielding Lady Banbury's movements? Attending to her after a distressing interview? Or was it something even worse?"

"That last possibility occurred to me as well," Isabella admitted.

At last, Gregory said, "I shall speak to Hargreaves again. Alone."

"And Lady Banbury?"

"I shall decide tomorrow whether to speak with her directly, and, if so, how."

Isabella folded her hands in her lap. "Then I was right to come to you."

"Yes," he said simply. "You were. Though you should have done so sooner." He then offered her a small smile. "Regardless, you have uncovered invaluable evidence, and I am grateful."

The relief that passed through Isabella was overwhelming.

"However," he continued, "do not take that as encouragement to continue as you have been."

She ought to have anticipated the reprimand. Even so, she felt herself stiffen slightly.

"I cannot have you and your maid conducting an unofficial inquiry throughout the household. You have been fortunate so far. That is not the same as being prudent."

"I understand."

"Do you?" His voice was not harsh, merely tired. "A murderer who realises you are no longer a useful scapegoat and instead a genuine inconvenience may behave very differently towards you."

His words chilled her more than she cared to admit.

"I had not considered it in those terms."

"Then think of it now." He held her gaze. "If you happen to learn anything more, you will bring it directly to me. You will not send your maid to fish for it, nor corner people in their rooms, nor wander the grounds with anyone you do not fully trust."

At that last line, it was impossible not to think of Shrewsbury leading her round the pond and up the folly tower.

"I give you my word," she said.

He seemed to consider whether her word was likely to prove equal to the circumstances. Apparently deciding it was the best he would get, he inclined his head.

"Good. Then we understand each other."

Inspector Gregory rose, signalling that the meeting was over. Isabella stood as well.

As Isabella left the library, it occurred to her that the case had not narrowed as much as she had hoped. Instead, it had shifted, and somehow that felt more dangerous.

CHAPTER 27

It had been a restless night. All Isabella could think about was Inspector Gregory's admonishments. While she'd been expecting him to be unhappy that she had been investigating, the specifics of his displeasure had been jarring. Of course, she had realised that allowing Polly to waylay Hargreaves carried risks, but the idea that it might appear she had knowingly put a member of her staff in harm's way, creating a situation where the young woman might feel she had no choice but to comply, was dreadful.

Her worries and tiredness must have shown on her face when she entered the breakfast room, for Shrewsbury immediately approached.

"Are you quite alright, Miss Hartwell?" he asked, his voice concerned.

"I didn't have the best night's sleep," she admitted.

Shrewsbury steered her to the table. "Let me get you some coffee and something to eat."

While the very independent Isabella might have chafed at any suggestion of frailty under normal circumstances, this offer felt merely kind and, given how exhausted she was, very welcome.

"Perhaps just some toast and jam," she said.

"Your wish is my command," he said with a slight bow. Again, a gesture that might have seemed a ridiculous attempt at chivalry in other circumstances felt like nothing more than gentlemanly good manners.

Ten minutes later, Isabella was drinking her second cup of coffee and had finished a slice of toast.

"You look better than when you walked in," Shrewsbury said with a gentle smile. He had been sitting at her side, saying very little as she fortified herself.

"It is a good thing that I am not a vain woman," she teased. "Saying that I looked anything other than wonderful earlier might have caused quite offence."

"Yet another asset to add to your list of charms," he replied.

As she started on her second slice of toast, Shrewsbury asked, "Might I enquire as to the cause of your poor night's sleep?"

Isabella sighed. "It was pointed out to me that I had been high-handed with a servant, something I strive never to be."

"And who dared to make such an accusation? I cannot imagine it was Lady Pembroke; she strikes me as someone who considers imperiousness, particularly towards servants, de rigueur."

This made Isabella chuckle. "You seem to have a good understanding of the dowager countess."

"I have a grandmother just like her. To this day, she terrifies me."

"Lady Pembroke's bark is worse than her bite," Isabella assured him.

"I was worried about you last night when the gentlemen returned to the drawing room after dinner, and you were not there," Shrewsbury said anxiously. "Did your disquiet begin yesterday evening?"

It was an innocent question, asked in a concerned tone, and Isabella saw no reason to demur.

"Indeed. The conversation I spent half the night worrying about took place then."

Very casually, Shrewsbury continued, "I noticed that Inspector Gregory also retired early for the evening. I do hope he is not persecuting you again."

The astuteness of Shrewsbury's observation caught Isabella off guard.

"I am not being persecuted," she assured her friend.

"But he was the cause of your unease?"

Was there any point in continuing to deny what she had already effectively given away?

"I did have a conversation with the inspector, and yes, that was part of why I had trouble sleeping."

"The cad!" Shrewsbury exclaimed passionately.

The vehemence of the remark was almost enough to make Isabella smile, despite her lingering unease.

"Inspector Gregory is not a cad," she said. "He was severe with me, yes, but not unjustly so. He believed I had overstepped."

Shrewsbury's expression softened to something more rueful. "Then I must amend my statement. He is not a cad, but perhaps not quite a gentleman if he interrogated you so roughly."

"That is neither wholly unexpected nor unreasonable for a policeman," Isabella pointed out. "His job is not to treat me with kid gloves."

"No, perhaps not." He leaned back slightly in his chair and regarded her carefully. "Still, I dislike the idea of his troubling you. You have suffered enough already from this business without being made to answer for every rumour and whisper in the house."

His tone was kind, yet Isabella could not help but notice how deftly he had shifted the subject from her abstract distress to the details of her conversation with Inspector Gregory.

Shrewsbury added, as though the thought had only just occurred to him, "I trust he has not resumed considering you as a possible suspect. He must realise that you are one of the least likely people to commit murder in this house."

Isabella was caught off guard by this statement; why was she one of the least likely people? While she hoped she was seen as morally upright and decent, she was young and strong, so certainly more physically capable of stabbing a man than many of the older guests.

Finally, she shook off her concern and assumed that, yet again, the statement was made more out of gallantry than anything else.

"He no longer considers me a likely culprit, if that is what you mean," she conceded. "I imagine none of us is entirely free of suspicion until the actual killer is caught."

"I am relieved to hear it." Shrewsbury reached for his coffee. "Though I confess I should like even more to hear in which direction his suspicion has turned, so as to reassure myself that you are entirely safe from the finger of accusation pointing in your direction."

"I can assure you that I have no fear of being accused of murder. However, where the inspector might be looking is hardly for me to say."

"No," he said at once, with a small smile. "Of course not. You must forgive me. I do not mean to pry."

Isabella buttered the last corner of toast on her plate more carefully than necessary and said, "I asked to speak with the inspector privately to share an observation of my own, nothing more. The inspector asked questions, and I answered them. That is all."

Shrewsbury inclined his head as if accepting the explanation. "Then let me ask you no more about Gregory," he said. "Let me ask instead about yourself. Why are you so upset that you cannot sleep?"

There was enough sincerity in the question that Isabella found herself answering more candidly than she had intended to.

"I do not like the idea of having behaved carelessly towards someone in my employ," she said. "To risk one's own comfort or reputation is one thing. To discover, after the event, that someone else may have felt obliged to take a risk because of one's wishes is quite another."

Shrewsbury's face changed very slightly. The idle social smile did not vanish, but a more serious look settled beneath it.

"You are speaking of your maid?"

"I am."

"And the inspector made you feel you had been careless with her?"

"He suggested, not unreasonably, that my judgement on the matter may have been less than perfect."

Shrewsbury looked down at his plate for a moment, then back at her. "For what it is worth, I think there is a great difference between using a servant carelessly and trusting one who chooses to act out of loyalty and intelligence."

"That is a generous distinction, one I had persuaded myself of initially. The inspector prompted me to reevaluate my thinking, and on reflection, I realised that his point was valid."

"You acted with good intent; there can be no doubt of that. Your upset at the situation speaks to both your good heart and your care for your maid."

He said this with such certainty and kindness that, for a moment, Isabella almost let herself be comforted by his words.

Then Shrewsbury added, in a tone that, though still mild, might have been just a shade too casual, "Though one wonders what the inspector hopes to gain by frightening you in that way, unless he has reached a conclusion of his own and is anxious to keep you clear of it."

Isabella set down her toast. There was something in that remark that made her look at him more closely. "You are very interested in Inspector Gregory's conclusions this morning."

"Would you have me be indifferent?" he asked, sounding faintly amused. "My sister's serenity, my brother-in-law's reputation, and the security of everyone in this household all seem closely entangled with his conclusions. To say nothing of your own peace of mind."

The answer was reasonable. Too reasonable, perhaps.

"And yet," Isabella said, "I have not mentioned your sister."

Shrewsbury's gaze did not waver, though something in it became a little more intense.

"No," he said. "You have not. But the whole house has done little else for two days. It would require unusually wilful blindness not to see where suspicion has settled."

There was no offence in his voice. If anything, there was weariness. That, more than anything, made Isabella listen.

He went on, "Ravensthorpe had a singular talent for turning every weakness in others into an instrument to use against them. Money, vanity, fear, affection, pride, he used them all in much the same way. Once he perceived a vulnerable point, he pressed it until the person in question either yielded or broke."

Isabella looked at him more closely. "You speak as if you knew that from experience."

"I knew him for most of my life. I have had the measure of him for many years now."

"But you said yesterday that he had nothing to hold over you personally."

"I said nothing he knew of," Shrewsbury corrected softly. "That is not quite the same thing."

"And is this something that might affect your position?" Isabella asked lightly.

That earned her a mirthless smile. "My own position is one of decorative uselessness, as Lady Pembroke has no doubt already observed. Perhaps that is why I was of no interest to Ravensthorpe; he had nothing to gain from me."

Shrewsbury stirred his coffee but never raised the cup to his lips. "My sister has been under strain that would have shaken many stronger people than she. Ravensthorpe knew it and preyed upon it. He knew precisely where to apply pressure and never once paused to consider the harm he did, so long as he moved matters an inch nearer to his own satisfaction."

"Yet, you seem very certain that your sister could not have killed him."

At that, something in his expression sharpened in a way Isabella had never seen before.

"My sister," he said with sudden emphasis, "may have been unwise. She may have shown poor judgement in maintaining old associations. She may have been frightened and indecisive when decisiveness was required. But she is not vicious, Miss Hartwell. She is not cold-blooded. And she is certainly not the kind of woman to creep into a gentleman's room and butcher him in his sleep."

The force of the statement made Isabella sit back slightly. Shrewsbury had raised his voice somewhat during his fervent endorsement of his sister, and Isabella was glad the breakfast room was mostly empty.

"I did not say she was guilty," Isabella pointed out.

"No. You did not." He drew a breath and immediately moderated his tone. "Forgive me, but it has become impossible to hear her name spoken in this house without feeling that everyone is quietly drawing the same conclusion."

"And are they?"

"Some of them." His smile returned, though it was thinner. "Others are less quiet."

There it was again, that over-readiness to defend Lady Banbury against accusations that had not been levelled. Of course, Isabella had wondered about Lady Banbury. Yet it was striking how determined her brother was to cast the situation in a particular light.

After a moment, he said in a quieter voice, "Did Gregory seem to believe in Antonia's innocence? Did he understand?"

The question was almost pleading.

"Understand what?"

"That fear is not the same as violence. That the wish to avoid a scandal, however ugly it might be, does not always lead to murder."

She considered the question. In truth, Inspector Gregory seemed to understand that very point extremely well. But it didn't seem her place to say so.

"The inspector seems a thoughtful man," was all Isabella felt comfortable admitting.

Shrewsbury gave a short, almost self-mocking laugh. "You will fit in very well with British upper-class society if you choose to settle in these Isles. You have learned the art of saying something and nothing at once."

"I prefer to believe I have learned discretion."

"Then Gregory did ask about my sister."

Isabella pressed her lips together firmly and said nothing more.

He held her gaze for a second longer, then smiled with a frankness that might almost have disarmed her, had it not seemed so deliberate.

"I apologise again," he said. "When one's family is under strain, curiosity becomes difficult to control. However, I have crossed a line this morning, and it is unconscionable that I have added to your strain rather than relieved it."

Before Isabella could relieve him of his culpability, Lady Banbury entered the breakfast room. She was pale again, particularly wan, as if she had slept as badly as had Isabella. Shrewsbury rose at once.

"My dear Antonia," he said. "You ought not to be down so early."

Lady Banbury gave him a look in which affection and impatience were mingled.

"If I stayed in bed every time you advised it, I should never rise at all," she said. Her gentle tone took any bite from the words.

Shrewsbury briefly took her hand, then let go. "At least let me get you some coffee."

"I am perfectly capable of pouring my own."

"I have no doubt of it. Miss Hartwell also slept poorly and allowed me to perform this small service for her."

He had already turned towards the coffeepot before his sister could protest any further.

Isabella watched the exchange in silence. On the surface, there was nothing odd about it. Nothing, indeed, that could not be explained by ordinary sibling concern in a household under strain. Yet the speed with which he had risen, the ease with which he had taken charge, and the anxious undercurrent of all his previous questions sat uneasily in her mind.

Shrewsbury returned with Lady Banbury's coffee and set it before her with exaggerated care.

As the room filled and the conversation broadened, Isabella found her appetite had deserted her again. Shrewsbury had asked many questions, and they all seemed to centre on one point: what did Inspector Gregory know, and how much more did he suspect?

By the time she rose from the table, Isabella had begun to wonder how much of Shrewsbury's apparent solicitude towards her was merely a prelude to learning more about her conversation with Inspector Gregory.

CHAPTER 28

Isabella had drunk three cups of coffee, but they hadn't woken her as much as she'd hoped. She still felt groggy, and her thoughts were fuzzy. She hadn't had a chance the previous evening to debrief the dowager about her conversation with Inspector Gregory. She knew she would get no thanks for holding onto that information any longer than necessary.

When the dowager hadn't come down for breakfast, which was unsurprising given her penchant for leisurely mornings, Isabella decided to call on her in her bedchamber. She only hoped she wouldn't catch the woman in her nightgown.

Looking at the grandfather clock in the hall, she saw it was past ten o'clock; surely that was a reasonably civilised hour.

A few minutes later, she knocked on the dowager's door, trepidatiously. The door was opened by the dowager's maid, Withers, who looked surprised to see a visitor at that hour.

"I apologise for disturbing her ladyship," Isabella said. "However, I have news I believe she would wish to hear as soon as possible."

The dowager's voice rang out from within the room. "Who is that, Withers?" The maid, who had not fully opened the door, now closed it a little more and said something to her mistress.

"Miss Hartwell? Well then, do not just stand there, woman. Let her in!"

In no time, Isabella was seated comfortably in an armchair opposite a, thankfully, fully dressed and coiffured dowager countess.

"Are you feeling quite well, my dear?" the dowager inquired.

"I slept poorly," Isabella explained. She then relayed her full conversation with Inspector Gregory.

Against form, the dowager made no interruptions. However, once Isabella indicated she was finished, the dowager had much to say.

"How dare that officious little man speak to you in such a manner?" she stormed. "And who does he think he is, telling you how to treat your lady's maid?"

Turning to Withers, who was standing nearby pouring tea, the dowager said, "Withers, tell Miss Hartwell how thrilled you were when I deigned to include you in an investigation, even in a small way."

While the truth was a little more complicated than that, and Withers' involvement, even such as it was, had ended up being minimised even further by the dowager, the maid had little choice but to agree.

"See!" the dowager said, turning back to Isabella. "While the enthusiasm in her answer was a little lacking, if you ask me, I have no doubt that her pleasure at the time in being included was genuine. From the sounds of things, your girl, Polly, has far more going for her than Withers here does. The last thing you should do is berate yourself for involving her. Instead, you should pat yourself on the back for hiring and encouraging such an enterprising young woman."

As much as Isabella didn't entirely agree with the dowager's pronouncement, she appreciated it, particularly because she knew how heartfelt the sentiment was.

Isabella had been contemplating whether to tell the dowager about her conversation with Shrewsbury at breakfast. Part of her hesitation stemmed from uncertainty about her own feelings. At the time, she'd sensed he'd hoped to encourage her to share the details of her conversation with Inspector Gregory, but now she wondered if she was making too much of it.

Even if her instincts had been correct, what did that mean? Shrewsbury had made clear that he resented the strain the investigation was putting on his sister. If he knew about her condition, how much more might a loving brother feel such resentment? Was it really surprising if he wanted to understand how the inspector viewed the Banburys?

Finally, deciding that her head was too thick to ponder such questions alone and that she'd welcome the dowager's opinion, she shared everything.

Again, the dowager heard Isabella out to the end, her expression growing ever more intent as the account of breakfast unfolded. When Isabella finished, there was a brief silence as the older woman sat back in her chair and tapped one finger thoughtfully against the armrest.

At last, she said, "Well."

It was a deceptively mild response. Isabella knew better than to take such mildness at face value.

"Well?" she repeated.

"Well," the dowager said again, her tone suggesting she might be trying to temper her instinctive response. "I agree that was an interesting conversation to have so early in the morning."

Isabella almost smiled. "So, you think I was right to find the exchange a little odd?"

"A little odd?" the dowager repeated. "My dear girl, the man was not merely making conversation. He was fishing, and not very subtly, by the sound of things. The question is: for what, precisely, and why?"

Isabella leaned back in her chair. It was a relief to hear someone else say it plainly. "That was my impression too, though by the time I came upstairs I had begun to wonder whether I was making too much of it."

"Nonsense. If he had truly wished only to console you, he would have been content to say the inspector had no business upsetting you. Instead, he circled and circled, with decreasing delicacy. Is he merely concerned for his sister's reputation and peace of mind? Or is there something else?"

"That is what I have been struggling with," Isabella admitted. "Certainly, if he knows that his sister is with child and fears for her, perhaps his questions are entirely understandable. Even if he doesn't know, it is obvious she is not coping well with the strain of the investigation."

The dowager took the cup of tea Withers offered her, then added a little more cream. "However, perhaps there is a difference between brotherly concern and strategic curiosity. Mr Shrewsbury strikes me as a man keen to know which way the wind is blowing, particularly if that wind threatens his ability to continue feeding at Banbury's table."

Isabella thought of Shrewsbury's words during their walk, of the loss of the roof over his head, the estate, the household, the future.

"He certainly seems deeply attached to Banbury Hall," she agreed.

"Yes," the dowager replied tartly. "I am sure that attachment is only increased by the man's lack of responsibility for paying the butcher's bill."

This made Isabella laugh despite her tiredness. Even so, she could not fully enjoy the joke; the earlier conversation had left an aftertaste of unease she had not yet shaken off.

"Do you think I told him too much?" she asked, unable to keep the self-doubt from creeping into her voice.

The dowager considered this. "I believe you handled it as well as possible, given the situation. Short of rudely refusing to answer the question, your response was suitably empty of content."

The words settled heavily on Isabella's mind. She had, in truth, told Shrewsbury nothing concrete. Yet she had confirmed that the inspector's questions had troubled her. In a house where every stray comment could be damning, perhaps that was enough.

"Even so, I feel foolish," Isabella said in a quiet voice.

The dowager's expression softened by a degree. "No. You are merely tired. There is a difference. Besides, it is hardly the first time in history that a woman has succumbed to flattery and flirtation and then regretted it." She paused. "Of course, I am entirely immune to such masculine wiles, but you should hardly hold yourself to the standard I set."

Withers, who had just finished arranging the tea tray, made a sound at this, which she managed to convert into a cough just in time.

The dowager finished her tea and continued, "Now then, the more pressing question is what, precisely, Mr Shrewsbury fears the inspector may learn. It cannot be only that his sister quarrelled with Ravensthorpe. Half the house already knows as much, or suspects it. Nor can it be merely the state of the estate. If Gregory wished to know the state of Banbury's finances, I cannot imagine that would be difficult to uncover. No, there is something else. Whatever other secrets might the woman be keeping? Is it nothing more than that she carries Ravensthorpe's child?" Then, answering her own question, she said, "Though that is a sufficient secret to be concerned about."

Before Isabella could answer, there came a discreet knock at the door.

"Withers!" the dowager called irritably, as if the woman weren't already halfway to the door.

The long-suffering maid finished crossing the room and opened the door. A footman stood outside. He was younger and broader-shouldered than Hargreaves. Isabella thought this was Andy Carter, the other footman who was on duty the night of Ravensthorpe's murder.

"I beg your pardon, your ladyship," he said. "Inspector Gregory asked whether Miss Hartwell might be willing to speak with him in the library."

The dowager drew herself up. "And did Inspector Gregory offer any explanation for this request?"

"No, your ladyship. Only that it concerns the inquiry."

"Well, one would have hoped as much." She turned to Isabella. "I suppose you had better go. Heaven knows what the man wants now. But if he intends to scold you again, tell him I shall have him horsewhipped."

The footman looked alarmed. Isabella rose, suppressing a smile.

"I doubt that will be necessary," she said. Turning to the footman, she added, "Please tell Inspector Gregory that I will come at once."

Once the door had closed behind the servant, the dowager said, "Do not forget what we have just discussed. If Mr Shrewsbury is questioning what the inspector knows too closely, it is because there is something in the house that he does not wish Gregory to hear. You might want to consider mentioning as much."

"I will consider it," Isabella assured her.

CHAPTER 29

As she descended to the library, Isabella's mind was whirling, even though her head still felt heavy from her poor sleep. When she entered the room, Inspector Gregory stood by the mantelpiece, a notebook in one hand, while one of his constables stood by the writing desk, sorting papers.

"Miss Hartwell," Gregory said. "Thank you for coming so promptly."

His manner was neither warm nor cold, but it was undeniably serious. Isabella took the chair he indicated.

Gregory continued, "I thought you should know I have just spoken to Hargreaves again."

Isabella sat up a little straighter. "And?"

"And his account has changed." Gregory glanced down at his notebook. "Not completely. But enough."

"That sounds like progress," Isabella observed. She wondered why he was deigning to inform her, but didn't want to say so. Instead, she waited to hear what else the inspector would say.

"Possibly." His expression suggested he was less satisfied with the footman's new account than she might have hoped. "He now admits what you told me: that the bell story was false."

Isabella did not hide her surprise. "He admitted it so readily?"

"Well, I would not say readily. However, he is young and sufficiently ambitious to worry about how a run-in with the law might affect his future prospects." Underlying the words was a suggestion of what threat might have been made to prompt the footman to tell the truth.

Gregory moved to the desk, set down his notebook, and rested both hands on the edge of the leather blotter. "He clung to the bell story for a while longer, then abandoned it when it became clear that I knew it had been contradicted. I should add that I didn't implicate your maid. He now says he used it merely to explain why he was upstairs longer than he should have been."

"And why was he upstairs so long?" Isabella asked, though she suspected she knew the answer.

"He says he took Lady Banbury her hot milk at half past ten and found her upset. Distressed, in his words. He did not wish to leave her ladyship in such a state. He says he stayed a little while to make sure she was settled." Gregory's tone suggested he objected far less to this part of the story than to what followed. "He then found himself with more time gone than he could easily account for, and used the bell as a convenient explanation that didn't implicate her ladyship in any way."

The story, if true, suggested a possibility that hadn't crossed Isabella's mind before: did Hargreaves's concern for her ladyship extend beyond what his position strictly required? Was that why he had stayed in her room longer than necessary? She wondered whether such a question had crossed the inspector's mind.

"Did he say how upset Lady Banbury was?" she asked, reluctant to be the one to make the rather outrageous suggestion.

Gregory's eyes narrowed a fraction. "Not in any useful detail. He described her as shaken and not herself. When I pressed him for the cause, he replied that it was not his place to speculate on the emotions of his betters." He looked unimpressed. "A neat answer, but not a helpful one."

Isabella thought of the marchioness's reaction to Ravensthorpe's drunkenness at dinner, then of the argument she had overheard, which she was now sure involved Lady Banbury. It was certainly plausible that Hargreaves had found his mistress distressed after all that.

She hesitated, then decided there was no point in hiding it. "My maid heard from the kitchen staff that Hargreaves had offered to take up the milk himself, saying he was already going upstairs to do something, even though that was not his assigned task for the evening."

At that, Gregory's expression changed slightly. Not exactly surprised, but curious. "Did she indeed?"

"She did."

He made a note in the margin of his page.

"Do you believe that he is telling you the truth?" Isabella asked.

Gregory took a moment before answering. "I believe him in part. The question is, what is he hiding or lying about? Why was he there? What did he discover when he entered his mistress's room? Is there another reason for the falsehood he's not saying?"

He tapped his fingers on the blotter absentmindedly. "The revised account explains why he was upstairs. It even, to an extent, explains why he later lied. A servant might well prefer to invent a bell rather than admit he found his mistress in tears and stayed to comfort her. Such a thing could fuel gossip, particularly in a house already brimming with it." Then, with a knowing look, he added, "Particularly if there were some prior familiarity he did not wish noticed."

So, the same thought had crossed the inspector's mind.

"Yes," Isabella said. "But it does not explain everything."

"No, it does not," Gregory agreed at once. "It certainly does not explain the handkerchief."

At that, Isabella felt the faintest shiver. Gregory had put his finger on what had been troubling her, even though she had not quite known how to articulate it.

"Hargreaves denied taking it?" she asked.

"Flatly." Gregory's mouth tightened. "If he is telling the truth, someone else in this house took it from the servants' hall and carried it to Ravensthorpe's room. If he is lying, I have not yet discovered why he thinks that lie is worth the cost."

"And what do you intend to do?"

"What I always intended to do," he said. "Keep asking questions until I reach the truth."

For a moment, neither of them spoke.

Finally, Gregory said, "I thought you ought to know, because you and I discussed Hargreaves yesterday, and because your maid's account appears to align with what he has now admitted. If nothing else, while I didn't mention her name, I wanted you and she to be aware that Hargreaves might now suspect she spoke to me."

Then, in a slightly different tone, he added, "I do not consider him cleared by this. Nor, for that matter, do I consider him condemned by it. At present, he strikes me as a man protecting something, but not necessarily as the man who wielded the knife."

Isabella found the distinction reasonable, though it also deepened the mystery.

She was about to rise and leave. "Thank you for telling me," Isabella said in farewell.

Gregory inclined his head. "Miss Hartwell. If anyone in this house suddenly becomes more interested than before in what you have or have not said to me, I suggest you take notice."

The words were spoken neutrally, but they landed with force. Isabella instantly thought of breakfast, of Shrewsbury's careful questions, his concern artfully turned into inquiry.

"In that case, Inspector, I ought to tell you about a rather interesting conversation I had with Mr Shrewsbury this morning," she said carefully. Even as she spoke, Isabella wasn't entirely sure how she wanted to characterise the interaction.

"Interesting in what way, Miss Hartwell?" he asked.

Isabella realised that, to set the conversation in context, she had to continue to engage in the kind of gossip she hated.

"As I suggested last night, I do believe it is possible that the marchioness is with child, and that it is not Lord Banbury's. I think that her brother, Mr Shrewsbury, might also know, or at least suspect both these things."

The inspector nodded. She then told him the details of her conversation with Mr Shrewsbury that morning.

When she had finished, he sat back and steepled his fingers. Isabella had already noticed that he did this when he was thinking deeply.

"I assume you believe Mr Shrewsbury's questioning of you was nothing more than concern for his sister, if she is indeed expecting," he said finally.

"Exactly." She felt compelled to add, "Although Mr Shrewsbury himself has made it quite clear to me that he is wholly dependent on his brother-in-law for somewhere to live. And so, it seems likely that his concern extends beyond his sister and encompasses Lord Banbury's welfare, if only for selfish reasons."

Inspector Gregory stood, and Isabella followed.

"Thank you, Miss Hartwell," he said with a smile. "It can't be pleasant to imagine yourself spreading what might be construed as tattle about your hostess and her family. But I am glad you told me all this. You've given me a lot to think about. It probably goes without saying, but I must ask that you keep the substance of our conversations to yourself."

When Isabella stepped out into the hall a few minutes later, she found it empty. Then, at the far end, near the turn towards the morning room, she saw Hargreaves exiting the service passage. He moved with his usual composure, but when he saw her leave the library, his face lost some of its colour. As he passed through a sunbeam filtering through a tall window, Isabella saw that his mouth was set in grim tension.

Noticing her gaze on him, he bowed slightly but didn't smile.

There was nothing in the gesture that could have been called insolent or even strange. Yet Isabella was suddenly certain of something: Hargreaves no longer looked merely uneasy. He looked like a man clinging to a story that he knew had already begun to split at the seams.

CHAPTER 30

Isabella was already exhausted; now she was also discombobulated. Part of her wondered whether, in her state of weariness, she was reading far too much into her brief interaction with Hargreaves. Nonetheless, she couldn't shake the idea that he'd witnessed her leaving what was obviously a private conversation with Inspector Gregory, and that he'd been less than pleased about it.

She remembered how tense he had seemed when she questioned the housekeeper in the kitchen days earlier, and she concluded that the man wouldn't have had to be particularly observant to realise she had been making inquiries into the circumstances of the murder.

Furthermore, despite the inspector's assurances that he hadn't revealed the source of his information and that the footman had been lying about hearing a bell ring, if Hargreaves remembered admitting as much to Polly, it wouldn't be a stretch to believe that the maid had told her mistress, who had then relayed it to the police.

If it was in fact the case that Hargreaves's closeness to Lady Banbury went beyond what was expected in a relationship between a servant and his mistress, then he might even have been aware of Isabella's awkward confrontation with the marchioness the day before.

Certainly, any combination of these might explain why the man had been wary of evidence that Isabella was continuing to liaise with the inspector about the murder.

Isabella wished she could return to her room and try to rest, but she'd never been very good at napping. She'd always envied people who could lie their heads down at any time of day and fall asleep. She always found that, no matter how tired she was, it was impossible to stop the gears of her mind from turning.

As people drifted into breakfast that morning, they'd been informed by the butler that luncheon would be a picnic on the lawn near the rose garden. Isabella was unsure how much more of this forced frivolity she could take. The house party had two more days before it was supposed to end. Inspector Gregory hadn't said what would happen if the murderer hadn't been apprehended by then. Would they all be compelled to remain at Banbury Hall, playing out this charade of upper-class, elegant idleness indefinitely?

While Isabella was tempted to skip the picnic altogether, she knew that her best chance of escaping this particular purgatory was to help Inspector Gregory solve the case, and that observing her fellow guests and their hosts was part of that. Reluctantly, she decided she had no choice but to try to revive herself, change into a more appropriate outfit, and smile through the picnic.

Before she'd left the dowager earlier, Isabella had mentioned the outing. The old woman hadn't been pleased at the idea of yet another al fresco meal and had prevaricated about attending. Given Isabella's own feelings about the proposed activity, she hadn't attempted to persuade her otherwise.

Given this, Isabella was surprised when, a little later, there was a knock at her door, and she found the dowager ready to accompany her out to the lawn.

"I wasn't expecting you to come to the picnic," Isabella admitted.

"My dear girl, have you not heard me berate Tabitha and Wolf repeatedly for the sin of trying to anticipate my actions?" the dowager scolded. "I should be regarded as a sphinx-like enigma at all times."

Isabella assured her that she'd take note, and the two women made their way downstairs and out into the grounds.

When she was a child, Isabella's father often took her on picnics in

Central Park. They'd sit on a blanket in the shade of a tree, eating all sorts of treats their cook had packed in a wicker hamper. It appeared this was not what the Banburys meant by "picnic".

Instead of a blanket, tablecloths covered tables set with china, crystal, and silver, dotted the lawn. And instead of a wicker basket, a large group of servants bustled around, ready to serve a multi-course meal.

"This isn't what I would call a picnic," Isabella observed to the dowager. "Rather, I would call it a formal luncheon held outdoors."

"What on earth did you expect? That I be forced to squat on the grass like a peasant working in the fields?" The genuine horror in the dowager's tone was almost comical.

Many people were already seated when the two women arrived at the "picnic". Isabella had been considering whether she wished to seek out Shrewsbury as a dining companion. While she thought she understood his questioning at breakfast, Isabella wasn't sure whether she felt up to a possible second round. Seeing a table with only two empty seats left, Isabella decided she wasn't ready for further interrogation and that it might behove her to get to know the other guests a little better. After all, she couldn't discount the possibility that Ravensthorpe had been killed by someone she hadn't considered at all up to then.

Isabella pointed out the table to the dowager, who looked almost as horrified by the suggestion as she had been by the thought of a real picnic.

"Really, my dear. Do you truly wish me to waste two hours of my life, already near its end, listening to the vicar ramble on about the merits of tile over slate for roof repairs, while that gauche Mrs Humsby declaims every word as if she has to project to be heard in the gods?"

"There are only two seats left," Isabella explained quietly. "And I do not feel up to sitting with Mr Shrewsbury after our conversation this morning."

"Ah, I see. Well, under those circumstances, I will forbear to listen to another round of complaints about how the church roof has been leaking for five years. However, I refuse to be the one to sit next to Baron Rice. I found the man to be a pompous blowhard, which, given the company we are in this week, is quite the achievement."

In the end, Isabella took the seat between the vicar and Baron Rice, and the dowager settled in between the deaf older gentleman and a man of middle years whom Isabella thought she remembered being introduced as Sir Gerald, who lived two counties away.

Baron Rice seemed deeply engaged in a conversation with Lady Brinkley about her views on the evils of duck shooting, and so Isabella turned her attention to the vicar.

If she'd been hoping to use the time to observe her fellow guests without talking directly about the investigation, she was to be disappointed; it seemed that the vicar had other ideas.

"I cannot tell you how relieved I was when your name was cleared, Miss Hartwell," he assured her. The vicar must have been in his late sixties, a short, rotund man with an almost entirely bald pate.

"As was I, reverend," Isabella replied.

"Let us hope that this time the culprit is caught," the vicar continued. "I know that many of my parishioners could not sleep easily at night, knowing that yet again a killer was at large."

It took Isabella a moment to realise what the man had said. "I am sorry. I am not sure I heard you correctly. Are you saying that this is not the only murder to have occurred recently?"

"Well, I wouldn't say recently," he said. "Let me see now. It must have been about five years ago. Nasty business. Banbury had just brought in a new land agent. From what I heard at the time, the man considered himself something of an innovative thinker and had all sorts of plans to make the estate more profitable. He hadn't been here more than two months when he was attacked crossing the grounds at dusk. In the end, the police decided it must have been a poacher."

The vicar leaned in and said in a confidential tone, "I have always believed it was gipsies. There were some camping not far away. I heard that the inspector on the case, not this Gregory fellow, someone else, had questioned them, but nothing ever came of it."

Isabella wondered whether anyone had told Inspector Gregory about this incident. Of course, it was hard to see how there could be any connection between a random killing on the grounds years before and a very specific murder in the house itself; nevertheless, she thought he should be told.

Twenty minutes later, when Baron Rice had steered the conversation away from Lady Brinkley's views on duck shooting to regaling them with tales of the proper breeding of pointers, Isabella was already regretting her decision to attend the picnic. From the look on the dowager's face as she sat across the table, she seemed even less happy.

The vicar seemed determined to continue his account of the murder that had occurred five years ago, yet each time he approached anything of real interest, Sir Gerald interrupted with a remark about county magistrates or the appalling state of rural roads. Across the lawn, Lady Banbury sat very straight-backed beneath the shade of a striped awning, speaking in low tones to Mrs Madison as if nothing in the world were amiss. Lord Banbury, seated two tables away, appeared equally at ease.

While Isabella was wondering whether she might reasonably plead sunstroke and retreat to the house, a maid approached her chair.

The girl was one of the younger housemaids, fair-haired and pink-cheeked; Isabella remembered her name was Tilly. Bending slightly, she said in a low voice, "Beg pardon, miss. Mr Hargreaves asked me to tell you something."

Isabella turned her head, instantly attentive. "Indeed?"

"Yes, miss. He said he remembers something else about the handkerchief and fears the inspector has the wrong end of the stick. He would be obliged if you'd step as far as the small gate beyond the rose walk, where the gravel path gives way to the servants' yard. He says he daren't speak in the house."

For a moment, Isabella said nothing. The murmur of conversation, the clatter of food being served, even the dowager's unmistakable voice, seemed to recede.

The maid, perhaps mistaking her hesitation for displeasure, added hurriedly, "He said to tell you it concerns what he told the inspector this morning, miss."

That settled it. It was exactly the sort of message a frightened servant might send, particularly one who had just altered his account under police pressure and found himself in even greater difficulty than before. This could explain the look he'd shot her earlier.

"Thank you," Isabella said quietly. "Did he say he would wait there for me?"

"Yes, miss."

The girl dipped in a small curtsey and moved away at once, pausing only to collect an empty dish from the next table.

Isabella took up her napkin and laid it beside her plate. She was aware that the dowager, despite seeming fully engaged in a scathing aside to Sir Gerald, had noticed the exchange and raised her eyebrows in query. Isabella gave a quick shake of her head. If she delayed leaving to explain matters to the dowager, Hargreaves might lose his nerve and vanish.

"I apologise," Isabella said, addressing no one in particular but loudly enough for the others at the table to hear, "You must all excuse me. I find I have had rather too much sun."

"We British get little enough of it to know better than to rush indoors at the first hint of warmth," the dowager declared.

The remark drew enough laughter to ease Isabella's departure, which was perhaps the dowager's intention. With her expression composed and her pace unhurried, she made her way across the lawn towards the rose walk, hoping everyone was too involved in their various pontifications to wonder why she wasn't returning to the house.

Chapter 31

It was a very warm, sunny day, and Isabella was glad she had worn a wide-brimmed straw hat. In fact, the sun shone so brightly that she wished she'd thought to bring her parasol. For a moment, she considered returning to the house for it, but again, she didn't wish to risk Hargreaves not waiting.

Why did the man wish to speak with her in particular? Isabella wondered. Then she considered that she might have been seen entering to speak to the inspector the previous evening as well, and that Hargreaves might have formed the opinion that the policeman was particularly interested in her perspective.

By his own account, Gregory had already leaned rather hard on the young footman, so it wasn't surprising that Hargreaves would rather explain himself more fully through an intermediary.

The walk to the meeting point was pleasant. It seemed as if every flower had exploded into full bloom since the day before, and the air was heady with their perfume. Isabella would have liked to take her time and enjoy the sweet floral scent and the bright array of colours, but she was mindful of the time and didn't allow herself to tarry. Perhaps when she had finished with Hargreaves, she would allow herself the luxury of a leisurely stroll back along the path.

It didn't take Isabella long to reach what she took to be the little service gate beyond the rose walk, but Hargreaves was nowhere to be seen. The gate stood on a narrow gravel path, screened from the servants' entrance by yew trees and secluded from the main path Isabella had been following by an old stone wall covered in rose bushes not yet fully in bloom. The sound of voices from the lawn was faint and intermittent. The spot was very secluded and made sense as a place for a discreet, clandestine meeting. Even so, for a moment, Isabella shuddered despite the afternoon sun.

Almost immediately, she realised how foolish she was being; there were many reasons a servant might be delayed. It was even possible that Hargreaves had already been here, waiting for her, but had then been called away.

She was tempted to call out to him, but didn't want to risk being overheard. Suddenly, Isabella heard a noise. It sounded like someone moving carefully along the gravel path.

"Hargreaves?" she said in a low voice. "Is that you?"

There was no answer. She thought she saw a shadow move just around the wall's corner. Was it possible that Hargreaves was here but afraid to reveal himself in case he was seen from the house? But then, why choose this spot to begin with?

Deciding she couldn't just stand there and wait all afternoon, Isabella went through the gate to where she thought she'd heard the noise and seen the shadow.

She had not even taken her first step when a gloved hand clamped over her mouth, and an arm grabbed her around the torso, pulling her back and causing her to lose her footing. Isabella's hat fell off her head, and as she tried to catch herself, she was shoved forward. She fell onto the path, striking her head on one of the rocks lining it. Isabella fell awkwardly, twisting her ankle. As she landed, her palms scraped harshly on the gravel.

The last thing she remembered was a harsh voice snarling as she fell, "Leave well enough alone."

Then she slipped into brief unconsciousness. The next thing she knew, a kind voice was whispering in her ear, "Miss Hartwell. Miss Hartwell, can you hear me?"

She was gently moved into a seated position, with a pair of strong arms around her shoulders for support.

It took a moment for the world to come back into focus, but once it did, she realised Mr Shrewsbury was seated on the path, holding her in his arms.

"Whatever happened, Miss Hartwell?" he asked, his voice filled with concern. "I was out for a walk on my way to the picnic when I came across you lying here. Did you trip? You are bleeding. You must have hit your head as you fell."

He produced a handkerchief and pressed it against her head wound.

It seemed oddly fortunate that he had come that way at all, Isabella thought, though in her dazed state she was too grateful to dwell on it.

"Do you think you can stand?" he asked.

Isabella's head was throbbing, and she felt very dizzy. She wanted to insist she was fine and could stand up, but wasn't sure that was true.

"Perhaps I can sit here for a few moments longer," she said.

"Take all the time you need, Miss Hartwell," Shrewsbury assured her.

Just then, a maid turned the corner.

"Millie, go and call the doctor. Miss Hartwell has fallen and hurt herself," he ordered.

"I don't think I need a doctor," she protested, even as a wave of nausea washed over her.

"Nonsense. That wound needs looking at, and who knows what other injuries you might have sustained?" Even as Shrewsbury said this, Isabella felt her ankle throbbing. Perhaps it wouldn't be a bad idea to see a doctor.

"I think I can stand now, if you help me," she said.

With Shrewsbury's help, she managed to get to her feet, but realised she couldn't put any weight on her right foot.

"I think I might have twisted my ankle too badly to walk," Isabella admitted.

"Then let me carry you into the house," Shrewsbury offered. Before she could answer, he swept her into his arms and followed the maid inside.

For such a delicate-looking man, Mr Shrewsbury was surprisingly strong, and Isabella felt quite safe, if a little absurd, being carried through the servants' entrance in his arms.

Luckily, most of the servants were out tending the picnic, but the cook and Mrs Patrick were there, and they both looked shocked as Shrewsbury strode into the kitchen, Isabella in his arms.

"Miss Hartwell fell and hit her head. She also seems to have twisted her ankle," he explained. "I have asked Millie to send for the doctor."

Mrs Patrick recovered herself first.

"Good heavens," she exclaimed. "Cook, fetch clean cloths and some cold water at once. And, Millie, do not stand gaping. Off with you and see to the doctor, as Mr Shrewsbury said," she commanded the maid.

The maid, still hovering in the doorway, gave a start and flew off to get the carriage to send down to the village.

Cook, muttering under her breath, hurried to do as she was told. Meanwhile, Mrs Patrick came forward and peered anxiously at Isabella's face and at the handkerchief Shrewsbury still held to her head.

"She is as white as a sheet," the housekeeper declared. "Mr Shrewsbury, you had best take her straight upstairs. I would have a footman take her, but they're all working at the picnic. There is no point leaving the poor young lady in the kitchen. I will send someone to alert her maid at once."

"I am sure I can walk," Isabella began weakly, though the room seemed to sway slightly around her.

"No, miss, you cannot," Mrs Patrick said with surprising firmness. "Not on that ankle, and not with your head as it is."

The practical wisdom of this was hard to deny, particularly as another surge of pain shot through Isabella's ankle.

Without ceremony, Mrs Patrick moved ahead of them and pushed open the baize door to the passage leading to the servants' staircase. "This way, sir. It will be quicker via the back stairs, and there will be fewer people to alarm."

Shrewsbury inclined his head and carried Isabella through. She was acutely aware of how ridiculous the situation must look, yet too dizzy to do much more than rest one hand against his shoulder and try not to jar herself as he climbed the narrow stairs. The service staircase was steep, enclosed, and far plainer than the grand front staircases the family and guests usually used.

"Are you comfortable enough?" Shrewsbury asked quietly as they reached the first landing.

"More so than you are, I'm sure," Isabella replied, trying to smile.

At the top of the stairs, they met Polly, who hurried along the corridor, pale with alarm.

"Oh, miss!" she cried. "Whatever has happened to you?"

"Miss Hartwell appears to have fallen and struck her head," Shrewsbury said before Isabella could answer. "Mrs Patrick has sent for the doctor."

Polly looked as though she had a dozen questions, but good sense prevailed over curiosity. She darted ahead, pushed open the door to Isabella's bedchamber, and hurried to turn down the bed.

"Lay her here, sir," she said, smoothing the counterpane with trembling hands.

Shrewsbury crossed the room and lowered Isabella onto the bed with great care. The moment her head touched the pillow, the pounding steadied into a duller, more persistent throb. Polly was at her side at once.

"Oh, your poor hands," the maid said, seeing the scraped palms. "And your gown and sleeve is torn. Miss, does your ankle pain you very much? Do you feel sick? I know a bad bump on the head can bring it on. Shall I bring a basin?"

"Hush," Isabella murmured, though not unkindly. "One would think I had been run over by a carriage."

"You might as well have been, by the look of you," Polly said.

Despite the pain, Isabella gave the faintest laugh. When she glanced up, she found Shrewsbury still standing by the bed, concern written plainly on his face.

"I will go and see how long the doctor is likely to be," he said. "Try not to move, Miss Hartwell."

And with that, he left her in Polly's care. For the first time since waking on the gravel, Isabella allowed herself to feel the full force of what had happened. Who had attacked her and why? Everything pointed to Hargreaves. She could think of no one else likely to have lured her there and warned her off in such terms.

"Polly, please ask Inspector Gregory to come to me as soon as possible," Isabella said. "And be discreet," she added.

Chapter 32

Inspector Gregory arrived fifteen minutes later and was shocked to find Isabella in bed, her hands grazed and her face still marked by the shock of her ordeal.

"Miss Hartwell, what happened?" he asked with genuine concern.

She had only just begun to tell her story when the doctor arrived. It seemed in the end, Millie had been very efficient in sending the carriage to the village to fetch the doctor. He looked to be not much older than Isabella, with kind eyes and a gentle smile.

"Miss Hartwell, I will step outside while the doctor examines you," Inspector Gregory said.

Isabella was eager to tell her story and worried that her attacker might panic and flee if too much time passed. However, a stern look from her maid made it clear that Isabella had little choice but to comply and accept medical attention.

Polly had done her best to wash Isabella's hands gently, so at least the gravel was no longer embedded, even if her palms were still raw and bloodied. A brief examination of her knees showed that her skirts and petticoats had shielded them from anything more than minor bruising. The maid had been reluctant to do much for the head wound before the doctor arrived, and now the first thing he did was inspect and dress it.

"Head wounds bleed a lot, and of course, there is always a concern that this may indicate something more serious, but I think that in this case, it really is quite superficial," he informed the patient.

"Now then, Miss Hartwell, I am going to ask you a few questions," the doctor continued, "and I must have you answer as plainly as you can. Do you know where you are?"

"In my bedchamber at Banbury Hall."

"Very good. And do you know how you came to be here?"

"I fell," Isabella said, then frowned. "Or I was pushed. I am not entirely certain."

"Quite so. Do not strain your memory. Is your head hurting badly?"

"Yes. It's a dull, throbbing ache."

"Do you feel sick?"

"A little."

"Have you vomited?"

"No."

"Do the room and the light trouble you?"

"The light does. If I move too quickly, the room seems to sway."

He nodded and gently touched the side of her head. "Tender there?"

She winced. "Very tender."

"Have you any double vision? Any ringing in the ears? Any numbness in your limbs?"

"No."

After a moment, he straightened. "You have had a knock to the head and, I think, a slight concussion. You are to lie quietly, avoid reading, conversation, and excitement, and not attempt to rise unless necessary. If the headache worsens, if sickness increases, or if you grow confused or difficult to rouse, I am to be sent for at once."

He then examined her ankle, pronounced it sprained, and re-wrapped it. Once he had left, Polly took advantage of the lack of visitors to help her mistress out of the dress she'd been wearing and into a nightgown.

"Is this really necessary?" Isabella complained. "I feel like a dying granny, dressed for bed in the middle of the afternoon."

Draping a shawl about her mistress's shoulders, Polly answered in a motherly yet stern tone, "Miss, you heard the doctor. You are not leaving this bed anytime soon. You will be far more comfortable in your night-gown and out of your stays."

Isabella knew she was right, but even so, she chafed at the confinement this implied.

Finally, Polly plumped her pillows, declared Isabella ready to resume her conversation with Inspector Gregory, and invited him back into the room.

"The doctor said Miss Hartwell needs to rest," Polly warned the inspector, wagging her finger. "I am going down to the kitchen to get some tea, and when I return, this interview needs to be over."

"I will be as brief as I can," he assured her.

Once Polly had left, the inspector brought a chair to Isabella's bedside and sat down.

"She is quite the fierce protector," he observed. "We'd better get started, because I don't dare risk her wrath by staying too long."

Isabella smiled. "Polly is a little overprotective," she admitted. "However, I do not wish to rush this conversation." She then continued from where they'd left off, describing how she received a message from the maid that Hargreaves wished to meet her. She left the picnic and made her way to the service gate, only to find no one there on her arrival.

At this juncture, Gregory felt compelled to point out that he had specifically asked her to suspend her investigative efforts. "Indeed, I believe I explicitly requested that you not wander the grounds with anyone you did not fully trust. And yet here you are, only hours later, accepting an invitation to meet a man whom we have already discussed as a person of interest."

Isabella accepted his admonishments contritely. Under other circum-stances, she might have pushed back against the criticism, but given her current situation, it seemed pointless to protest.

Instead, after conceding his point, she said, "It must have been Harg-reaves who lured me there and then attacked me."

"Tell me exactly what happened after you arrived for the rendezvous."

"I waited for a few minutes, then heard a noise and thought I saw a shadow. I made my way towards where it seemed to be, and the next thing I knew, I had been grabbed from behind and a gloved hand clamped over my mouth. I stumbled, then was pushed forward onto the path, where I struck my head."

"And was anything said?"

Isabella thought for a moment. The attack had happened so quickly, and her head still felt groggy.

Finally, she said, "I think he said, 'Leave well enough alone,' or something like that. I must have hit the ground and blacked out right after that, so I am not entirely sure. But I believe that is what he said."

"Well, if you're right, it wasn't a random attack. Those words seem to be quite pointedly about this investigation."

Talk of a random attack made Isabella recall her earlier conversation with the vicar.

"Has anyone mentioned to you the other murder that took place here, perhaps five years ago?" she asked.

The look of surprise on the inspector's face was all the answer she needed.

However, confirming her suspicions, he replied, "No, they have not. What murder?"

Isabella gave him an outline of what the vicar had told her, then added, "I am surprised none of your constables mentioned anything."

"Well, they're both quite young and might not even have been officers back then. And of course, there's no reason to believe the two murders have anything in common," he pointed out.

"And yet," Isabella mused. "That killer was never found, so it has to be possible that, rather than being a poacher or a gipsy as the vicar claimed, it was someone in this household who just killed again."

"So, the murdered man was the new land agent for the estate, was he?" Inspector Gregory considered this for a moment. "I will certainly ask Lord Banbury about this. My first task is to have Hargreaves found and brought to me at once. If he has any sense, he won't attempt to abscond."

"Everything points to Hargreaves having been my attacker," Isabella said. "But why?" Then she remembered the odd encounter earlier that morning and described it to the inspector. "It was nothing more than the way he looked at me, yet I do not believe I was imagining his disquiet."

"This was as you were leaving the library after our talk this morning?" Isabella nodded. "While it doesn't prove he's our killer, it does suggest that

Mr Hargreaves was unhappy with what he perceived as your tale-telling on him."

It certainly suggested as much, Isabella agreed. Gregory stood to leave.

Before he could, Isabella made a request she assumed would be denied. "I would like to be in the room when you talk to him."

For a moment, it seemed as if she were right in her assumption. Then the inspector surprised her. "If you do not mind the interview being conducted in your bedchamber, I will allow it. It may tell us something to have him answer before you, if you are equal to it."

Isabella laughed. "So, from that, I take it I should try not to revive too much in the interim."

Gregory chuckled and left the room.

When he had gone, Isabella settled back against her pillows. What was she to do while she was thus confined? If she weren't even able to read, she might go out of her mind with boredom. She'd never been good at just relaxing and doing nothing. Now she wished she could at least knit or crochet, though perhaps those would be banned as well.

She tried not to think about the attack, yet it kept coming back to her. Isabella replayed those few minutes over and over, but her throbbing head kept her from finding any clarity.

Finally, Isabella felt her eyes getting heavy. She fought the overwhelming urge to close them for a few minutes, then finally gave in and drifted off to sleep. The last thought that went through her mind was the leather glove over her mouth.

Chapter 33

Isabella wasn't sure how long she'd slept, but even with the curtains closed, she could tell it was still daylight outside. The first thing she thought was how much better her head felt. The second thought was the memory she'd had as she'd drifted off to sleep.

She needed to speak to Inspector Gregory. Immediately.

As she tried to prop herself up, a wave of dizziness washed over her, and she slumped back against her pillows. Her attempt to sit up must have alerted Polly, who had been sewing in the sitting room, loath to go far in case her mistress woke and needed anything.

The maid hurried into the room. "You lie yourself back down, Miss," she demanded.

"You are very bossy for a maid," Isabella said with a grin.

"And I will keep being bossy until you follow the doctor's orders and rest." Polly moved to the bed and took a glass from the bedside table.

"Would you like some water? Just take a few sips to begin with," she said, holding the glass out.

Isabella raised her head, but found she wasn't in a good position to drink.

"Polly, please help me sit up first."

It was clear the maid would have preferred to refuse and insist that her mistress remain prone, but she realised how impractical that would be. So, she put the glass back down and helped Isabella sit up.

"What time is it?" Isabella asked.

"It's just gone five o'clock. But don't you worry about the time. Whenever you're peckish, I'll bring something light up for you to eat."

"Have you heard anything from Inspector Gregory?"

Polly's instinct was to reply to this question by saying that this wasn't something Isabella needed to worry about either, but a glare from the invalid put paid to that.

"He sent word that they have Hargreaves," the maid admitted, "and he's being held in the library for now under guard. Whenever you're feeling up to it, the inspector will bring him up."

Before Isabella could reply, Polly added sternly, "Was it not enough that this investigation almost got you killed? Let the police handle this from here on!"

"Polly, I know you mean well, but I cannot. I can neither be the cause of an innocent man's condemnation nor risk a killer escaping justice."

The maid sighed and shook her head in exasperation. "And why are either of those your responsibility?"

Before Isabella could answer, there was a soft knock at the door. Polly went to answer it and returned with the dowager.

"Isabella! What on earth happened?" the old woman said in a tone of genuine concern. "You left the picnic, and the next thing I heard was that you had been hurt and that the doctor had called."

Curious about the story circulating, Isabella asked, "You didn't hear about the attack?"

"Attack? Heaven help us. I heard that you had fallen, hit your head, and twisted your ankle, and that Mr Shrewsbury had found you and, rather gallantly, carried you inside and up here. I must say, that young man improves in my estimation by the hour."

"Yes," Isabella agreed. "It was fortunate he was walking by. I cannot imagine how long I might have lain there otherwise. I certainly don't think I would have been able to stand on my own. I was very dizzy."

"Well," the dowager said sagely. "A goose egg on your head will do that."

Isabella put her hand to her forehead and found the dowager wasn't exaggerating; there was an enormous lump that must have been visible even under the bandage.

Turning to Polly, Isabella said firmly, "Please go down to the library and tell Inspector Gregory that I am ready for the interview." Before the girl could protest, Isabella added, "Now, please, Polly."

As the maid reluctantly left to deliver the message, the dowager took the chair still by the bed, and Isabella brought her up to date on all that had happened.

When she had finished, the dowager couldn't contain herself. "So, it was the footman after all! Well, I cannot say I am surprised."

Given that the woman had been ready to be judge and jury for the Banburys only the day before, Isabella was unsure how she could take such credit, but was wise enough not to say so.

For the next ten minutes, the dowager brought Isabella up to date on everything she'd missed at the picnic. It was a relief to lie back and just listen for a few minutes. Isabella knew the upcoming interview with Hargreaves would be difficult and draining, and was grateful for a chance to listen to mindless gossip, at least for a short while.

"That Baron Rice really is a self-important ass," the dowager pronounced. "As if anyone cares about breeding pointers. I would rather listen to Lady Brinkley twitter on about pigeons."

It was an amusing way to pass the time until Polly returned with the inspector.

This moment came soon enough. Her maid entered first to check that Isabella was still awake and determined to proceed with the meeting. Once assured on both counts, Inspector Gregory entered. He looked surprised to see the dowager already in attendance. For a moment, it seemed he was considering asking her to leave, but he then thought better of such a dangerous move.

Lastly, Hargreaves was brought into the room, handcuffed and accompanied by both constables. The man looked confused and scared. He was still in his footman's uniform, and it was incongruous to see his white cotton-gloved hands constrained by the cuffs.

Suddenly, Isabella found herself caught up in this idle thought. The gloves. There was no doubt in her mind that the man who had attacked her had been wearing leather gloves. And if she thought about it, soft leather gloves. She remembered having this fleeting thought at the time, in the middle of her panic during the attack, that they were so soft.

Was it possible that a servant owned such a pair of gloves? She supposed it was possible, though unlikely. More to the point, why would Hargreaves go to the trouble of changing in and out of the white gloves worn by all the footmen? If anything, they would have been far more noticeable if he'd run into a member of the household coming to or from the service gate.

Then she thought back to the moment when she had been grabbed and pulled back against her attacker's chest before being pushed onto the path. She remembered the top of her head grazing what must have been the man's chin.

Now, looking at Hargreaves, she realised the footman must be well over six feet tall. If she stood in front of him, she guessed the top of her head would barely reach his breastbone.

These two insights could only mean one thing. Without considering the implications of what she was about to say, Isabella blurted, "Inspector, it couldn't have been Hargreaves who attacked me."

Her words shocked everyone.

The dowager was the first to recover. "Isabella, you have had a nasty bump to the head and do not know what you are saying. My dear, the man wished to speak with you, you went, and you were attacked. The conclusion is hardly difficult to reach."

Hargreaves was next to speak. Isabella's words had jolted him out of the stupor he'd fallen into since being apprehended and handcuffed.

"I did wish for a word with Miss Hartwell; that much is true," the man insisted. "I knew you'd been asking questions, which is why Inspector Gregory called me back in for an interrogation. I thought that if I could explain myself a little better, perhaps matters might not go so hard."

This was addressed to the inspector, but the footman spoke directly to Isabella. "But I never asked that you be sent to the service gate, nor that you come alone, nor that anyone tell you it concerned the handkerchief. I said only that, if there were a chance, I should be obliged to speak with you quietly. Someone took that and made more of it than I did."

"Who did you say that to?" Isabella asked cautiously.

"I was in the drawing room, helping Tilly dust the high shelves earlier, and I mentioned it to her. Just as I said. Nothing more."

"And did anyone overhear you say this?" Gregory asked, making no effort to hide his scepticism.

"There was no one else in the room, though the door was open, so someone might have."

The inspector addressed Isabella. "How can you be so sure this wasn't the man who attacked you?"

"For two reasons," Isabella explained. "My attacker was much shorter than Mr Hargreaves. He was of middling height, certainly not a man as tall as he is. When he pulled me against him, I felt his chin graze the top of my head. I suspect that if I were to stand next to Mr Hargreaves, my head would barely reach his breastbone."

Inspector Gregory looked as if he might question her logic, but held back.

Instead, he asked, "And what is the second reason?"

"The man who attacked me put his hand over my mouth, and I could feel he was wearing the sort of soft leather gloves a gentleman might wear. I doubt a footman could afford such a luxury, but even if he could, why would he change into them in the middle of his duties? As we can see, Mr Hargreaves is wearing the white cotton gloves worn by all the footmen."

"He certainly could have switched them," the dowager pointed out, echoing Isabella's earlier brief thought.

"But why? That would be quite conspicuous if he ran into another servant or into Lord and Lady Banbury. Why go to the trouble?"

No one had a good answer to this. Finally, with a resigned sigh, Inspector Gregory turned back to Hargreaves.

"I know you haven't been entirely honest about everything you know. If you want me to believe you now, that needs to change. So, let's start with an explanation of why you lied about hearing the bell."

CHAPTER 34

Hargreaves looked down at his bound hands. For a few seconds, Isabella thought he might refuse to answer. Then he said quietly, "Because I had been upstairs longer than I ought to have been, sir."

"We already know that," Gregory said. "The question is why."

"Because I took Lady Banbury her hot milk."

"That too we know."

Hargreaves lifted his eyes, and for the first time, there was a hint of desperation in them. "She was upset, sir."

Everyone was silent. Inspector Gregory waited.

The footman hesitated. Isabella could almost see the struggle cross his face, the calculation of what might be admitted and what must still be concealed.

"She was not herself," he said at last. "I did not think it right to leave her in that condition."

Gregory's eyes narrowed. "You did not think it right as a servant? Or for some other reason?"

Hargreaves flushed. "As a servant, sir."

Isabella was not certain she believed him. Neither, she suspected, did Inspector Gregory. But he let that pass for the moment.

"And when you left Lady Banbury's room?"

"I realised I had been absent too long. When I got back downstairs, I said I thought I had heard a bell, so there would be some explanation for where I had been."

"You told me this when we spoke earlier. Yet, I suspect that is not all."

Hargreaves said nothing.

Gregory's voice hardened. "Do not trifle with me. If that were all, you would not have gone pale every time the matter was raised. If that were all, Miss Hartwell's handkerchief would not have found its way into Lord Ravensthorpe's room. If that were all, someone would not have used your name to lure Miss Hartwell to a secluded gate."

At the mention of the handkerchief, Hargreaves's composure slipped visibly.

The inspector saw it too. "Ah," he said softly. "We are closer to the truth there, are we?"

Hargreaves looked from Gregory to Isabella, then to the dowager, and finally looked away altogether. "I do not know who attacked Miss Hartwell," he said. "But I swear to God, sir, I did not."

"And the handkerchief?"

Still, he would not answer.

Gregory stepped closer. "If you were merely protecting Lady Banbury's good name, say so plainly and be done with it. But if you were protecting someone else, you had better decide whether they will protect you in return."

That landed. Isabella saw it in the sharp, involuntary twitch of Hargreaves's head.

Someone else.

The dowager, sensing it too, said, "Pray, who else was there to protect? Lord Banbury?"

Hargreaves said nothing. The pained look on his face almost made Isabella feel sorry for him. It seemed to go beyond the strain of a loyal servant forced to betray his employer; it felt deeply personal.

"Who are you protecting, Jimmy?" Isabella asked gently, using the man's given name. "It must be someone you care about very much to risk the gallows to protect them."

That landed a blow; Isabella could see it had. She almost expected the footman to howl in agony.

Gregory took the chance to thrust and parry. "Who asked you to stay upstairs? Were you to keep watch?"

For a moment, it seemed the man would crack. Then, with almost a shudder, he said, "No one, sir. I swear I didn't kill anyone, but if you don't believe me and I hang for that, then that will be my fate."

"Do not be a fool," Gregory said, though without heat. "You have already admitted enough to sink yourself if I choose to press the point. The only question now is whether you intend to sink alone."

Hargreaves's jaw clenched, and he pressed his lips together tightly. It seemed the man was not going to break that easily.

Gregory studied him for a long moment. To Isabella's surprise, he did not press further.

"Then consider yourself under arrest." Turning to the constable, he said, "Put him in the cellar for now, and have one of you guard the door at all times. No one is to speak to him without my say-so. That includes Lord and Lady Banbury."

Hargreaves looked, for the first time, openly afraid, but said nothing.

As the constables led him away, he glanced once over his shoulder at Isabella. There was appeal in the look, shame, and something else she could not quite name. Not gratitude, exactly. Perhaps it was a plea for help. Yet without his full testimony, what assistance could she offer?

When the door had closed behind him, the dowager let out a sharp breath.

"Well," she said. "That was most unsatisfactory."

Gregory did not answer that directly. He turned to Isabella. "How certain are you about the gloves?"

"Absolutely certain."

"And the height?"

"As certain as I can be about anything that happened in a moment of panic. But yes."

He nodded once. "Then the attack is no longer the simple matter it seemed."

"Which means?" Isabella asked.

"It means," he said, "that I now have at least two conversations to conduct."

"With whom?" the dowager demanded.

Gregory began to enumerate. "The maid, Tilly, who brought Miss Hartwell the message, to begin with. If Hargreaves truly spoke only a quiet word to her earlier, I must know why she delivered such a specific message to Miss Hartwell. Someone made the request. Then I want to speak to Lord Banbury about the murder five years ago that I was never informed of and that I only know about thanks to Miss Hartwell."

At that, the dowager's eyebrows shot up. She glanced at Isabella, who nodded, indicating she'd tell her all later.

Then he turned back to Isabella. "You have been an invaluable source of information and insight, Miss Hartwell, and I am grateful. I will return after these conversations, and I would appreciate your thoughts." Then he bowed and departed.

When they heard the door close behind him, the two women looked at each other.

"Well, I suppose I should feel flattered that the inspector has gone from berating me for interfering to asking for my help," Isabella said.

"Indeed," the dowager agreed, though from the look on her face, Isabella suspected the woman was offended that she hadn't been included in the thanks and invitation.

Just then, there was another knock on the door. They heard Polly go to answer it.

A moment later, she entered the room and said, "It is Mr Shrewsbury, miss. He has come to make sure you are alright. Should I admit him?"

While it wasn't the done thing to allow a single man to enter the bedroom of a woman he wasn't related to, there were extenuating circumstances; he had saved her, the dowager was still in the room, and Polly remained by the door.

Isabella wasn't a vain woman, yet even she worried about how she might look. Polly, sensing her hesitation, took a hairbrush, came over, and brushed the stray hairs from her face.

Realising that there was only so much that could be done to make her presentable, Isabella indicated that Polly should show him in.

Shrewsbury swept into the room, bowed briefly to the dowager, then crossed the room and, before she could protest, clasped Isabella's hand, bringing his head down over it. It was all quite improper, yet she was disinclined to rebuke the man who had rescued her.

"Miss Hartwell, I cannot tell you how good it is to see you sitting up and looking so well. You had us all quite worried for a moment. I heard from one of the servants that you were awake and had to come and assure myself of your good health."

"I never had the chance to thank you properly. You were my saviour, yet again. I cannot imagine how much worse I might have been if you hadn't been passing."

The man stepped back to a more appropriate distance from the bed and placed one hand on his heart. "It does not bear thinking about. So, it seems the footman is the culprit. The blackguard, attacking an innocent woman. If I could get my hands on him, well, I would not use such language in front of two ladies, but suffice it to say, he would be begging for the gallows once I was through with him."

Isabella had to suppress a smile at the thought of the rather slight Mr Shrewsbury taking on the tall, muscular footman. Yet she appreciated the sentiment.

For a moment, she almost told Shrewsbury that she had realised Hargreaves hadn't been her attacker. However, something made her hold back.

Polly, who had been standing in the doorway, caught Isabella's eye, and the look on her face was enough to cut the conversation short.

"Mr Shrewsbury, I do appreciate you taking the time to make sure I was well, but the doctor said I need to rest, and I fear that all this excitement is not what he had in mind."

"Of course, of course," Shrewsbury said. "I have set my mind at ease that you are recovering. That is enough." He stepped forward, caught her hand once more, and kissed it as if overcome.

At that moment, a gentle breeze blew through the slightly ajar window, and Isabella caught the aroma wafting off the man: verbena and hair pomade. And then she remembered the last time she had smelled that scent.

CHAPTER 35

It took all of Isabella's self-control not to react to her epiphany. Doing her best to make her smile seem sincere, she thanked Shrewsbury again. For a moment, the man seemed not to be ready to leave, but when she said nothing to stop him, he bowed again to both women and left the room.

Isabella waited until she had heard the main door close behind him, and even then, indicated to Polly that she should close the door to the sitting area.

"Whatever is it, my dear?" the dowager exclaimed. "You look as if you have seen a ghost."

"Worse," Isabella replied. "I believe I have seen a killer."

"What on earth does that mean? Who is the killer?"

Trying to get her thoughts straight while her head was still fuzzy, Isabella took a moment. She considered the scent she suddenly recognised, the height of her attacker, and her certainty that he had been wearing fine leather gloves. Then she thought about the lucky coincidence that Mr Shrewsbury happened to be walking to the picnic late and had taken a route that led him past the service gate. Where had he been coming from? Certainly, that wasn't the direction he would have taken if he'd left by the front door.

And suddenly, through the fog that had filled her mind since waking that morning and had only been exacerbated by hitting her head, she saw it all. The pieces of the puzzle swam before her and then slid together to form an almost perfect picture. There were still some holes in the puzzle, some information she was missing, but she had the corners and edges, and those were always the most important.

It seemed she'd been thinking too long, because the dowager repeated, "Am I never to know what you mean?"

"I am sorry," Isabella told her. "But I just need to understand something else." Reaching for the bell beside her bed, she rang for Polly.

"Is it possible you know roughly how long Lord and Lady Banbury have been married?" she asked her maid.

"Well, you could have asked me that," the dowager said in a huff. "I remember it well. I took note of the wedding announcement because of the earlier, unsuccessful attempt to hook Jonathan. Let me see now, it must have been five years ago, maybe a little longer. Yes, that would be right. Jonathan married Tabitha in February of '95, which is just over four years ago. So, I believe the Banburys were about a year before that."

"That is very helpful," Isabella said. Then, turning once more to her maid, she asked, "Polly, do you know how long Mr Shrewsbury has been living at Banbury Hall?"

The maid considered the question. "Well, not precisely. But I have become quite friendly with Miss Bowen, Lady Banbury's maid. She mentioned that not long after her ladyship married his lordship, her brother came to visit and never left."

"So, he was almost certainly living here five years ago, when the land agent was killed."

"What is all this about the land agent? The inspector mentioned it earlier, and it seems you were the first to inform him."

Isabella realised she risked the dowager's ire if she didn't explain the earlier murder at the estate. She gave an outline of what had happened, as relayed by the vicar during the picnic.

"And why do you believe Mr Shrewsbury's tenure as a houseguest is relevant?" the dowager asked, confused.

Isabella took a deep breath before speaking. "I believe Mr Shrewsbury was the man who attacked me earlier," she explained.

"What nonsense!" the dowager replied. "Perhaps you hit your head even harder than we realised. Polly, it may be necessary to send for the doctor again." In a patronising tone, the dowager added, "Isabella dear, Mr Shrewsbury rescued you after you were attacked."

"I realise this, Julia. However, I believe he did both. I think he attacked me, then acted as if he were my rescuer." She then explained the smell of verbena.

The dowager looked unconvinced. "Certainly, he is not the only man to use such a scent," she insisted.

Isabella could tell the dowager was unwilling to be persuaded and realised that her acceptance was not what she needed.

"Polly, please go down and ask the inspector to come back up as soon as possible. And Polly," she insisted, "be discreet."

The maid nodded and left immediately to find Inspector Gregory.

"What on earth is this all about, Isabella?" the dowager demanded. "I thought you were growing quite fond of Shrewsbury."

"My feelings are unimportant. And the truth is the truth. Let us talk about something else until the inspector arrives. Tell me more about the picnic."

It looked as if the dowager were going to argue, but she shrugged and related an amusing anecdote she'd been told about the vicar.

It couldn't have been more than ten minutes later when Polly returned with Inspector Gregory. The poor girl must have run downstairs and dragged the man out of whatever interview he was conducting.

"Miss Hartwell," the inspector said, a hint of annoyance in his voice. "Whatever is the matter? Your maid insisted I come immediately. I was just finishing my talk with Tilly Coates and hadn't even spoken to Lord Banbury yet about the other murder."

"I believe, no, I am certain, that Mr Shrewsbury attacked me, and I believe he killed Lord Ravensthorpe, and I strongly suspect that he also murdered the land agent five years ago."

Whatever the inspector had expected her to say, it wasn't that. The man looked so stunned that the dowager almost stood and offered him her chair.

It took him a few moments to compose his thoughts before answering. Finally, he asked, "Why would he do such things?"

In the five minutes or so that the dowager had been gossiping, more of the puzzle pieces had fallen into place. Isabella still didn't understand why Hargreaves was protecting Shrewsbury, but that was the least important point at that stage.

Confident in her conclusions, she replied, "Because both men threatened his place at Banbury Hall. I expect that when you have a chance to speak with Lord Banbury, he will confirm that the land agent had been tasked with setting the estate to rights. I suspect that part of the report he was never able to deliver would have noted that one of the first obvious economies was to stop maintaining an idle dependant in comfort at Banbury Hall."

"And you believe that Shrewsbury suspected what the man was going to report and killed him before he could?" Gregory asked in stunned amazement.

"I doubt you will ever be able to prove it; far too much time has passed. However, Ravensthorpe's murder fits the pattern; he was also threatening Shrewsbury's easy life as one of the estate's dependents. This time, the peril was very different; he knew enough to bring Banbury to financial ruin. Shrewsbury may have believed the man would carry out his threats, particularly once Lady Banbury seemed unwilling to yield to his will. I suspect he decided to take advantage of the house party to rid himself of the meddlesome lord."

She thought about what Shrewsbury himself had admitted to her. "He told me he saw Ravensthorpe outside his chamber after the argument I heard. He claimed he was using the facilities. But what if none of that is true? What if he only said that to absolve his sister of blame, when actually he was the one who entered Ravensthorpe's room that night, probably found him passed out from drink, and stabbed him?"

Saying this aloud made her consider something else. "Inspector, you still haven't found the murder weapon, have you?"

"No," Gregory admitted. "We've searched the house and grounds as far as we can, but it's nowhere to be found. I wondered why the killer took it with him and concluded that it was either taken in the confusion of the moment, or there was something about the knife that could be linked to our murderer, and he never found a safe time to dispose of it."

"You need to ask Lord Banbury for his permission to search Shrewsbury's room."

"Are you certain of this, Miss Hartwell?" the inspector said nervously. "This is quite a serious accusation to make if it isn't true. Even if Mr Shrewsbury was your attacker, that doesn't prove he murdered a man, let alone two of them. If I make this accusation and am wrong, the marquess could have my job."

"I am more certain of it by the minute," Isabella declared with conviction. "It all makes sense." Then she realised that Gregory had been speaking with Tilly, the maid, when Polly had interrupted him. Now she asked what the girl had said.

"Well, as it happens, that does corroborate your theory that he was your attacker. She said she was just leaving the house to come out to the picnic when Mr Shrewsbury stopped her. He said that Hargreaves wanted her to give you a message that he was waiting by the little service gate beyond the rose walk."

Now the dowager interrupted, exasperated, "And the silly girl never thought to wonder why a member of the family was running errands for the footman?"

"Well, that was the interesting thing. She seemed very shy about explaining the exact purpose, but I got the sense that she imagined Mr Shrewsbury had a familiarity with Hargreaves that made the errand seem unremarkable."

Then another piece of the puzzle fell into place. Isabella shivered; she had long believed that Hargreaves was lying to protect someone he cared deeply for. Now she suspected that person had never been Lady Banbury.

CHAPTER 36

"I'm coming with you to speak to Lord Banbury." Isabella began to get out of bed.

"No, you are not, Miss Hartwell!" the inspector said decisively. "I am more than capable of handling the marquess, and you need to stay in bed. Besides, even if I agreed, you'd never get past your maid."

"I just worry he may be reluctant to give his permission for his brother-in-law's room to be searched, particularly without hard evidence," Isabella explained. "I could lend you my support."

The dowager rose. "While your concerns are entirely valid, my dear, your answer is insufficient. There is no reason to believe that Lord Banbury will take your concerns any more seriously than he will Inspector Gregory's. You are, after all, a young, unmarried American woman. However, what he will not do, what he will not dare to do, is brush my views aside. I will accompany the inspector and ensure that he is granted the permission he requires."

She was right, of course, Isabella realised.

"He will not dare," she repeated with a smile.

With that, the dowager accompanied the inspector downstairs to find Lord Banbury and make the shocking request of him.

Once they were gone, Isabella realised how exhausted she was and sank back against her pillows. Perhaps, she thought, she would just close her eyes again for a few minutes.

It took the dowager and the inspector little time to find Banbury. After the picnic, he'd sought sanctuary in his study for a few hours. They found him seated in an armchair by the fire, a glass of brandy in one hand, a book in the other.

They had expected him to be shocked by the accusation against Shrewsbury. They had expected him to push back against the request to search his room. What no one could have anticipated was how little the accusation that his brother-in-law might be a murderer, and not for the first time, would unsettle him.

"It would not surprise me at all," he said, shaking his head. "I should have thrown him out years ago, but Antonia always pleaded with me to let him stay, saying he was such a comfort to her, particularly when I was in town." As he said this, Banbury looked a little guilty, and the dowager suspected he was thinking of Mrs Ashwin.

"And so, what of Hargreaves?" he asked. "I heard from Myers that you have him locked up in the cellar."

"We believe he was involved, if not in the murder itself, certainly in helping to cover it up. He must have taken Miss Hartwell's handkerchief. Whether he planted it at the scene of the murder or merely gave it to Shrewsbury, he was involved. At the very least, he will be charged with accessory after the fact to murder."

Lord Banbury looked genuinely upset at this, far more so than he had been at the prospect of his brother-in-law being arrested. "Damn shame. Good man, Hargreaves. Good man. He hoped to follow in his father's footsteps and become a butler one day. And he might have done just that."

"So, I have your permission to search Shrewsbury's room," the inspector confirmed.

"Yes, yes," Banbury said with a dismissive wave of his hand.

The dowager was quite put out that there had been no need to bully the man into submission.

Rather sullenly, she asked, "And where is that ne'er-do-well brother-in-law of yours now?"

"No idea. Last I saw him, he was heading upstairs."

Just then, the door opened and Myers, the butler, entered with that evening's newspaper.

"Good timing, Myers," Lord Banbury said. "Do you happen to know where Mr Shrewsbury is?"

"I believe he called for the carriage about thirty minutes ago, sir."

"The carriage?"

Lord Banbury might not have known what that meant, but Inspector Gregory did.

"He's bolting!" he said with certainty. "Must have felt the net closing in."

Addressing the butler, he asked, "Do you know where he was headed?"

"I do not, sir."

"May I use your telephone, Lord Banbury?" the inspector asked. "I need to send men to the local railway station."

Inspector Gregory made the call.

"Well, I must say, this is all quite thrilling!" the dowager exclaimed, her eyes shining with excitement.

Inspector Gregory ignored the dowager's delighted pronouncement entirely.

Turning back to Lord Banbury, he said, "Until we know more, no one is to leave this house without my permission, your lordship. That includes your guests and the rest of the household. Myers, I assume Mr Shrewsbury's room remains as he left it?"

"Yes, sir," the butler replied. "As far as I know, he only had a Gladstone bag with him when he left."

"Good. Before I set off after him, I intend to search it."

Banbury rose at once, setting aside his brandy and book. "Very well. If the fellow has taken only one small bag, he must have left something behind. The man has lived here almost six years and is a popinjay; I doubt he could have fit all his cravats into one Gladstone. I will join you for the search."

The dowager gave him an appraising look; she hadn't seen the marquess as galvanised into action as he seemed to be by the prospect of finding incriminating evidence against Shrewsbury.

Myers led them upstairs. At Gregory's request, one constable remained below to guard Hargreaves in the cellar, while the other joined the search. They took the back stairs, partly for speed, but mostly for discretion.

Shrewsbury's room was pleasant enough, though evidently not one of the Hall's best, since it overlooked the stable yard and kitchen garden. Myers opened the door with a passkey and stepped aside.

Even though its occupant had left in a hurry, the room was still excessively tidy. The curtains had been drawn against the late-afternoon light, and everything seemed in its place. There were no shaving items on the washstand, but a silver-backed brush and comb lay side by side on the dressing table. The bed had been made perfectly. There was no sign of haste or disorder anywhere.

"How very like him," Banbury muttered. "Even absconding with fastidiousness."

Gregory began his search in the obvious places. He crossed to the dressing table and opened the drawers one by one. Handkerchiefs, collar studs, gloves, and letters tied with ribbon were lifted, examined, and set aside. Banbury moved restlessly about the room while the dowager watched with narrowed eyes from an upright chair by the hearth. She was determined to be in the thick of the action, but wouldn't stoop to rifling through a man's undergarments.

There was nothing in the escritoire except stationery and more than a few unpaid bills. Gregory set those aside for Lord Banbury's later perusal and then went to the wardrobe.

A selection of coats and jackets, neatly brushed and arranged, hung inside. Beneath them stood two pairs of boots, a leather valise, and, pushed right to the back, a square travelling case that seemed too small to be of much use and too carefully hidden to be innocent.

Gregory crouched to inspect it. He drew the case out. It was locked. The inspector took a small penknife from his pocket and tried to jimmy the lock. At first, it seemed he couldn't break into the case. Then, just as he was about to despair, the lock gave way.

For a moment, no one spoke. Inside the case lay a folded towel, once white, now stiffened and stained with old brown marks. Gregory lifted it carefully by one corner. Within the stained towel lay a gentleman's clasp knife, narrow and sharp, with a dark handle of polished horn. There had been an attempt to wipe it clean, yet dark residue remained where the blade met the hilt.

Banbury stared at the knife in disbelief; it was one thing to hear that Shrewsbury had killed a man, quite another to see such gory proof.

"So, it is true," he said at last. Banbury dragged a hand over his face. "Enough to hang him, is it?"

Gregory replied. "It is more than enough to justify his arrest, and perhaps enough to secure his conviction."

He wrapped the knife again at once and closed the case. "Constable, you will carry this. Carefully."

"Now," Gregory said, "let us hope my men were able to apprehend Shrewsbury before he gets on a train."

Inspector Gregory paused at the door. "First, I must tell Miss Hartwell what we have found."

He departed the room so quickly that it took a moment for the dowager to realise she had been left behind and to rise and follow. Lord Banbury remained in the room, wondering how he was going to break this news to his wife.

By the time they reached Isabella's room, Polly was just emerging from the dressing room carrying a tray of tea and broth.

The maid started at the sight of the inspector and the dowager at the door.

"Is she awake?"

"She is, sir. She closed her eyes for a few minutes, but I just went in to check on her and she was up."

Gregory entered without waiting to be announced. Isabella, who had been lying back with her eyes closed, opened them at once at the sound of the door. One look at the inspector's expression, and she pushed herself upright against the pillows.

"Well?" she asked.

"Lord Banbury gave permission. We searched Mr Shrewsbury's room."

"And?" Isabella pressed.

Gregory crossed to the foot of the bed. "Your assumptions were correct. We found a locked case at the bottom of his wardrobe," he said at last. "Inside was a knife, imperfectly cleaned and wrapped in a towel stiff with old blood. Mr Shrewsbury has fled the Hall. I have sent word to the station and set every available man on him. We'll find him before he can get far."

Isabella felt quite stunned. Although she had been so certain of Shrewsbury's guilt in theory, the reality of it was still a harsh blow.

"It was him," she whispered.

"Yes," Gregory said quietly. "It was."

"And what of Hargreaves?" Isabella asked.

The inspector's expression shifted slightly. "I will talk to him again. I hope that this physical evidence of the crime and the news that he was abandoned to shoulder all the blame will finally persuade him to tell all he knows. While the knife would seem to be incontrovertible proof, Hargreaves's testimony will tie everything together in a way that no jury will be able to ignore."

For a moment, Isabella considered whether to share her more speculative, sensitive suspicion with the inspector.

Then, realising he would need all the ammunition at his disposal, she said, "I believe Hargreaves harbours deep feelings towards Mr Shrewsbury. Of course, I have no idea what the precise nature of their relationship was, but he may need to be confronted with just how completely he has been sacrificed."

The inspector acknowledged her advice. He began to turn to leave, then said, "As soon as we have Shrewsbury in custody, I will send word."

"Thank you, Inspector," Isabella replied.

"No. Thank you, Miss Hartwell. We might never have cracked this case if it weren't for your meddling." The words were spoken with a lightness that made it clear no offence was intended. None was taken.

The dowager had been standing quietly in the doorway. Now she said, "Let us not forget my oversight of the meddling, Inspector."

"Indeed, your ladyship," he said, with only a brief smile in Isabella's direction.

Polly had entered the room with the tea tray and now handed Isabella a cup. "Drink this while it is hot, miss. I think you've had more than enough excitement for one day. I can only imagine what the doctor would say about all this."

Isabella took the teacup obediently, though her mind was elsewhere. A hunt for a murderer was underway, and his accomplice was about to be grilled. Yet she could do nothing but remain propped against her pillows and wait. Until the inspector returned with news of Shrewsbury or Hargreaves broke at last, all she could do was lie still and wonder what would finally force the truth into the open.

CHAPTER 37

For nearly half an hour after Inspector Gregory left her, Isabella could do nothing but rest, the teacup cooling in her hands, thinking about all that had transpired. She wondered what was happening downstairs. Had Shrewsbury been apprehended? Had Hargreaves finally broken down and confessed? The suspense was so unbearable that she was tempted to brave Polly's ire, get out of bed, get dressed, and go down to see for herself what was happening.

Perhaps suspecting the direction of her mistress's thoughts, Polly hovered nearby. The dowager sat for a time in the chair by the bed, saying little. At last, she rose, declared she would go downstairs to see whether there was any news worth hearing, and swept out, leaving Isabella even more frustrated by her enforced impotence.

Polly looked after her, then turned back to Isabella. "Would you like a little broth, miss?"

"No."

"You must eat something."

"I cannot."

The maid frowned, but said nothing further. Rather than arguing, she folded the shawl more securely around her mistress's shoulders and moved to the window.

Isabella had assumed the inspector would interrogate Hargreaves alone. She was therefore shocked when, less than an hour later, Gregory was once more in her room, with one of the constables escorting a still-handcuffed Hargreaves.

The footman looked markedly altered from the man who had stood in Isabella's room earlier. Then he had been frightened and defensive. Now he looked hollowed out. His face had gone grey, and his eyes, when they lifted to Isabella, showed how close he was to total defeat.

Gregory addressed the cowed footman, "Mr Shrewsbury has fled Banbury Hall. A knife wrapped in a bloodstained towel has been found in his room. It is my belief that it is the murder weapon and that Shrewsbury killed Lord Ravensthorpe. It is also my belief that he let suspicion of the attack on Miss Hartwell settle upon you, in the hope that this would cause me to accuse you of the murder as well."

Hargreaves seemed genuinely stunned by the news. Yet he did not comment.

The inspector continued, "Mr Hargreaves, if you have anything more to say, this is the moment to say it. I should add that you will be arrested for concealing evidence and misleading the police, at the very least. However, if you tell the full truth now, I will ensure your cooperation is taken into account."

Hargreaves shut his eyes briefly. Then Isabella saw something shift in his face, not dramatically, but enough. It was the change that comes when a man has told himself one story for too long and is suddenly forced to face reality.

She spoke before she had fully decided what to say. "He used your words," she said quietly. "You wanted a chance to explain yourself. He must have overheard your conversation with Tilly and turned it into a trap. Then he viciously attacked me and led everyone to believe you were the perpetrator. Whatever regard you believed Mr Shrewsbury had for you, it was never what you thought. He used and then abandoned you. You owe him nothing."

For several seconds, the only sound in the room was the faint hiss of the fire.

Then Hargreaves said, almost too softly to hear, "At first, I didn't think he meant to let it go so far."

He drew a deep breath. "I wanted only to spare the house from disgrace."

"I know you did," Isabella assured him.

"When I took her ladyship the milk that night," he said, "she was in great distress. I had never seen her like that. She was crying, and I... I could not bring myself to leave her at once."

"Go on," Isabella encouraged him. Gregory said nothing; it seemed the inspector was willing to let Isabella draw Hargreaves out.

"When at last I left her ladyship, I encountered Mr Shrewsbury in the corridor. He asked what I was doing there. I said her ladyship was upset that Lord Ravensthorpe was going to expose everything. He swore under his breath and told me to stay where I was for a few minutes and make sure no one came up from below. He said he must see Lord Ravensthorpe before he drank himself insensible and made everything worse."

"And you obeyed," said Gregory.

"Yes, sir."

"Did you know why he wanted to see him?"

"I could tell at dinner that night how angry Peter, I mean Mr Shrewsbury, was with Lord Ravensthorpe about his behaviour. He's a very protective brother, and I thought..." He swallowed. "Well, I thought he just meant to warn him off, or beg him to leave her ladyship alone. Something of that kind."

"But not to kill him."

"No, sir." The words came with sudden force.

"And did you see Mr Shrewsbury enter Lord Ravensthorpe's room?"

"I saw him go that way."

"Did you see him come out?"

Another pause. Hargreaves lifted his head slightly, enough for Isabella to see the misery plainly in his eyes.

"Yes."

Gregory's voice stayed level. "What state was he in?"

"He looked... not anxious, exactly, but tense. He asked if anyone had passed. I said no. Then he told me to go downstairs at once and to make an excuse if anyone asked where I'd been."

"And did nothing strike you as odd?" Isabella asked. The footman paused, and she encouraged him. "Remember, Jimmy, that your honest account now will make all the difference to how you are charged."

Hargreaves nodded.

Then, his face showing the pain the admission was causing, he said, "He was carrying something wrapped in a white towel."

Isabella exchanged a look with the inspector; this was the missing piece that would ensure Shrewsbury's conviction.

"I did not see the blow struck," Hargreaves admitted. "But when I later learned that his lordship had been found stabbed in his bedchamber, I knew... I knew what it must mean."

Gregory let the confession sink in.

"So, from that moment onward, you knew or strongly suspected that Mr Shrewsbury had killed him."

Hargreaves pressed his lips together.

"Yes," he said at last.

"And yet you lied."

"Yes."

"And then there was the handkerchief."

At that, Hargreaves drew a shuddering breath. "Yes, sir."

"Tell us."

"It was later. Much later. Mr Shrewsbury found me in the passage behind the servants' hall. He held Miss Hartwell's handkerchief. I do not know where he got it. He said everything was coming apart, that her ladyship would be ruined and the whole house brought down if I didn't help him. He said it was only to confuse matters, only to buy time. He gave it to me and told me to put it in Lord Ravensthorpe's room when there was a chance."

"And you did this?" Gregory asked.

"Yes, sir."

The footman went on, more quietly, "He said no real blame would fall anywhere if the matter were only muddled a little. He said the police often seize on what is nearest to hand, at least at first."

Isabella suddenly felt cold.

"Then you helped him cast suspicion on me," she said.

Hargreaves turned towards her. "I never meant you any harm, miss. I swear it. I thought only that it might send the investigation in circles for a few hours."

Whether this was true or not, Isabella immediately spotted the contradiction in what Hargreaves had said moments earlier.

"But if you dropped my handkerchief in Lord Ravensthorpe's room, you knew he had been killed long before he was found the following morning. Is that not so?" she demanded.

Caught in the lie, the man's expression changed to pure terror. His only answer was a dejected nod.

Gregory said nothing at first. Then, in a stern, formal tone, he asked, "Do you understand what you have now admitted?"

"Yes, sir."

"That you assisted after the fact, concealed evidence, and misled the police," Gregory said, spelling out the crime.

"Yes, sir."

"And that Mr Shrewsbury used you from the beginning to the end."

Hargreaves flinched again, but did not deny it.

Before Gregory could speak further, there was a sharp knock at the door. One of the constables entered and stood respectfully at the threshold. Everyone in the room turned.

"Beg pardon, sir. A message came from the station."

"Well?" Gregory demanded.

"We have him, sir. He had got as far as Oxford, but the stationmaster detained him after the call came through. He is being brought to the station now."

For the first time since entering the room, Hargreaves seemed to lose the last of his strength. He sank to the ground as if his knees could no longer hold him.

Isabella looked at Hargreaves and saw not merely a servant who had lied, nor even a man who had helped cover up a murder. She saw someone who had, step by step, descended into ruin because of misplaced loyalty and devotion.

Gregory turned to the constable. "Good. We will be bringing Mr Hargreaves to join him in the cells."

The constable withdrew.

The inspector faced Hargreaves once more. "You will be taken to the police station. But understand this, Mr Hargreaves, what happens next depends very much on whether you maintain this honesty when you put your statement into proper form."

"I will," Hargreaves said dully.

The inspector nodded to the other constable, who stepped forward.

As Hargreaves rose, he looked at Isabella once more. There was no plea on his face now. Only desperation, shame, and, more than anything, grief.

When they had all left, Isabella didn't feel triumphant, only sad.

Polly, who had stood stiff and silent throughout the whole scene, moved at once to her mistress's side.

"You are done with all this for tonight," she said in a voice that brooked no argument.

Isabella might once have protested. Now she only leaned back against the pillows and listened as footsteps receded along the corridor and down the stairs, taking a young man with once-bright prospects towards the cells that now awaited him.

At last, she understood the full shape of the betrayal. Shrewsbury had not merely used a gullible accomplice. He had betrayed the trust of someone who loved him.

EPILOGUE

The next morning, Banbury Hall had grown noticeably emptier. In theory, the house party still had two days to go. However, once Inspector Gregory made it clear that the culprit had been apprehended and that he had no further need of the remaining guests, the house party began to dissolve with remarkable speed. Isabella would have happily joined them, but when the doctor visited, he allowed her to get up and dress, though he insisted she remain at least one more day before travelling. While she might have been inclined to ignore his advice, the combination of Polly and the dowager proved a force Isabella couldn't resist.

With the help of one of the dowager's walking sticks, Isabella made it downstairs in time for luncheon, only to find the dining room almost entirely empty, except for the deaf older gentleman, who seemed oblivious to the chaos that had transpired.

As she took a seat beside the dowager, Isabella asked, "Has there been any word as to how Lady Banbury is taking the news of her brother's arrest?"

Even though their companion was deaf, she kept her voice low, and the dowager followed suit in her reply. "She has kept to her room and has not been seen or heard from since last night."

Isabella could only imagine the terrible shock the news of her brother's culpability had been to the already fragile woman. For all their deep flaws, the marchioness had now lost the only three men who, in their different ways, seemed to care for her: Ravensthorpe, Hargreaves, and Shrewsbury. Now she was left with a philandering husband she clearly despised, and a child whose likely parentage could only deepen the misery of her position.

"What will become of the estate's finances now?" Isabella wondered aloud.

"Well, whatever debt Banbury owed Ravensthorpe has now passed to his heirs," the dowager surmised. "Let us hope they are kinder and more forgiving toward him."

While it was difficult to feel much sympathy for the bombastic, unfaithful man, Isabella felt genuine compassion for his wife and hoped the dowager's words proved true.

Despite her insistence on leaving her bedchamber, once downstairs, Isabella found the atmosphere of the Hall so oppressive that she chose to return to her room for the rest of the day and evening, intending to leave as early as possible the following morning.

Isabella had arrived at Banbury Hall, trepidatious about why she'd been invited. As the carriage that would take them to the station pulled away the next day, she could only reflect on how trivial those concerns now seemed.

As they turned the bend in the driveway and the house fell out of sight, she was no longer thinking about Ravensthorpe, Lady Banbury, or even poor, foolish Hargreaves. Instead, Isabella was thinking about Mr Shrewsbury's smile, his careful gallantry, and how nearly she had mistaken his performance for genuine admiration. She would not soon forget the lesson, nor would she mistake charm for character again.

For bonus content, extra mysteries, and news about upcoming releases, join my newsletter at sarahfnoel.com.

Want a sneak peek at book 2, A Coveted Woman? Keep reading...

Set in 1890s London, this Victorian historical mystery follows Isabella Hartwell, a sharp-witted American heiress, as she investigates a murder at Harrods, uncovering hidden debts, secret deals, and dangerous high-society deception.

London society may still be deciding what to make of Isabella Hartwell, but Isabella has little interest in conforming to expectations. When she attends an exclusive private event at Harrods, she expects spectacle, gossip, and perhaps a little matchmaking. She does not expect to find a man dead within the store's glittering walls.

At first, the killing appears linked to luxury goods and discreet business dealings. But as Isabella investigates, she uncovers concealed debts, secret bargains, and rival ambitions hidden beneath polished counters and respectable smiles. In a world where everything and everyone seems to be assessed for value, murder may be the price of keeping ruin out of sight.

With suspicion spreading through drawing rooms, showrooms, and back corridors alike, Isabella must discover who wanted the victim silenced before the killer turns their attention to her.

AFTERWORD

Thank you for reading An Impertinent Heiress. I hope you enjoyed it. If you'd like to see what's coming next for Isabella, here are some ways to stay in touch:

SarahFNoel.com
Facebook
@sarahfNoelAuthor on BlueSky
sfnoel on Instagram
@sfnoel on Threads

If you enjoyed this book, I'd very much appreciate a review (but, please no spoilers).

ABOUT SARAH F. NOEL

Originally from London, Sarah F. Noel now spends most of her time in Grenada in the Caribbean. Sarah loves reading historical mysteries with strong female characters. The Tabitha & Wolf Mystery Series and its spin-off, The Continental Capers of Melody Chesterton, are exactly the kind of books she loves to curl up with on a lazy Sunday.

Visit Sarah's website (sarahfnoel.com/) to join her mailing list, connect with her on social media, and see what's coming next!